TOM FAIRFIELD'S HUNTING TRIP

BY

ALLEN CHAPMAN

TOM FAIRFIELD'S HUNTING TRIP

CHAPTER I

THE BIG SNOWBALL

"Well, Tom, it sure is a dandy plan!"

"That's right! A hunting trip to the Adirondacks will just suit me!"

"And we couldn't have better weather than this, nor a better time than the coming holiday season."

Three lads, who had made the above remarks, came to a whirling stop on their shining, nickeled skates and gathered in a small ring about the fourth member of the little party, Tom Fairfield by name. Tom listened to what was said, and remarked:

"Well, fellows, I'm glad you like my plan. Now I think——"

"Like it! I should say we did!" cried the smallest of the three lads grouped about the one in the centre. "Why, it's the best ever!" and he did a spread eagle on his skates, so full of life did he feel that crisp December day.

"Do you really think we can get any game?" asked Jack Fitch, as he loosed his mackinaw at the throat, for he had warmed himself by a vigorous burst of skating just before the little halt that had ended in the impromptu vote of thanks to Tom.

"Get game? Well, I should say we could!" cried another of the lads.

"What do you know about it, Bert Wilson?" demanded Jack. "Were you ever up there?"

"No, but I'm sure Tom Fairfield wouldn't ask us up to a hunter's camp unless he was reasonably sure that we could get some kind of game. I'm not very particular what kind," Bert went on, "as long as it's game—a bear, a mountain lion, a lynx—I'm not hard to suit," he added magnanimously.

"Well, I should say not!" laughed Tom.

"But say!" exclaimed the youngest member of the quartette—George Abbot by name. "Do you really think we can bag a bear? Or a lynx, maybe? Or even a fox? Are there really any big animals up there, Tom? What sort of a gun had I better take? And what about an outfit? Do you think——"

Tom reached out and gently placed a gloved hand over the mouth of the questioner, thereby cutting off, for the time being, the flow of interrogations.

"Just a moment, Why, if you please," he said, giving George the nickname his fellow students at Elmwood Hall had fastened on the lad who seemed to be a human question mark.

"Well, I—er—Buu—er—gurg——"

But that was the nearest semblance to speaking that George could accomplish. His companions laughed at him. He finally made a sign that he would desist if Tom removed the hand-gag, and when this had been done, Jack proposed a little sprint down to one end of the small lake on which they were skating.

"No, we've had enough racing to-day," declared Bert Wilson. "I vote Tom tells us more about this hunters' camp, and what we expect to do there."

"All right, I'm agreeable," Jack said.

"Are they——?" began Why, but a look from Bert warned him, and he stopped midway in his question. His chums well knew that if George once got started it was hard to stop him.

"Well, there isn't so much to tell that you fellows don't know already," began Tom slowly. "In the first place, there are three hunters' camps, not one."

"Three!" exclaimed Jack and Bert, while George looked the questions he dared not ask.

"Yes. You see they belong to a party of gentlemen, a sort of camping club. The camps are about five miles apart, in the wildest part of the Adirondacks."

"Why—three?" came at last from George. Really he could not keep it back any longer. Tom did not seem to mind.

"Oh, I suppose they wanted to change their hunting ground," he answered, "and they found it easier to make three camps, or headquarters, than to come all the way back to the first one. And the club is pretty well off, so it didn't mind the expense."

"But you don't mean to say we can use all three of 'em?" cried Jack, incredulously.

"That's the idea," Tom said. "We're just as welcome to use all three camps as one. They're all about alike, each with a log cabin, nicely fitted up, set in the midst of the big woods."

"That's jolly!" cried Bert.

"And aren't the men themselves going to use them?" George wanted to know. Again he went unrebuked.

"Not this season," Tom Fairfield explained. "The club is sort of broken up for the time being. Some of the men want to go, but they can't get enough together to make a party, so they had to give up their annual holiday outing this year.

"A business friend of my father's belongs to the club, and he mentioned to Dad that there was a chance for someone to use the camps. Dad happened to speak of it to me, and I—well, you can imagine what I did! I jumped at the chance, and now you know almost as much as I do about it.

"I'll tell you later just where the camps are, and how we are to get to them. We want to get together and have a talk about what we'll take with us. School closes here day after to-morrow, and then we'll be free for nearly a month."

"And won't we have some ripping old times, though!" cried Jack.

"Well, I should say yes!" chimed in Bert.

"Tell you what let's do, fellows!" broke in George. "Let's go up to the top of that hill and have a coast. Some of our lads from Elmwood are there with the bobs, and they'll give us a ride. I've had enough of skating."

"So have I," chimed in Jack.

"I'm with you," agreed Bert, stooping to loosen his skates, an example followed by Tom Fairfield.

"I hope this snowy weather holds," spoke Jack. "But are you allowed to shoot game when there is tracking snow?"

"I don't just know all the rules," said Tom, "but of course we will do what is right. I guess we'll have plenty of snow in the mountains, and cold weather, too."

"It's getting warm here," observed Bert. "Too warm," for the variable New Jersey climate had changed from freezing almost to thawing in the night, and the boys were really taking advantage of the last bit of skating they were likely to have in some time.

There were not many besides themselves on the ice of the lake when they started from it, heading for the big hill not far away—a hill whereon the youth of Elmwood Hall, a boarding school near the Jersey state capital, had many jolly times.

When Tom Fairfield and his chums, talking about the camping and hunting trip in prospect, reached the hill, they found it deserted—that is, by all save a few small town boys with their little sleds.

"No coasting to-day," observed Jack, ruefully.

"No, it's getting too soft," added Bert, digging his foot into the snowy surface of the hill. But the small boys did not mind that. With the big lads out of the way, smaller fry had a chance.

George Abbot picked up a handful of snow and rolled it into a ball. As he noticed how well it packed, he exclaimed:

"Say, fellows, another idea!"

"Ha! He's full of 'em to-day!" laughed Jack.

"Get rid of it, Why," advised Tom. "Don't keep ideas in your system."

"Let's roll a whopping big snowball," proposed George, "and send it down hill. It will roll all the way to the bottom, and pick up snow all the way down."

"It will be some snowball when it gets to the bottom," observed Tom. "This snow does pack wonderfully well," he added, testing it.

"Come on!" cried George, and he started to roll the ball. In a few minutes he had one so large that it needed two to shove it about, and as it gathered layer after layer of snow, it accumulated in size until the strength of the four lads was barely sufficient to send it slowly along.

"Now to the top of the hill with it!" cried Tom, and it was placed on the brink. The boys held it at a point where it would not interfere with the small coasters. It was poised on the brink a moment.

"Let her go!" cried Tom.

"There she goes!" echoed Jack Fitch.

They shoved the ball down the slope. On and on it rolled, gaining in momentum and size with every bound.

"Look at it!" cried George. "Say, it sure is going!"

"And it's getting as big as a house!" excitedly shouted Bert.

"It will roll all the way across the lake," said Tom, for the frozen body of water was at the foot of the hill, and it did seem as though the snowball had momentum enough to carry it over the ice.

A moment later the ball was at the foot of the hill, and rolling along with increasing speed. And then, so suddenly that the boys were startled with fear, something happened.

Out on the ice drove a horse and a cutter, containing a man. He had left the road and taken a short cut across the ice. And now he was directly in the path of the immense, rolling snowball.

"Stop! Stop!" cried Tom Fairfield. "Look out!"

But it was too late to stop, even if the man in the cutter had heard him.

On rushed the great ball directly toward the horse and vehicle.

CHAPTER II

A SURPRISE

"Say, it's going to hit him, sure as fate!" cried Tom.

"No help for it," half-groaned Jack.

"And there will be some smash!" murmured Bert. "Oh, what did you do it for, George?"

"Me do it? Why, say, you fellows had as much to do with it as I did! I didn't do it all!" and the smaller lad looked indignantly at his companions.

"Come on!" cried Tom, as he started on a run down the snowy side of the hill.

The others followed.

"We can't do anything!" shouted Jack.

"Of course not," agreed Bert. "By the time we get there——"

He did not finish the sentence. All this while the big snowball had been rushing on. The man in the cutter had seen it, but too late. He tried to whip up the horse and get out of the way, but even as Bert spoke the mass of snow struck fairly between the horse and cutter.

In an instant the vehicle was overturned.

The boys, running to the rescue, had a confused vision of a man flying out to one side, head first, toward a snowbank. They also saw the horse rear up on his hind legs, struggle desperately to retain his balance and then, with a fierce leap, break loose from the cutter and run on, free, across the ice.

As the boys hastened on, they saw the man slowly pick himself up out of the snowbank, and gaze wonderingly about him, as if trying to fathom what had happened, whether it had been an earthquake or an avalanche. Indeed, so large was the snowball, and so strong was the force of it, for it had gained speed by the rush down the steep hill, that it really was a small avalanche.

The ball had split into several pieces on hitting the cutter, the shafts of which were broken and splintered, showing how the horse had been able to free himself.

"We'll have to—to apologize," murmured Tom, as he and his companions kept on toward the man who was now gazing down disconsolately at the ruin wrought.

"Yes, I guess we will," agreed Jack. "We—why, Cæsar's corn-plasters!" he cried. "Look who it is—Professor Skeel!"

"The old tyrant of Elmwood Hall!" murmured Bert. "Who'd have thought it?"

"Now we are in for it," added Tom, grimly.

"Burton Skeel!" said George in a whisper as he caught sight of the angry-looking man, gazing at his smashed cutter and staring off over the ice in the direction taken by the runaway horse. "Skeel, the man who made so much trouble for Tom Fairfield. And we upset him! Oh—good-night!"

Those of you who have read the first volume of this series, entitled "Tom Fairfield's Schooldays," do not need to be introduced to Professor Skeel. The unpopular instructor of Elmwood Hall, where Tom and his chums attended, had been the cause of a rebellion, in which Tom was a sort of leader, and, later, a pacifier. Tom Fairfield, the son of Mr. and Mrs. Brokaw Fairfield, of Briartown, N. J., had made himself popular soon after coming to Elmwood, where he had been sent to board while his parents went to Australia about some property matters.

And now to find that the man upset from his cutter was this same unpopular teacher, Professor Skeel, was enough to give pause to any set of lads.

But Tom Fairfield was no coward. He proved that when the Silver Star was wrecked, an account of which you may read of in my second volume, called "Tom Fairfield at Sea," for the days that followed the foundering of that vessel were trying ones indeed, and the dreary days spent in an open boat, when Mr. Skeel proved himself not only a coward, but almost a scoundrel, showed Tom fully what sort of a man the professor was.

Tom finally reached Australia, and set out on another voyage in time to rescue his parents from some savages on one of the Pacific islands. So it was such qualities as these, and those developed when Tom had other adventures, set forth in the third book, "Tom Fairfield in Camp," that made our hero keep on instead of turning back when he found what had happened to Mr. Skeel.

In camp Tom and his chums succeeded in clearing up the mystery of the old mill, though for a time it seemed that they were doomed to failure. But Tom was not one to give up easily, and this, I think, was more fully shown, perhaps, in the volume immediately preceding this, called "Tom Fairfield's Pluck and Luck."

True, Tom did have "luck," but, after all, what is luck but hard work turned to the best advantage? Almost any chap can have luck if he works hard, and takes advantage of every opportunity.

And now, after many weeks of tribulations, Tom found himself at the beginning of the Christmas holidays, and he and his chums had in prospect a very enjoyable time.

But just at the present moment they would have given up part of anticipated pleasures, I believe, not to have had the snowball accident happen.

"It is Skeel," murmured Tom, as though at first he had doubted the evidence of his own eyes.

"Of course it is," said Jack.

"And we're in for trouble, or I miss my guess," added Bert.

"I wonder what in the world he is doing in these parts?" came from George. "You thought you'd seen the last of him, didn't you, Tom, after the wreck of the Silver Star?"

"I certainly did."

"And yet he bobs up again," went on George. "What does he want? Is he trying to get back on the faculty of Elmwood Hall?"

No one answered his questions, nor did Tom, or any of the others, rebuke Why for his queries. They had too much else to think about.

"Well, young men, well!" began Professor Skeel in his pompous voice. "Well, are you responsible for this?"

"I—I'm afraid we are," said Tom. He did not add "sir," as once he would have done. He had lost the little respect he had for the former teacher, and when a man loses the respect of a manly youth, it is not good for that man.

"Humph! Yes, you certainly have done mischief enough," went on Mr. Skeel, in snarling tones. "My cutter is broken, I am thrown out, and may have sustained there are no telling what injuries, my horse has run away and may be killed, and you stand there like—like blithering idiots!" he cried, with something of his old, objectionable, schoolroom manner.

"We—we didn't mean to," said Tom.

"We just made a big snowball and rolled it down," George said, determined to take his share of the blame.

"Hum! Yes, so I see—and so I felt, young men!" cried the irate man, as he brushed the snow off his garments.

The boys had not yet gotten over the surprise of identifying Professor Skeel. They could not understand it.

"We will do anything we can to make amends," Tom said, slinging his skates over his shoulder with a jangling of steel. "We will try to catch your horse, and we can get you another cutter. We are——"

Something in Tom's voice caused the man to look up quickly. As he did so Tom noticed that his right ear appeared as though it had been recently injured. The lower part was torn and hung down below the other lobe.

"Ha! So it's you, is it!" fairly snarled Mr. Skeel. "It's you, Tom Fairfield?"

"Yes, Mr. Skeel. And I can only say how sorry I am——"

"Don't tell me how sorry you are!" interrupted the former teacher, in a voice filled with passion. "I don't want to listen to you. I've had enough of you. Don't you dare to address me!

"This was done on purpose. It was a deliberate attempt to injure me, perhaps kill me, for all I know. But I will not submit. I will at once go to town and cause your arrest, Tom Fairfield. The arrest of yourself, and those rascals with you. I'll have you all arrested."

George turned pale under his ruddy cheeks. He was not afraid, but he was thinking of the disgrace. But Tom Fairfield was master of the situation.

"Oh, I wouldn't have anyone arrested if I were you, Mr. Skeel," he said, in easy tones.

"Yes, I shall, too!" blustered the man. "I'll have you all arrested! The idea of rolling a snowball on me and almost killing me. I'll have everyone of you arrested."

"Oh, I wouldn't," Tom said. "You forget that little matter of the forgery, Mr. Skeel. That indictment is still hanging over you, I believe. And if you were to go to the authorities, it might come out, and there would be some other arrests than ours. So if I were you——"

He did not need to finish. Mr. Skeel turned pale and uttered an exclamation under his breath.

At that moment George created a diversion by crying:

"Here comes your horse back."

CHAPTER III
THE PLOT

George Abbot was not exactly correct in saying that the runaway horse was coming back. The animal was being brought back, and he seemed quiet and docile enough. Perhaps he had lost his fright in the run he had taken after being freed from the cutter.

"Who's leading the horse?" asked Bert Wilson, while Tom turned to look, after having faced the angry professor until the latter turned aside his head. Well he knew that Tom spoke the truth. A shady transaction, while a member of the Elmwood faculty, had placed Professor Skeel under the ban of the law, and he realized that he could not appeal to it without bringing himself into its clutches.

"That's Morse Denton with the animal," said Jack.

"Morse must have caught him before he went very far, or he wouldn't be back so soon," spoke Bert, waving his hand toward the former Freshman football captain.

"Does that horse belong there?" Morse called across the ice.

"Yes, bring him over here," said Tom. "Perhaps we can patch up the shafts and send you on your way again, Professor Skeel," Tom went on, for he did not hold enmity, and he was willing to let bygones be bygones, if the professor did not push matters too far.

"Um!" was all the answer the former teacher vouchsafed. He was arranging his garments, which had been rather twisted, to say the least, by his sudden exit from the cutter.

"What happened?" asked Morse, when he led the horse up to the little group standing partly on the ice of the lake and partly on the shore, for the accident had happened close to the edge.

"It was a big snowball," volunteered George. "We rolled it down the hill, and Professor Skeel ran into it."

"Be correct, young man. Be correct!" growled the former instructor. "The snowball ran into me, but I'll have satisfaction. I'll——"

He caught Tom's eye on him, and fairly quailed.

"Why, it's Professor Skeel!" cried Morse. "Where did you——"

But Tom gave Morse a quick and secret sign to cease questioning, and the newcomer, still holding the captured horse, acquiesced.

"Is the animal hurt?" demanded the former teacher.

"Doesn't seem to be," Morse replied. "I saw him coming at a slow canter across the ice, and I had no trouble in stopping him. I guessed it was a runaway and I started him back in just the opposite direction to that he was going. Then I saw you fellows," he added to his chums.

"I have told Professor Skeel how sorry I am that the accident occurred," went on Tom, "and I have assured him that we will do all that we can to repair the damage." He was speaking slowly and with reserve, and choosing his words carefully.

"Repair the damage!" snapped the man.

"The shafts are all that seem to be broken," proceeded Tom. "I know a farmer near here, and I'm sure he will lend you another pair of shafts for your cutter. The harness is not damaged, the cutter itself is all right, and the horse is not hurt. There is no reason why you should not continue your journey, Professor Skeel."

"Well, do something then, don't stand there talking about it!" burst out the irritated man.

Tom did not answer, and his chums rather marveled, for Tom was not the youth to take abuse quietly. But Tom realized that, through no fault of his own, Professor Skeel had been put to serious inconvenience, and it was no more than just that the lads should make good the damage they had unwittingly done.

"Let's set up the cutter, fellows," proposed Tom, after a pause, "and then we'll see about getting another pair of shafts. We can't use these, that's certain." They were splintered beyond repair.

The boys of Elmwood Hall were used to doing things quickly, especially under Tom's leadership. In a trice the cutter was righted, and the robes and the scattered possessions of Professor Skeel were picked up and put into it. Then while Morse, George and Bert remained to adjust the harness on the now quieted horse, Tom and Jack went to a farmhouse near the lake to borrow a spare pair of shafts.

Tom knew the farmer, of whom he had often hired a team in the summer, and the man readily agreed not only to loan the shafts, but to adjust them to the cutter.

He made a quick and neat job of it, and soon the horse was once more hitched to the righted vehicle.

"There you are, Professor Skeel," said Tom. "Not quite as good as before, but almost. You can keep on, and once more I wish to tell you how sorry I am that it happened."

"Um!" sneered Mr. Skeel.

"You may not believe it," Tom went on. "We did not see you coming until we had started the ball down hill, and then it was too late to stop it. We never thought anyone would cross the lake on the ice at this point, as no one ever does so."

"I had a right to, didn't I?" demanded the irate professor.

"A right, certainly," agreed Tom. "But it is unusual. Teams go down on the lake about a mile farther on, and you would have been perfectly safe there."

"Humph! I guess I can cross this lake where I please! And the next time you roll a snowball on me, I'll——"

"I told you," said Tom, and his voice was cuttingly cool, "that we did not roll the ball on you. It was unintentional, but if you persist in thinking we did it purposely, we can't help that. Now, is there anything more we can do for you?" and he looked about the snow to make sure all the contents of the cutter had been picked up and returned to it.

The professor did not answer, but busied himself getting into the vehicle, and taking the reins from Morse Denton.

"You can send them spare shafts back any time," said the farmer who had kindly loaned them.

"We'll pay for 'em if he doesn't," said Jack in a low voice, anxious to preserve peace. "It's getting off cheap as it is," he added.

"That's right," agreed Bert. "I thought he'd raise no end of a row."

"So he would have—only for Tom. Tom closed him up in great shape, didn't he?"

"He sure did."

Without a word of thanks, Professor Skeel drove off over the ice. He never looked back, but the boys could hear him muttering angrily to himself, probably giving vent to threats he dared not utter aloud.

"I wonder what he is doing in this neighborhood?" ventured Bert.

"It's certainly a puzzle," admitted Tom Fairfield. "He's up to no good, I'll wager."

"That's right," agreed Jack. "Well, I'm glad he's gone, anyhow. That sure was some upset!"

"Say, did you notice his ear?" asked George. "It wasn't that way when he was teaching school here. Looks as if a knife had cut him."

"Was his ear like that when he was shipwrecked with you, Tom?" asked Bert.

"No. That's a new injury," was the answer. "Rather a queer one, too. He might have been in a fight."

The lads remained standing together, for a little while, gazing at the now fast-disappearing cutter and its surly occupant.

"Well, let's get back to school," proposed Jack. "It will soon be grub-time."

"And Tom can tell us more about that hunting trip," suggested Bert.

"All right," agreed our hero, but as he walked along he was puzzling his brain, trying to think what Professor Skeel's object was in coming back to Elmwood Hall.

Perhaps if Tom could have seen Mr. Skeel a little later, as the cutter drew up at a road-house some miles away—a road-house that did not have a very enviable reputation in the neighborhood—Tom would have wondered still more over his former teacher's return.

For, as the cutter drew up in the drive, there peered from a window two men, one with a more evil-looking face than the other, which was his only claim to distinction.

"There he comes," murmured the man with the less-evil countenance.

"Yes, but he's late," agreed the other. "Wonder what kept him?"

"He looks mad—too," commented his companion.

A few moments later Professor Skeel entered the rear room of the road-house. The two men arose from the table at which they had been sitting.

"Well, you kept your word, I see," muttered Skeel to the man with the evil face. "You're here, Whalen. And you too, Murker."

"Yes. We're here, but you didn't say what you wanted of us," spoke the one addressed as Whalen.

"You'll know soon enough," was the rejoinder. "We sha'n't want anything—at least not for a while," Mr. Skeel went on to the landlord, who had followed him into the room. "You can leave us alone. We'll ring when we want you. And close the door when you go out," he added, significantly.

The landlord grunted.

"Well, now, what's the game?" asked Whalen, when Mr. Skeel had seated himself at the table.

"Revenge! That's the game!" was the fierce answer, and a fist was banged down on the table. "I want revenge, and I'm going to have it!"

"Who's the party?" demanded Murker.

"Someone you don't know, but whom you may soon. Tom Fairfield! I owe him a long score, but I'm going to begin to pay it now. I want you to help me, Whalen."

"Oh, I'll help you quick enough," was the ready answer.

"He was instrumental in having you discharged from Elmwood Hall, wasn't he?" went on the former instructor.

"That's what he was."

"Something about beating one of the smaller boys, was it not?" and Skeel smiled in a suggestive way, as though he rather relished, than otherwise, the plight of Whalen.

"Naw, I only gave the kid a few taps 'cause he threw a snowball at me," the discharged employee went on, "but that whelp, Fairfield, saw me, and complained to Doc. Meredith. Then I was fired."

"And you'd like a chance to get even, wouldn't you?"

"That's what I would!" was the harsh answer.

"Well, I want to square accounts with him also, and, at the same time, make a little money out of it. I thought you and Murker could help me, and that's why I asked you to meet me here. I'm a bit late, and that's some more of Fairfield's doings. Now to business. This is the game!"

And the three plotters drew their chairs closer together and began to talk in low, mumbling voices.

CHAPTER IV

HOLIDAY FUN

"Jolly times to-night, fellows!" exclaimed Jack Fitch as he, with Tom and the other chums, walked along the snowy road on their way back to Elmwood Hall. "No boning to do, and we can slip away with some eats on the side and have a grub-fest."

"That's right," chimed in Bert Wilson. "Maybe you'd better put off telling us about the hunting trip, Tom, until we all get together. Suppose we meet in my room—it's bigger."

"All right," agreed Tom. "Anything suits me as long as you fellows don't grab all the crackers and cheese before I get there."

"We'll save you a share," promised Morse Denton.

"I've got part of a box of oranges my folks sent me," volunteered George Abbot.

"Bring 'em along," advised Jack. "They'll come in handy to throw at the fellows if any of 'em try to break in on us."

"What! Throw my oranges!" cried George. "Say, they're the finest Indian Rivers, and——"

"All right. If they're rivers, we'll let 'em swim instead of throwing 'em," conceded Bert. "Anything to be agreeable."

"Oh, say now!" protested George, who did not always know how, or when, to take a joke.

"It's all right, don't let 'em fuss you," advised Tom in a low voice. "But, fellows, we'd better hustle if we're going to have doings to-night."

"That's right!" chorused the others, and they set off at a rapid pace toward Elmwood Hall, which could be seen in the distance, the red setting sun of the December day lighting up its tower and belfry. The skates of the students jangled and clanked as they hurried on, making a musical sound in the frosty air, for it was getting colder with the approach of night.

"Seasonable weather," murmured Jack. "It'll be a lot colder than this up in the Adirondacks, when we start hunting deer and bear."

"What's all this?" asked Morse, with a sudden show of interest.

"Some of Tom's schemes," answered Jack. "We're going on a hunting trip."

Morse looked to Tom for confirmation.

"That's the idea," Tom said, briefly sketching his plan. "Bert, Jack and George are going with me. Like to have you come along."

"I'd like to, first rate, old man," was the answer, given with a shake of the head, "but the governor has planned a trip to Palm Beach for the whole family, over Christmas, and I have to go along to keep order."

"I'm sorry," voiced Tom, but his words were lost in a gale of laughter from his chums as they sensed the final words of Morse.

"You keep order! You're a fine one for that!"

"The fellow who tied the cow to Merry's back stoop!"

"Yes, and the lad who put the smoke bomb in the furnace room! A fine chap to keep things straight!"

"Oh, well, you don't have to believe me!" said Morse, with an air of injured innocence that ill became him.

"They evidently don't," commented Tom dryly.

"Say, what was the row about just before I came back with that horse?" asked Morse, as though he wanted to change the subject.

"Snowball and old Skeel," explained Tom briefly. "It was sort of a case of a perfectly irresistible force coming in contact with a perfectly immovable body—but not quite," and he went more into the details of the accident on the ice.

"Humph! He must have been pretty mad," commented Morse.

"He was. Threatened arrest and all that. But Tom calmed him down," said Jack with a chuckle. "I guess Skeel didn't want to see the police very badly."

"What gets me, though," spoke George, in his perpetually questioning voice, "was what Skeel was doing around here."

"I'd like to know that myself," voiced Tom. But he was not to know until later, and then to his sorrow.

As the group of lads progressed, they were joined, from time to time, by other students from Elmwood, who had been out enjoying the day either by skating, coasting or sledding, and it was a merry party that approached the gate, or main entrance to the grounds, passing through the quadrangle of main buildings, and scattering to their various dormitories.

The holiday spirit was abroad. It was in the air—everywhere—the glorious spirit of Christmas, the day of which was not far distant. The boys seemed to know that the school discipline would be somewhat relaxed, though they did not take too much advantage of it.

Various engagements were made for surreptitious parties to meet here and there, to enjoy forbidden, and, therefore, all the more delightful, midnight lunches. The lads had been saving part of their allowances for some time, just for this occasion, and some had even arranged to bring away with them, from the refectory, some of their supper that night.

In due time a merry little party had gathered in the room of Bert Wilson in one of the larger and newer dormitories. The boys slid in, one by one, taking reasonable care not to meet with any prowling professor or monitor. But they knew that unless the rules were flagrantly violated, little punishment would be meted out. Each lad who came brought with him a more or less bulky package, until Bert's room looked like the headquarters of some war, earthquake or flood-relief society, as Tom said.

"And are these the oranges George boasted of?" asked Jack, taking up one and sampling it.

"Aren't they dandies?" demanded George.

"Whew! Oh, my! Who put orange skins on these lemons?" demanded Jack, making a wry face.

"Lemons?" faltered George, a look of alarm spreading over his expressive countenance.

"Lemons?" cried Tom. "Let me taste. Whew! I should say so," he added. "They're as sour as citric acid."

"And he said they came from Indian River," mocked Morse.

"Let's throw 'em out the window," proposed Joe Rooney.

"And him after them!" added Lew Bentfield.

"No, let's save them to fire at Merry in chapel in the morning," was another suggestion.

"I say, you fellows," began the badgered one, "those oranges——"

"They're all right—the boys are only stringing you," whispered Tom. "Don't get on your ear."

The advice came in good time. The arrival of other revelers turned the topic of conversation.

"Oh, here's Hen Watson. What you got, Hen?"

"A cocoanut cake!" cried someone who looked in the box Hen carried. "Where'd you get that?"

"Bought it—where'd you s'pose?" asked Hen. "Here, keep your fingers out of that!" he cried, as Jack took a sample "punch" out of the top of the pastry.

"I wanted to see if it was real," was the justifying answer.

"Oh, it's real all right."

"Here's Sam Black. What you got, Sam?"

"Why, he's all swelled up as though he had the mumps."

Sam did indeed bulge on every side. He did not speak, but, entering the room, began to unload himself of bottled soda and root beer. From every pocket he took a bottle—two from some—and others from various nooks and corners of his clothes, until the bed was half covered with bottled delight.

"Say, that's goin' some!" murmured Jack enviously.

"It sure is," agreed Tom. "We won't die of thirst from my olives now," for Tom had brought a generous supply of those among other things.

Someone leaned against the bed, and the bottles rolled together with many a clatter and clash.

"Easy there!" cautioned Bert. "Do you want to bring the whole building up here? Remember this isn't the dining-hall. Go easy!"

"I didn't mean to," spoke George, the offending one.

Gradually the room filled, until it was a task to move about in it, but this was no detriment at all to the lads. Then in the dim light of a few shaded candles, for they did not want the glimmer of the electrics to disclose the affair to some watching monitor, the feast began.

It was eminently successful, and the viands disappeared as if by magic. The empty bottles were set aside so their accidental fall would not make too much noise.

Gradually jaws began to move more slowly up and down in the process of mastication, and tongues began to wag more freely, though in guarded tones.

"This sure is one great, little Christmas feed!" commented Jack.

"All to the horse-radish," agreed Tom. "But it's nothing to what we'll have when we get up in the Adirondack camp, fellows. I wish you were all coming."

"So do we!" chorused those who were not going, for various reasons.

"Hark! What's that?" suddenly cried George. Instantly there was silence.

"Nothing but the wind," said Tom. "Say, fellows," he went on, "I have an idea."

"Chain it!" advised Jack. "They're rare birds these days."

"Let's hear what it is," suggested Bert. "If it's any good, we'll do it."

CHAPTER V

OFF TO CAMP

Tom Fairfield disposed himself comfortably on the bed before replying. There was room there, now, for the food and drink had been disposed of. Tom stretched out, finished a half-consumed sardine sandwich, and went on.

"You know old Efficiency, don't you?" began Tom, with tantalizing slowness.

"I should say we did!" came in a whispered chorus.

"The prof who's always lecturing on improving your opportunities, isn't he?" asked a student who had not been at Elmwood very long.

"That's the one," resumed Tom. "You know he claims we all eat and drink too much. He holds that a person should find the minimum amount of food on which he can live, and take no more than that."

"I've had more than my share to-night, all right," comfortably murmured Jack.

"And Efficiency, as we call him," went on Tom, "is a hater of feasting of any sort, unless it be a feast of reason. I think he lives on half a cracker and a gill of milk a day, or something like that."

"Well, what's the idea?" asked Bert, impatiently.

"This," answered Tom, calmly. "We will take the remains of our herewith feast, the broken victuals, the things in which they were contained, the empty tins, the depleted bottles, and deposit them on the doorstep of the domicile of Professor Hazeltine, otherwise known as Old Efficiency. When they are seen there it will show to the world that he does not practice what he preaches."

There was silence for a moment following Tom's announcement, and then came chuckles and smothered laughter.

"Say, that's a good one all right!"

"It sure is!"

"Ha! Ha! Ha! It takes Tom Fairfield to think 'em out!"

"Easy there!" Bert cautioned them. "You'll give the whole snap away, if you're not careful."

"Well, shall we do it?" asked Tom.

"I should say we will!" declared Jack.

"Then gather up the stuff and come along, a few at a time," advised the ringleader. "We don't want to make too much noise."

A little later dark and silent figures might have been observed stealing across the school campus, carrying various objects. The front stoop of the professor, who was such a stickler for efficiency and the maximum of effect with the minimum of effort, was in the shadow, and soon it was piled high with many things.

Emptied sardine tins, olive bottles which contained only the appetizing odor, pasteboard cartons of crackers or other cakes, ginger-ale bottles with only a few drops of the beverage in the bottom, papers and paper bags, the pasteboard circlets from Charlotte russes—these and many more things from the forbidden midnight feast were piled on the steps. Then the conspirators stole away, one by one, as they had come.

Tom Fairfield lingered last to make a more artistic arrangement of the empty bottles; then he, too, joined his chums.

"I rather guess that'll make 'em lie down and close their eyes," he said, in distinction to the process of "sitting up and taking notice."

"It sure will," agreed Jack, with a chuckle.

There were whispered good-nights, pre-holiday greetings and then the students sought their rooms, for there was a limit beyond which they did not want to stretch matters.

In the morning they were sufficiently rewarded for their efforts—if rewarded be the proper word.

Professor Hazeltine, going to his front door to get his early morning paper, saw the array of bottles and debris. At first he could not believe the evidence of his eyesight, but a second look convinced him that he could not be mistaken.

"The shame of it!" he murmured. "The shame of that disgraceful gorging of food. They must be made an example of—no matter who they are. The shame of it! I shall report them! Oh, the waste here represented! The shameful waste of food! I suppose all that is here represented was consumed in a single night. It might have lasted a month. I shall see that they are punished, not only for their disgraceful action in thus littering my stoop, but for gorging themselves like beasts!"

But the professor forgot one thing, namely, that to punish a culprit one must first know who he is, and how to catch him. It was the old application of first get your rabbit, though doubtless the professor would have changed the proverb to some milder form of food.

However, he took up his paper, ordered the servant to remove the debris, and then proceeded to his simple breakfast of a certain bran-like food mingled with milk, a bit of dry toast and a cup of corn-coffee. After which, bristling with as much indignation as he could summon on such cold and clammy food, he went to Dr. Meredith and complained.

The Head smiled tolerantly.

"You must remember that it is the holiday season," he said. "Boys will be boys."

"But, Doctor, I do not so much object to the disgraceful exhibition they made of me. I can stand that. No one who knows me, or my principles, would think for a moment that I could consume the amount of food represented there."

"No, I think you would be held guiltless of that," agreed the President.

"But it is the fact that the young men—our students—could so demean themselves like beasts as to partake of so much gross food," went on Professor Hazeltine. "After all my talks, showing the amount of work that can be done, mental and physical, on a simple preparation of whole wheat, to think of them having eaten sardines, smoked beef, canned tongue, potted ham, canned chicken—for I found tins representing all those things on my steps, Dr. Meredith. It was awful!"

"Yes, the boys must have had a bountiful feast," agreed the President with a sigh.

Was it a sigh of regret that his days for enjoying such forbidden midnight "feeds" were over? For he was human.

"I want those boys punished, not so much for what they did to me as for their own sakes," demanded Professor Hazeltine. "They must learn that the brain works best on lighter foods, and that to clog the body with gross meat is but to stop the delicate machinery of the——"

"Yes, yes, I know," said Dr. Meredith, a bit wearily. He had heard all that before. "Well, I suppose the boys did do wrong, and if you will bring me their names, I will speak to them. Bring me their names, Professor Hazeltine."

But that was easier said than done. Not that "Efficiency" did not make the effort, but it was a hopeless task. Of course none of the boys would "peach," and no one else knew who had been involved.

Professor Hazeltine came in for some fun, mildly poked at him by other members of the faculty.

"I understand you had quite a banquet over at your house last night," remarked Professor Wirt.

"It was—disgraceful!" exploded the aggrieved one, and he went on to point out how the human body could live for weeks on a purely cereal diet, with cold water only for drinking purposes.

So the boys had their fun; at least, it was fun for them, and no great harm was done. Nor did Professor Hazeltine discover who were the culprits.

The school was about to close for the long holiday vacation. Already some of the students, living at a distance, had departed. There were the final days, when discipline was more than ever relaxed. Few lectures were given, and fewer attended.

Then came the last day, when farewells echoed over the campus.

"Good-bye! Good-bye!"

"Merry Christmas!"

"Happy New Year!"

"See you after the holidays!"

"Get together now, fellows, a last cheer for old Elmwood Hall! We won't see her again until next year!"

Tom Fairfield led in the cheering, and then, gathering his particular chums about him, gave a farewell song. Then followed cheers for Dr. Meredith, and someone called:

"Three cheers for Professor Hazeltine! May his digestion never grow worse!"

The cheers were given with a will, ending with a burst of laughter, for the professor in question was observed to be shaking his fist at the students out of his window. He had not forgiven the midnight feast and its ending.

"Well, we'll soon be on our way," said Tom to Bert, Jack and George, as they sat together in the railroad train, for they all lived in the same part of New Jersey, and were on their way home.

"What's the plan?" asked George.

"We'll all meet at my house," proposed Tom, "and go to New York City from there. Then we can take the express for the Adirondacks. We go to a small station called Hemlock Junction, and travel the rest of the distance in a sleigh. We'll go to No. 1 Camp first, and see how we like it. If we can't get enough game there, we'll go on to the other camps. As I told you, we'll have the use of all three. None of the members of the club will be up there this season."

"But will whoever is in charge let us in?" asked Jack.

"Yes, all arrangements have been made," Tom said. "There is grub up there, bedclothes, and everything. All we'll take is our clothes, guns and cameras."

"Yes, don't forget the cameras," urged Bert. "I expect to get some fine snapshots up there."

"And I hope we get some good gun-shots," put in Tom. "We're going on a hunting trip, please remember."

The time of preparation passed quickly, and a few days later, and shortly after Christmas, the boys found themselves in the Grand Central Station, New York, ready to take the train for camp.

They piled their belongings about them in the parlor car, and then proceeded to talk of the delights ahead of them, delights in which their fellow passengers shared, for they listened with evident pleasure to the conversation of our friends.

CHAPTER VI
DISQUIETING NEWS

Three men sat in the back room of the road-house, talking in whispers, a much-stained table forming the nucleus of the group. Two of the men were of evil faces, one not so much, perhaps, as the other, while the third man's countenance showed some little refinement, though it was overlaid with grossness, and the light in the eyes was baleful.

The men were the same three who foregathered as Tom Fairfield and his chums left the scene of the snowball accident, and it was the same day as that occurrence. It must not be supposed that the men had been there during all the time I have taken to describe the holiday scenes at Elmwood Hall.

But I left the three men there, plotting, and now it is time to return to them, since Tom and his chums are well on their way to the winter camps in the Adirondacks.

"Well, what do you think of that plan?" asked Professor Skeel, for he was one of the three men in the back room.

"It sounds all right," half-growled, rather than spoke, the man called Murker.

"If it can be done," added the other—Whalen.

"Why can't it be done?" demanded the former instructor. "You did your part, didn't you? You found out where they were going, and all that?"

"Oh, yes, I attended to that," was the answer. "But I don't want to get into trouble over this thing, and it sounds to me like trouble. It's a serious business to take——"

"Never mind. You needn't go into details," said Professor Skeel, quickly, stopping his henchman with a warning look, as he glanced toward the door through which the landlord had made his egress.

"But I don't want to be arrested on a charge of——" the other insisted.

"There'll be no danger at all!" broke in the rascally teacher. "I'll do the actual work myself. I'll take all the blame. All I want is your help. I had to have someone get the information for me, and you did that very well, Whalen. No one else could have done it."

"Yes, I guess I pumped him dry enough," was the chuckling comment.

"It's a pity you had to go and get yourself discharged, though," went on Mr. Skeel. "You would be much more useful to me at Elmwood Hall than out of it. But it can't be helped, I suppose."

"I didn't go and get myself discharged!" whined he who was called Whalen. "It was that whelp, Tom Fairfield, who was to blame."

The man did not seem to count his own disgraceful conduct at all.

"Well, if Tom Fairfield was to blame, so much the better. We can kill two birds with one stone in his case," chuckled the professor. "Now I think we understand each other. We needn't meet again until we are up—well, we'll say up North. That's indefinite enough in case anyone hears us talking, and I don't altogether like the looks of this landlord here."

"No, he's too nosey," agreed Murker. "Well, if that's settled, I guess we're ready for the next move," and he looked significantly at Mr. Skeel.

"Eh? What's that?" came the query.

"We could use a little money," suggested the evil-faced man.

"Money. Oh, yes. I did promise to bring you some. Well, here it is," and the former instructor divided some bills between his followers and fellow plotters.

"Now I'll leave here alone," he went on. "I don't want to be seen in your company outside."

"Not good enough for you, I reckon," sneered Whalen.

"Well, it might lead to—er—complications," was the retort. "So give me half an hour's start. I'm going to drive back where I hired this cutter, and then take a train. You follow me in two days and I rather guess Tom Fairfield will wish he'd kept his fingers out of my pie!" cried Mr. Skeel, with a burst of anger.

The three whispered together a few minutes longer, and then the former instructor came out of the road-house alone and drove off.

"What do you think of him?" asked Murker of Whalen.

"Not an awful lot," was the answer. "But he'll pay us well, and it will give me a chance to get square with that Fairfield pup. I owe him something."

"Well, I don't care anything about him, one way or the other," was the rejoinder. "I went into this thing because you asked me to, and to make a bit of money. If I do that, I'm satisfied. Now let's get cigars and slide out of here at once."

And thus the plotters separated.

Meanwhile, Tom and his friends were a merry party. They talked, laughed and joked, now and then casting glances at their pile of baggage, which included gun cases and cameras. For they were to do both kinds of hunting in the mountain camps, and they were particularly interested in camera work, since they were taking up something of nature study in their school course.

The railroad trip was without incident of moment, if we except one little matter. It was when George Abbot mentioned casually the name of Whalen, one of the men employed at Elmwood Hall.

"I wonder why he left so suddenly?" George said, as they were speaking of some happening at school.

"I guess I was to blame for that," Tom explained, as he related the incident of the cruel treatment on the part of Whalen.

"I thought he looked rather sour," went on George.

"Why, were you talking to him lately?" asked Tom, a sudden look of interest on his face.

"Yes, the day before we left the Hall. He met me in town and borrowed a quarter from me. Said he wanted to send a telegram to friends who would give him work. Then he and I got talking, and I happened to mention that we fellows were going camping."

"You did!" exclaimed Tom.

"This Whalen was quite interested," resumed George. "He asked me a lot of questions about the location of the camps, and what route we were going to take."

"Did you tell him?" demanded Tom.

"Why, yes, I told him some things. Any harm?"

"No, I don't know that there was," spoke Tom more slowly and thoughtfully. "But did Whalen say why he wanted to know all that?"

"No, not definitely. He did mention, though, that he might look for a job somewhere up North, and I suppose that was why he asked so many questions."

"Maybe," said Tom, in a low voice. Then he did some hard thinking.

In due time Hemlock Junction was reached. This was the end of the train journey, and the boys piled out with their baggage, their guns and cameras. It was cold and snowing.

"I guess that's our man over there," remarked Tom, indicating a person in a big overcoat with a fur cap and a red scarf around his neck. "Does he look as though his name was Sam Wilson?" asked our hero of his chums.

"Why Sam Wilson?" asked Jack.

"Because that's the name of the man who was to meet us and drive us over to camp," Tom said.

The man, with a smile illuminating his red face, approached.

"Looks to be plenty of room in the pung," remarked Tom.

"What's a pung?" asked George.

"That big sled, sort of two bobs made into one, with only a single set of runners," explained Tom, indicating the sled to which were hitched four horses, whose every movement jingled a chime of musical bells.

"Be you the Fairfield crowd?" asked the man.

"That's us," Tom said. "Are you Sam Wilson?"

"Yes."

"Then, we are discovered, as the Indians said to Columbus," Jack murmured, in a low voice.

"Pile in," invited Sam Wilson, indicating the pung. "I'll get your traps. Ain't this fine weather, though?"

"It's a bit cold," Bert remarked.

"That's what a party said that I drove over to your camp the other day," spoke Sam. "He was from down Jersey way, too. You fellers must be sort of cold-blooded down thar! This chap complained of the cold. But pshaw! This is mild to what we have sometimes. Yes, this feller I drove over kept rubbin' his ears all the while. One ear was terrible red, and it wasn't all from the cold either. It had some sort of a scar on it, like it had been chawed by some wild critter. It sure was a funny ear!"

Tom looked at his chums with startled gaze. This was disquieting news indeed.

CHAPTER VII

AT CAMP

Seemingly by common consent on the part of Tom's chums, it was left for him to further question Sam Wilson and learn more about the man the caretaker had driven over to the hunting camp. And Tom was not slow to follow up the matter. He had his own suspicions, but he wanted to verify them.

"You say you drove someone over to our camp yesterday?" Tom asked.

"Not yesterday, the day before," was the answer. "And it wasn't exactly to your camp, but near it. Your camp is a private one, you know—that is, it belongs to an association, and I understand you boys are to have full run of all three places."

"Yes, the gentlemen who make up the organization very kindly gave us that privilege," assented Tom.

"Then you're the only ones allowed to use the camps," went on Sam. "I'll see to that, being the official keeper. I'm in charge the year around, and sometimes I am pretty hard put to keep people out that have no business in. So, naturally, I wouldn't drive no stranger over to one of my camps—I call 'em mine," he added with a smile, "but of course I'm only the keeper."

"We understand," spoke Tom, and his tone was grave.

"Well, then you understand I wouldn't let anyone in at the camps unless they came introduced, same as you boys did."

"Well, where did you drive this man then—this man with——" began George, but Jack silenced him with a look, nodding as much as to say that it was Tom's privilege to do the questioning.

"I drove this man over to Hounson's place," resumed the camp-keeper, as he saw that all the baggage was piled in the pung. "This man Hounson keeps what he calls a hunters' camp, but shucks! It's nothing more than a sort of hotel in the woods. Some hunters do put up there, but none of the better sort.

"The gentlemen who own the three camps you're going to tried to buy up Hounson's place, as they didn't like him and his crowd around here, but he wouldn't sell. That's where I took this Jersey man who complained of the cold. Kept rubbing his ears, and one of 'em was chawed, just as if some wild critter had him down and chawed him. 'Course I didn't say anything about it, as I thought maybe it might be a tender subject with him. But I left him at Hounson's."

"Did he say what his name was?" asked Tom, but he only asked to gain time to think over what he had heard, for he was sure he knew who the man with the "chawed" ear was.

"No, he didn't tell me his name, and I didn't ask him," Sam said. "Whoa there!" he called to his horses, for they showed an impatience to be off.

"Some folks are sort of delicate about giving out their names," went on the guide when the steeds were quieted, "and as I'm a sort of public character, being the stage driver, when there's one to drive, I didn't feel like going into details. So I just asked him where he wanted to go, and he told me. Outside of that, and a little talk about the weather, him remarking that he come from Jersey, that's all the talk we had.

"But maybe you boys know him," he went on, as a thought came to him. "He was from Jersey, and so are you. Do you happen to know who he is?" he asked.

"We couldn't say—for sure," spoke Tom, which was true enough.

"Well, maybe you'll get a chance to see him," went on Sam Wilson. "Hounson's isn't far from your first camp, where we're going to head for in a minute or so. You could go over there. You probably will have to, anyhow, if you want your mail, for the only postoffice for these parts is located there. And you'll probably see your man.

"To tell you the truth, I didn't take much of a notion to the feller. He was too sullen and glum-like to suit me. I like a man to take some interest in life."

"Didn't this man do that?" asked Tom, as he stowed his gun away on the straw-covered bottom of the pung.

"Not a cent's worth!" cried Sam, who was hearty and bluff enough to suit anyone, and jolly in the bargain. "This chap sort of wrapped himself up in one of my fur robes, like one of them blanket Indians I read about out West, and he hardly spoke the whole trip. But you'll probably see him over at Hounson's. Well, are you boys all ready?"

"I guess so," assented Bert, as he slung his camera over his shoulder by a strap. He hoped to get a chance at a snapshot.

"Well, then we'll start," went on Sam. "Pile in boys, and wrap them fur robes and blankets well around your legs. It's colder riding than it is walking. So bundle up. It'll be colder, too, when we get out of town a ways. We're in sort of a holler here, and that cuts off the wind."

"What about grub?" asked Jack. "Do we need to take anything with us? I see a store over there," and he indicated one near the small depot.

"Don't need to buy a thing," said Sam. "Every one of the three camps is well stocked. There's bacon, ham, eggs, besides lots of canned stuff, and I make a trip in to town twice a week. As for fresh meat, why, you'll probably shoot all that you want, I reckon," and he seemed to take that as a matter of course.

"Say, look here!" exclaimed Tom, determined not to sail under false colors, nor have his companions in the same boat. "We aren't regular hunters, you know. This is about the first time we ever came on a big hunting trip like this, and maybe——"

"Don't say another word!" exclaimed Sam, good-naturedly. "I understand just how it is. I'm glad you owned up to it, though," he went on, with a twinkle in his blue eyes. "Some fellers would have tried to bluff it out, but I guess me and some of the other natives around here, would have spotted you soon enough.

"But as long as you say you haven't had much experience, and as long as you ain't ashamed of it, I'll see that you get plenty of game. I'll take you to the best places, and show you how to shoot."

"Of course we know how to use guns, and we've hunted a little," Tom said, not wanting it to appear that they were absolute novices. And he added: "We're pretty good shots in a rifle gallery, too. But it's different out in the woods."

"I know!" cried Sam. "I understand. You don't need to worry. You won't starve, if that's what's troubling you. Now I guess we'll get along," and the horses stepped proudly out over the snowy road. Bells made a merry jingle as the party of boy hunters started for their first camp.

"Say, Tom," spoke Jack in a low voice to his chum, "do you think that was Skeel, the man with the 'chawed' ear, who was driven over to Hounson's?"

"I'm almost sure of it," was the answer.

"Well, what in the world is his object in coming away up here and at the same time we're due?"

"Give it up. We'll have to look for the answer later," was Tom's reply.

Out on the open road the horses increased their speed, and soon the pung, under the powerful pull of the animals, was sliding along at a fast clip. Much sooner than the boys had expected, they saw, down in a little valley clearing, a comfortable looking log-cabin, and at the sight of it Sam Wilson called out:

"There she is, boys! That's your first camp!"

CHAPTER VIII

THE FIRST HUNT

The pung came to a stop at the head of a driveway that led up to the log cabin, which was situated in a little clearing in the dense woods all about it. Tom and his chums gave one look at the structure which was to be their home, or one of them for several weeks, and were about to leap out of the sled, when Sam stopped them by a sudden exclamation.

"Hold on a minute, boys!" he said. "I want to take a look there before you step out in the snow."

"What's the matter? Are there traps set under the drifts?" asked Bert.

"No, but it looks to me like someone had been tramping around that cabin. I never made them footprints," and he pointed to some in the snow.

The snow on the driveway, leading from the main road through the woods, up to the hunting cabin itself, was not disturbed or broken by the marks of any sled runners or horses' hoofs. There were, however, several lines of human footprints leading in both directions.

"Just a moment now, boys," cautioned Sam, who was following a certain line of footprints, at the same time stepping in a former line, that he had evidently made himself, for his boots just fitted in them.

"What in the world is he doing?" asked George. "Has anything happened? Has a crime been committed? Is he looking for evidence? Why doesn't he go right up to the cabin?"

"Any more questions?" asked Jack, as the other paused for breath. "It seems like old times, Why, to hear you rattle on in that fashion."

"Aw——" began George, but that was as far as he got. Sam was ready now, to make an announcement.

"I thought so!" exclaimed the guide. "There has been someone else up here since I left this morning. Someone has been snooping around here, and they hadn't any right to, as this is private property."

"Did he get in?" asked Bert, thinking perhaps all the "grub" might have been taken.

"Don't seem to have gone in," replied Sam. "Whoever it was made a complete circle around the cabin, though, as if he was looking for something. You can see the tracks real plain," he went on. "Here is where I came up this morning, to see that everything was all right, for I expected you boys this afternoon," he went on. "And here is where I came back," and he pointed out his second line of footprints. "And here is where Mr. Stranger started up, went around the cabin, and came out on the main road again," the guide resumed. "No, he didn't get in, but he looked in the windows all right."

This the boys could see for themselves, for they were now out of the pung, there being no further need of not obliterating the strange footprints.

Tom and his chums noticed where the intruder had paused beneath several of the low cabin windows, as though trying to peer inside. And another thing Tom noticed; in the broad sole-impression of each boot-mark of the stranger's feet was the outline of a star, made in hob nails with which the soles were studded.

"I'll know that footprint if I see it again," thought Tom. "But I wonder who it was that was spying around this cabin?"

Sam, however, did not seem to be unduly alarmed over his discovery. George asked him:

"Who do you s'pose it was that made those marks?"

"Oh, some stray hunter," was the answer. "They often get curious, just like a deer, and come up to see what's going on. No use getting mad about it, as long as no harm's done, and they didn't try to get in. Of course, in case of a blizzard, I wouldn't find fault if a man took shelter in one of the cabins, even if he had to break in. A man's got a right to save his life."

"Do you have bad storms up here?" Bert wanted to know.

"I should say we did!" Sam exclaimed, "and from now on you can count on a storm or a blizzard 'most any day. So watch out for yourselves and carry a compass with you. But here I am chinning away when you want to get in and warm up and tackle the grub. Come on!"

He unlocked the door with a key he carried, and the boys gazed with interest at the interior of the shack. It suited them to perfection.

The cabin contained three rather large rooms. One was the kitchen and dining-room combined, another was sort of a sitting or living-room, made comfortable with rugs on the floor, and a fireplace in which big logs could be burned, while in the middle of the room was a table covered with books and magazines. The third room, opening from the living apartment, was where several bunks were arranged, and the momentary glimpse the boys had of them seemed to promise a fine place to rest at night.

A second glance into the kitchen showed a goodly stock of food. There was a stove, with a fire laid ready for lighting; and a pile of kindling and logs on the hearth was also prepared for ignition. In short, the place was as comfortable as could be desired, and with a blazing fire on the hearth, the knowledge that there was plenty of "grub" in the pantry, and with a blizzard raging outside, there was little more that could be desired—at least, the boys thought that would be perfect.

"Can you fellows cook?" demanded Sam.

"Well, we can make a stab at it," answered Jack.

"We've done some camping," spoke Tom, modestly enough. "I guess we can get up some sort of a meal."

"All right. Then I'll leave you, for I've got to get back to my farm," the guide explained. "Of course there isn't much to do in the Winter, but attend to the chores and feed the stock, but they have to be looked after. I live about seven miles from here," he explained, as he brought in the baggage, guns and cameras. "Now the two other camps, that go with this one, are several miles from here, almost in a straight line. There's a map showing just how to get to 'em," he said, indicating a blueprint drawing on the cabin wall. "Study that and you won't get lost. But if you can't find the other camps when you want to, I'll come and show you."

"Oh, I guess we can manage," said Tom, who was getting off his coat preparatory to helping start the fires and cooking.

"I'll stop and see you about once in four days, in case you need anything," Sam went on. "Just pin a note to the door of the cabin you last leave, saying where you're going, or whether you're coming back, so's I'll know where to look for you. My farm is located about half way between Camp No. 1, that's this one, and Camp No. 3, which is the farthest off.

"Well, now if you think you can manage, I'll leave you. It's getting on toward night, and my folks will be looking for me," and Sam prepared to start for home.

"We can get along all right," Tom assured him. "And may we begin hunting whenever we want to?"

"Start in now if you like, but I'd advise waiting until to-morrow," the guide said, with a chuckle.

"Yes, we'll wait," agreed Jack.

Though the four chums had never been to a real hunters' camp before, they had often shifted for themselves in the woods, or at some lake, and though they were perhaps not as expert housekeepers as girls, or women, they managed to get up a good meal in comparatively short time.

The fire was started in the kitchen stove, and another blaze was soon roaring up the big chimney in the living-room. This would take the chill off the bunk-room, for it was very cold in there, the windows being covered with a coating of ice.

"Baked beans—from a can—bacon and eggs—coffee and canned peaches, with bread and butter. How does that strike you for the first meal?" asked Tom, who had been looking through the cupboard.

"Fine!" cried Jack. "But what about bread? If there's any here, it will be as stale as a rock."

"Sam had some in the sled. His wife baked it, I guess," said Tom, indicating a bundle on the table. "I found some butter in a jar here."

"Then start the meal!" cried Bert. "I'm hungry."

They all were, and they did ample justice to the viands that were soon set forth. The cabin was filled with the appetizing odor of bacon and coffee, and wagging tongues were momentarily stilled, for jaws were busy chewing.

Rough and ready, yet sufficiently effective, was the dish-washing, and then came a comfortable evening, sitting before the crackling blaze on the hearth, while they talked over the experiences of the closing day.

They were all rather sleepy, from the cold wind they had faced on the sled ride, and soon were ready to turn in. Just before banking the fire for the night, Tom paused, and stood in a listening attitude near one of the windows.

"What's the matter?" asked Jack.

"I thought I heard something," was the reply.

"He's worried about the man whose footprints Sam saw in the snow," said George.

"Or the man with the 'chawed' ear," added Bert.

"No, it was the wind, I guess," Tom spoke. "But say, fellows, what do you think Skeel is doing up here?"

"Is he here?" questioned Jack.

"Well, that 'chawed' ear makes it sound so."

They discussed the matter for some time longer and then sought the comfortable bunks. Nothing disturbed them during the night, or if there were unusual noises the boys did not hear them, for they all slept soundly.

They awoke to find the sun shining gloriously, and after breakfast Tom got down his gun, an example followed by the others.

"Now for a hunt!" he cried. "Some rabbit stew, or fried squirrel, wouldn't go half bad."

"Or a bit of venison or a plump partridge," added Jack. "On with the hunt!"

CHAPTER IX

AN UNEXPECTED MEETING

Tom and his chums had no false notions about their hunting trip. They did not expect much in the way of big game, though they had been told that at some seasons bear and deer were plentiful. But while they had hopes that they might bag one of those large animals, they were not too sanguine.

"We'll stand better chances on deer than bears," said Tom. "For the bears are likely to be 'holed up' by now, though there may be one or two stray ones out that haven't fatted up enough to insure a comfortable sleep all Winter. Of course the deer aren't like that. They don't hibernate."

"What!" laughed Bert. "Say it again, and say it slow."

"Get out!" cried Tom. "You know what I mean."

"Well, we might get a brace of fat partridges, or a couple of rabbits," Jack said. "I'll be satisfied with them for a starter."

"Well, I know one thing I'm going to get right now!" exclaimed Bert, with a sudden motion.

"Do you see anything?" demanded Jack, bringing forward his rifle.

"I'm going to snapshot that view! It's a dandy!" Bert went on, as he opened his camera.

"Oh! Only a picture! I thought it was a bear at least!" cried Tom.

But Bert calmly proceeded to get the view he wanted. He was perhaps more enthusiastic over camera work than the others, though they all liked to dabble in the pastime, and each one had some fine pictures to his credit.

"Well, if you're done making snapshots, let's go on and do some real shooting," proposed Jack.

He and Tom each had a rifle, while Bert and George had shotguns, so they were equipped for any sort of game they were likely to meet. For an hour or more they tramped on through the snow-covered woods, taking care to note their direction by means of a compass, for they were on strange ground, and did not want to get lost on their first hunting trip.

As they came out of a dense patch of scrubby woods, into a little semi-cleared place, a whirr of wings startled all of them.

"There they go—partridges!" yelled Bert, bringing up his gun and firing quickly.

"Missed!" he groaned a moment later as he saw the brace of plump birds whirr on without so much as a feather ruffled.

"You don't know how to shoot!" grunted Jack. "You're not quick enough."

"Well, I'd like to see you shoot anything when it jumps up right from under your feet, and almost knocks you over," was Bert's defence of himself.

"That's right," chimed in George. "I couldn't get my gun ready, either, before they were out of sight."

"You've got to be always on the lookout," said Tom. "Well, the first miss isn't so bad. None of us is in proper shape yet. We'll get there after a while."

A little disappointed at their first failure, the boys went on again, watching eagerly from side to side as they advanced. No more did Bert use his camera. He wanted to make good on a real shot.

"Well, there's game here, that's certain," said Tom. "If we can only get it!"

Almost as he spoke there was a whirr at his very feet. He started back, and half raised his rifle, not thinking, for the moment, that it was not a shotgun. Then he cried:

"Bert! George! Quick, wing 'em!"

George was quicker than his companion. Up to his shoulder went his weapon and the woods echoed to the shot that followed.

"You got him!" cried Bert, as he saw a bird flutter to the snow. Bert himself fired at the second partridge, and had the satisfaction of knocking off a few feathers, but that was all. But George, who had not thought to fire his second barrel, ran forward and picked up the bird he had bagged. It was a plump partridge.

"That will make part of our meal to-morrow," he said, proudly, as he put it in the game bag Tom carried.

"Say, we've struck a good spot all right!" exclaimed Jack. "It's up to us now, Tom, to do something."

"That's what it is," agreed his chum.

But if they expected to have a succession and continuation of that good luck they were disappointed, for they tramped on for about three miles more without seeing anything.

"Better not go too far," advised Tom. "Remember that we've got to walk back again, and it gets dark early at this season."

"Let's eat grub here and then bear off to the left," suggested Jack.

They had brought some sandwiches with them, and also a coffee pot and tin cups. They found a sheltered spot, and made a fire, boiling the coffee which they drank as they munched their sandwiches.

"This is something like!" murmured Bert, his mouth half full.

"That's what," agreed George. "You wouldn't know from looking around here that there was such a place as Elmwood Hall."

The meal over, they again took up the march, and they had not gone far before Tom, who was a little in advance, started a big white rabbit. He saw the bunny, and then almost lost sight of it again, so well did its white coat of fur blend with the snow. But in another instant Tom's keen eye saw it turning at an angle.

He raised his rifle.

"You can't hit it with that!" cried Jack.

But Tom was a better shot than his chum gave him credit for being. As the gun cracked, the rabbit gave a convulsive leap and came down in a heap on the snow.

"By Jove! You did bag him!" cried Jack, admiringly.

"Of course," answered Tom coolly, as though he had intended doing that all along, whereas he well knew, as did his chums, that the shot was pure luck, for it takes a mighty good hunter to get a rabbit with a rifle bullet.

However, the bunny was added to the game bag, and then, for some time, the boys had no further luck. A little later, when they were well on their way back, Jack saw a plump gray squirrel on a tree. Bert was near him, but on the wrong side, and Jack, taking his chum's gun, brought down the animal, which further increased their luck that day.

"Well, we've got all we want to eat for a while. What do you say we quit?" suggested Tom. "No use killing just for fun."

"That's right," agreed his chums.

"We won't fire at anything unless it's a deer or a bear," went on Bert, laughing.

As they neared their cabin they were all startled by a movement in the bush ahead of them. It sounded as though some heavy body was forcing its way along.

"There's a deer—or bear!" whispered Jack, raising his rifle.

"Don't shoot at anything you can't see," was Tom's good advice. And the next moment there stepped into view of the boys the figure of Professor Skeel. He was almost as startled on seeing the four chums as they were at beholding him.

CHAPTER X

AT CAMP NO. 2

Professor Skeel might well have shrunk back at the sight which confronted him, for Jack stood poised, with raised weapon, as though he had it pointed at the former instructor. But Professor Skeel did not shrink back. He gazed at the boys, though there was evidence of surprise on his face.

"I—I beg your pardon," said Jack, for he could not forget the time when the crabbed man had been in authority over him. "I—I—didn't see you there," Jack went on.

"Evidently not," said the man, dryly. "You had better be careful what you do with a gun."

"I am careful," answered Jack, a trifle nettled at the words and manner of Mr. Skeel. "I wasn't going to fire until I saw you."

"Oh," said Mr. Skeel.

"I—I didn't mean just that," Jack went on. "I meant I was going to see what it was before I shot."

That was decidedly the better way of putting it.

"You—you are quite a ways from—from Elmwood Hall," said Tom, changing from his first intention of saying "home," for he recollected he did not know where Professor Skeel lived.

"Yes, I am up here on—business," went on the unpopular man. "And I trust there aren't any hills where you can roll down big snowballs," he added significantly.

"You seem to forget that was an accident," Tom said. He did not altogether like Professor Skeel's tone.

"Well, I don't want any accidents like that to happen up here," went on the former teacher. "And now another matter. Are you boys following me? If you are, I warn you that I will not tolerate it. You must leave me alone. I have business to do up here, and——"

"We most decidedly are not following you!" exclaimed Tom, with emphasis. "Besides, we are on private grounds, the use of which we were granted for this holiday season, and——"

"Is that a polite request for me to—get off?" asked Mr. Skeel.

"Well, no, not exactly," Tom answered. "We are not the owners, but we have the privilege of hunting here. It is possible that the caretaker may order you off. But you have no right to say that we are following you. We have a right here."

"I didn't say you were—I only asked if you were," said Mr. Skeel, who seemed to "come down off his high horse a bit," as Jack said afterward.

"Then I'll say that you are entirely mistaken," went on Tom. "We were out hunting, and we came upon you unexpectedly. We were as much surprised as you were, though we guessed you were in the neighborhood."

"You did?" cried Professor Skeel, with sudden energy. He seemed both startled and angry. "Who told you?" he demanded.

"Sam Wilson, the man who drove you over from the depot to Hounson's place," replied Tom, who had no reason for concealment, and who also wanted to show that he knew the whereabouts of Mr. Skeel.

"I never told him my name!" declared the former instructor.

Tom did not care to state that they had guessed the identity of the man by the description of his injured ear. The member was in plain sight as Tom looked—a ragged, torn lobe, of angry-red color, and it did look, as Sam had said, as though it had been "chawed by some critter."

"You seem to know considerable of my affairs," went on Mr. Skeel. "But I want to warn you that I will tolerate no spying on my movements, and if you try any of your foolish schoolboy tricks, I shall inform the authorities." He glared at Tom as he said this, as though challenging him to make a threat. Doubtless the professor knew that any charges which might lie against him in New Jersey would be ineffective in the Adirondacks. But Tom did not care to press that matter now.

"You need not fear that we will spy on you," said the leader of the young hunters. "And as for playing tricks, we have something else to do, Mr. Skeel."

"Very well; see that you keep to it."

He turned as though to go away, and, as he did so the boys saw two other men advancing up a woodland path toward the professor.

Mr. Skeel made a quick motion toward the men, exactly, as Bert said afterward, as though he wanted to warn them back. But either they did not see, or understand, the warning gestures, or else they chose to ignore them, for they came up the inclined snowy path, until they stood in full view of the four boys. At the sight of one of the men, Tom uttered an exclamation, that was echoed by his chums.

"Whalen!" he murmured, recognizing the discharged employee, for whose dismissal he was, in a great measure, responsible, since he had made a report of the man's cruelty to a young student at Elmwood Hall.

"We were looking——" began Whalen, speaking to the professor, when he happened to recognize the four young hunters, whom he had evidently failed to notice, as they stood somewhat in the shadow of a big pine tree, and were well wrapped up from the cold.

"Never mind now," said Mr. Skeel, quickly, as though to keep the man silent. "I was just going back to you. It seems we are on private grounds."

"Well, what of that?" jeered the other man, who had not yet spoken. He had a brutal, evil face.

"Lots of it, if you're not careful," snapped Tom, who did not like the fellow's tone, or manner.

"Oh, is that so, young feller? Well, I'd have you know——"

The man stopped suddenly, for Whalen had administered a quiet kick, and whispered something in his ear. What he said the boys could not hear, but they saw the warning and quieting chastisement.

"Oh," and the other man, who had been addressed as Murker, seemed to swallow the rest of his words.

"Come on," said Professor Skeel, and without a further look at the four chums he turned away, followed by the two men with evil faces.

"Whew! This is going some!" gasped Jack, when the trio was out of sight. "Who'd think of meeting Skeel and those two worthies up here in the wilderness?"

"Well, we practically knew Skeel was here," said Bert, "though we aren't any nearer than we were in guessing at what his object is. But it is a surprise to see Whalen and that other man, whoever he is. They must be trailing in with Skeel. What's the game, Tom?"

Tom Fairfield did not answer for a moment. He was busy looking at some tracks in the snow.

"Yes, they are just the same," he murmured, slowly.

"What is it? A bear?" asked George, eagerly.

"No, but look," and Tom pointed to some footprints. In the middle of the sole of each one was a star made in hob nails.

"Why—why, that's the same mark that was near our cabin," cried Jack.

"Exactly," Tom agreed coolly. "I thought it would prove so."

"But what does it all mean?" asked Bert. "What are they doing up here, and around our cabin?"

"Give it up," spoke Tom. "Maybe they're hunting, as we are."

"But they had no guns," Jack said.

"No. Well, we'll just have to wait and see what turns up," Tom went on. "I think we gave 'em rather a surprise, though."

"We sure did," agreed George. "But that Whalen surprised me, too. I wonder how he got here?"

"Didn't you say you told him where we were coming?" Tom asked.

"Yes, I did, after he pumped me with a lot of questions. I didn't realize what I was doing. I say, Tom, I hope I haven't done any harm!"

"Oh, no. There wasn't any secret about where we were going to spend the Christmas holidays," Tom said. "But it is rather odd to find those three so close after us. But maybe it will be all right. They know they are on private preserves—our private grounds—for the time being, and I guess they won't trouble us."

"Then it was those three, sneaking around the cabin?" asked Jack.

"Professor Skeel, at least," Tom went on, "though it may have been only ordinary curiosity that took him there. We'll take a little trip over to Hounson's some day, and see what we can pick up there."

It was getting late, so the young hunters made haste back to their cabin. They had supper, and then once more sat about the fire and talked through the long Winter evening. The next day they dressed their game and cooked it, finding it a welcome relief from the canned meats and bacon on which they had been living.

The rest of that week they remained in the vicinity of Cabin No. 1, having fair luck, but getting no big game. They saw one deer, but missed him. In this time they saw no more of Skeel or his cronies.

"What do you say we go over to Camp No. 2 for a change?" asked Tom, one night.

"We're with you," his chums agreed, and they made an early start, through the woods, locking up the place they left behind, for they might not be back for several days. They managed to bag several rabbits and squirrels on their march, but saw no signs of deer. Sam had told them they might not have much luck in this direction.

In due time, by following a copy of the blue print map they had made, they came to Camp No. 2. There had been a light fall of snow in the night, and as Tom approached the cabin, he cried out:

"Boys, they've been here ahead of us!" He pointed to footprints in the white blanket—footprints, one of which had a star in the middle of the sole.

CHAPTER XI

MORE PLOTTING

Impetuous George Abbot was about to rush forward when Tom, stretching out a hand, held him back.

"Hold on a minute," he said, and there was some strange quality in Tom's voice that made his chum obey.

"What's up?" he asked, glancing from Tom to the cabin.

"Nothing yet, but there may be," was the cool answer.

"You mean there may be someone in that cabin—Skeel or those other men?"

"That's about the size of it," Tom said.

"That's right—best to be on the safe side," put in Bert. "Those men, or Skeel, especially, have been here lately."

"But they haven't any right in our cabin—at least the cabin your friends gave us the use of, Tom," objected George.

"I know they haven't, and that's just where the trouble might come in. Those two men with Skeel look like ugly customers. If we cornered them in a cabin they had no right to enter, they might turn ugly. It's best to go a bit slowly until we find out whether or not they are in there."

"That's what I say," chimed in Jack. "Not that I'm afraid, but I don't want to run into trouble so early on our vacation. Of course it's possible," he went on, "that someone else besides Skeel and his cronies may have been here, or may still be here, for boots, with nail-marks like those on the sole, can't be so very rare. But I'm inclined to think Skeel wore those," and he nodded toward the marks in the snow.

"I agree with you," Tom said, "and we'll soon find out. Let's look about a bit before we rush up to the cabin," he went on.

Slowly the boys circled about it, gradually coming closer, to give those within, if such unwarranted visitors there might be, a chance to either make their presence known in a friendly manner, or take their departure.

But there was no sign from the cabin of Camp No. 2, and, after waiting a little while, Tom and his chums moved forward. As they came nearer, they could see that some two or three persons had made a complete circle about the cabin, and had even advanced up on the rough steps that led to the front door. Whether they had entered or not was something that could not be stated with positiveness.

"Well, the door's locked, anyhow," Tom said, as he looked at the padlock. "But of course they might have a duplicate key." He drew from his pocket the one Sam Wilson had given him, and a moment later Tom and his chums stood inside the cabin. They breathed a sigh of relief. No one opposed them.

Nor, as far as could be learned by a glance around the interior, had any uninvited guests been present. The place was in order, not as complete, perhaps as that of the first camp, but enough to show that it had been "slicked up," after its last occupancy by the hunting party of gentlemen to whom Tom and his friends were indebted for the use of the camps.

"Skeel and his cronies may have been here all the same, looking for us," said Jack, as he stood his gun in a corner.

"Why should they be looking for us?" inquired George.

"Now don't start that list of questions," objected Jack. "Ask Tom."

George turned a gaze on his other chum.

"Of course Skeel may have been here," admitted our hero. "We were never in this cabin before, and we don't know how it looked, or how it was arranged. But if they were here, they don't seem to have done much damage, and if they had a meal, they washed the dishes up after them."

A look in the kitchen showed that it was in order. This cabin was built just the same as was No. 1, and the arrangements and furnishings were practically similar.

"Well, Skeel or no Skeel, I'm going to have something to eat!" cried Tom. "Come on, fellows, make yourselves at home."

This they proceeded to do, making arrangements to get a meal, for there was plenty of wood for the stove as well as a pile of dry logs for the fireplace. A blaze was not unwelcome, for it was growing colder, and there were signs of a storm.

As our friends sat about the cozy, crackling blaze on the hearth they were unaware of three men, on the edge of the little clearing in which the cabin stood—three men who were gazing at the smoke curling up from the chimney.

"Yes, there they are!" grumbled the one known as Whalen. "There they are in their cabin, nice and warm, and with plenty to eat, and we're out in the cold. I don't like it, I say! I don't like it!"

"Now, don't get rash!" observed Professor Skeel, for he was of the trio. "What is a little discomfort now compared to the satisfaction we'll have later?"

"I wouldn't mind so much, if I was sure of that," said Whalen sullenly. "But it ain't noways sure."

"I'll make it sure," said the hoarse voice of the other plotter.

"Have you decided on a way to get him into our hands?" asked the former teacher eagerly. "Have you a plan, Murker?"

"Yes, and a good one, too!" was the answer. "It's come to me since we've been fiddling around here."

"And can we get him—get Tom Fairfield—where we want him?" asked Professor Skeel eagerly. "That's what I want to know."

"Yes, I think we can," answered Murker, an unpleasant grin spreading over his evil face. "I haven't all the details worked out yet, but when I get through, I think we'll have him just where we want him. Not that I want him particularly," he went on. "I never knew him before you fellows got me into this," and when he classed Professor Skeel as a "fellow," the latter did not object.

It showed to what depths the really talented man had fallen. For Professor Skeel was a brilliant scholar, and would have made his mark in educational circles, had he chosen to be honest. But he took the easiest way, which ends by being the hardest.

"I don't ask you to take any interest in Tom Fairfield, once you help me get him in my power," went on the former instructor. "I'll attend to the rest. But I want him alone. I don't want to have to handle any of the others."

"I should say not!" exclaimed Whalen. "We'll have our hands full, if we try to take care of all four of 'em."

"Oh, I wouldn't be afraid," was the sneering comment of Murker. "I guess we could persuade 'em to be good," and he leered at his companions.

"Four are too many to handle," decided Professor Skeel. "I want Tom Fairfield alone."

"And I'll get him for you," promised Murker. "But you've got to give me a share of the ransom money."

"Oh, I'll do that," readily agreed the former teacher. "I'm doing this as much to square accounts with him as for anything else."

"Well, I'm not working for love—or revenge," chuckled Murker. "I want the cold cash."

"So do I," chimed in Whalen, "but I want revenge, too. It's going to be a regular kidnapping, isn't it?" and he looked at Professor Skeel.

"It will be if he can carry it out," was the answer, with a nod at Murker.

"Oh, I'll do my part," was the assurance given.

"But won't it be risky—dangerous?" asked Whalen. "I don't want to get in trouble," and he looked rather anxiously about him, as though already he feared officers of the law might be after him.

"There's no more risk for you than for us," spoke Professor Skeel.

"There won't be any risk—not up in this lonesome place," Murker said.

"But how are you going to make sure of getting Tom into our hands alone?" asked the rascally professor.

"Leave that to me," was the chuckling answer. "I used to live in this region when I was a young fellow. Folks have forgotten me, but I haven't forgotten them."

"I say!" exclaimed Professor Skeel, "I hope you're not going to bring any more into this. The more there are the more risk there is, and the money I expect to get from Mr. Fairfield, for giving Tom back to him, won't go so far if we have to split it up——"

"Oh, don't worry! No one else but us three will be in it. I should have said I hadn't forgotten the country up around here—not so much the people. I don't care anything about them. But I know every cross-road and bridle-path through the woods, and it will be funny if I can't get this lad where I want him. They're strangers up here, and they have to depend on signposts, and what that guide tells them."

"But they are smart fellows," said Professor Skeel. "I know, for I taught them in school. If they have a signboard to go by, it will be as good to them as a printed book would be to most people."

"That may all be very true," chuckled Murker. "But tell me this. A wrong signboard isn't much use to anyone, is it? Not even to a smart lad."

"A wrong signboard? What do you mean?" asked the professor.

"I mean just what I said—'a wrong signboard'—one that gives the wrong direction. It's worse than none at all, isn't it?"

"Well, I should say it was," was the slow answer of the former teacher. "But are you going to get Tom Fairfield——"

"Now, don't ask too many questions," was the advice of his evil-faced crony. "When you don't know a thing, you can say so with a clear conscience in case the detectives get asking too many personal questions of you."

"That's so," agreed Professor Skeel, readily understanding what was meant.

"Detectives!" exclaimed Whalen. "Did you say detectives?

"But—er—I—they—I don't want to see any detectives," stammered the former employee of Elmwood Hall.

"I don't either," chuckled Murker. "But it's best to be on the safe side, and to prepare for emergencies. So what you and the professor don't know, you can't tell. Leave the details to me, and I'll fix 'em. Now I think we've been here long enough. We know what we came over to this cabin to find out—that they hadn't been here before until just now. And we're pretty certain they'll go next—to No. 3 Camp."

"What makes you think so?" asked Whalen.

"Because boys are like deer at times—mighty curious. They won't rest satisfied until they've tried all three camps. They'll go over to the last one in a few days, and then, Skeel, we may have Tom Fairfield just where we want him!"

"I hope so!" was the fervent exclamation, as the three plotters made their way off through the dense woods.

CHAPTER XII
A LUCKY SHOT

"Well, we're not going to stay in all the rest of the day, are we?" asked Jack Fitch, pushing back his chair from the table.

"I should say not!" exclaimed Bert. "There's plenty of time yet to go out and bag a deer or two."

"Nothing small about you," chuckled Tom, as he looked to his ammunition. "But I agree that there's no use wasting time indoors. It does look like a storm, so we won't go too far away from the cabin."

"Are we going to stay here to-night?" asked George.

"Sure," remarked Tom. "It's too far to tramp back to No. 1 Camp. This is just as well stocked up, and as there are plenty of bedclothes here, and lots of wood, we don't care how cold it gets outside."

They had finished their meal, and it was now early in the afternoon. It would soon be dark, however, for in December the days are very short. But, as Jack had said, the few remaining hours of daylight need not be wasted, and as yet the boys had not bagged any big game.

"It's too dark for photographs," suggested George, as he saw Bert getting out his camera.

"Not if I make a few as soon as I get out," was the answer. "I want to get some views around this camp."

A close search through the cabin had not revealed that Skeel and his companions had entered. The boys felt sure it was those men who had made the tracks in the snow about the little building. But, if they had entered, nothing had been unduly disturbed.

"I wish I knew what their game was," spoke Jack, as he shouldered his gun and followed Tom and the others outside.

"It is sort of a puzzle," our hero agreed. "We'll have to take a walk over to Hounson's some day this week, and see what we can learn. If those fellows think they can trespass all over these camps it's time we told Sam Wilson. He'll send them flying, I'll wager!"

"That's right!" declared Bert.

The boys followed a trail through the woods. Their friend, the guide and caretaker of the camps, had told them about it, advising them to follow it, as they might see some game along it. This they were now hoping for, keeping a bright lookout in every direction.

As they tramped along, the sudden rattle of a dried bush on the right of Tom attracted his attention. He looked in time to see a white streak darting along.

"A rabbit!" he cried and fired on the instant.

"Missed!" yelled Bert, as the echoes of the shot died away.

"No, I didn't!" cried Tom. "You'll find him behind that stump."

And, surely enough, when the other boys looked, there was the rabbit neatly bagged. He was needed for food, too, for they had no fresh meat at this camp, and already they were beginning to tire of the canned variety.

Except for the determination to each bring back a deer's head, and the pelt of a bear, our four boy hunters had made up their minds not to be wanton shots. They wanted to get enough game for food, and the head and skin for relics, after using such of the meat as they needed of the bear and deer.

"Of course we four can't eat all that meat in the short while we'll be in the woods," Tom said, "but we can give it to Sam, so it won't be wasted."

Tom and his chums had the right idea of hunting, and had no desire to slaughter for the mere savage joy of killing.

"Another rabbit and a few partridges and we'll have enough to keep the kitchen going the rest of the week," Bert said, as Tom put the bunny in his bag. "Then all we'll have to look for will be a bear or a deer."

But even small game was scarce, it seemed, and though several shots were tried at rabbits at a distance, and though some partridges were flushed, no further luck resulted.

It was growing dusk when Tom suggested that they had better return to camp, and they retraced their steps. However, the rabbit was a large one, and, made into either a stew or potpie, would provide the main dish for their next day's dinner.

Early in the morning the boys were on the move again. They hunted around the cabin, planning to come back to it at noon for the hot rabbit dinner, and this they did.

The only luck they had was that Bert and George got some fine photographs. But not a rabbit nor a bird fell to their guns that day. Tom scared up a fox, and took several shots at it, hoping he might carry home the skin. But if Reynard were hit he showed no signs of it, and went bounding on through the woods.

"We'll make a regular hunt of it to-morrow," decided Tom, as they sat about the cheerful fire in the cabin that night. "We'll get an early start, take our lunch, a pot to make some coffee over an open fire, and we won't come back until dark."

"That's the talk!" cried Bert.

"This is the best hunting ground, according to what Sam said," Tom went on, "and we want to put in our best licks here. So we'll take a whole day to it, and go as far as we can, working north, I think, as the woods seem to be thicker there."

This met with the approval of the others, and they started out the next morning, equipped for staying several hours in the open. They set out on a new trail, one they had not traveled before, but they had not gone far on it before Tom, who was in the lead, came to a sudden halt, and uttered an exclamation of surprise.

"What's the matter?" called Jack, who was directly behind him. "See some bear tracks?"

"No, these are Skeel tracks, I should say. Those fellows must be just ahead of us, for the marks seem quite fresh."

Tom pointed to some impressions in the snow. Among them were footprints showing that same star mark in hob nails.

"I wonder why they're trailing and following us?" remarked Bert. "It can't be just for fun."

"Maybe they don't know where to look for game, and are depending on us," suggested George.

"That might be so," agreed Tom. "But I wish they'd show their hands, and not keep us guessing all the while. It's getting on my nerves."

"Well, we'll keep a lookout for 'em now," suggested Bert, "and if we see 'em, we'll give 'em a bit of our minds."

"Yes, and I'm going to ask Sam Wilson to tell 'em to go," added Tom. "They haven't any right here. They may be scaring all the game away, and besides, it's risky. They may get in the way of our guns, or we come too close to theirs, though I haven't seen them with either a rifle or a shotgun yet."

"No they don't seem to be hunting, but if they aren't, what in the world are they up here for?" asked Bert.

"That's what gets me," remarked Jack. "Well, come on. Time's too valuable to waste in chinning."

Once more they took up the trail. The footsteps of the three men, on their mysterious errand, crossed the path of our friends at an angle, and they did not think it wise to follow the marks of the hob nails.

Luck seemed to be better to-day, from the very start, for, before they had gone three miles, they had bagged two rabbits, three squirrels and Jack had a partridge to his credit.

"Enough to keep us from starving," he said. "Now for bigger game—a deer, at least."

"I'd like to get a good deer picture," announced Bert, looking to see that his camera was in working order.

A little later the four boys stood in a small clearing in the woods, wondering which way to go next, for, so far, they had seen no signs of either bear or deer. They hoped it was not so late in the season that all the bears would be enjoying their winter sleep.

Suddenly there was a slight noise over in the underbrush to the left of the clearing.

"I'm going to see what that is!" cried Bert, starting forward with his camera.

"Probably nothing but a rabbit," said Jack. "And we've got enough of the bunnies."

"Then I'll take a snapshot; that won't hurt," Bert responded.

The others, not much interested, watched him. Softly he went forward, hoping he might get a picture of a rabbit in its native woodland. The sun was just right for a picture.

But, as Bert looked, a deer suddenly came out of the brush, and stood on the edge of the clearing, seemingly unconscious of the presence of the boys. They had seen the beautiful creature, however, and for the moment none of them raised his rifle. Bert's, indeed, was slung on his back out of the way while he used his camera.

Without speaking, Bert motioned to his chums not to shoot until he had a chance to make a picture. Tom and the others signified that they would hold their fire.

Bert crept up, the deer still unconscious of the presence of its enemies, and the youth soon had the animal in focus. It looked as though it would be a fine photograph.

Suddenly there was another crashing sound in the bushes, and as the boys, startled, turned, they saw a larger deer, with sharp, branching antlers, step from cover just behind Bert. The latter was so intent on getting the photograph that he did not turn to see how he was menaced from the rear.

The male deer, with a snort and a stamping of hoofs, and with lowered head, leaped toward Bert. The animal, evidently thinking its mate in danger, was going to her defense.

"Look out, Bert!" cried Jack, but the warning would have come too late. Bert did not even turn around, for he was on the point of pressing the shutter release of his camera. He had noticed a slight movement on the part of the female deer that indicated she was about to leap into the bushes.

"There, I've got you!" cried Bert, as he pressed the bulb.

The next instant he was startled by a snort behind him. He heard a rattle of hoofs, and the voices of his chums crying a warning.

Bert turned to run, but he would not have been in time, except for what happened. A lucky shot on the part of Tom probably saved his friend from severe injury, if not death.

With a sudden motion Tom threw his rifle to his shoulder, took quick aim, and fired.

The male deer went down in a heap, actually turning a somersault, so great was its speed. And it came to rest, breathing its last, almost at Bert's feet.

CHAPTER XIII

THE CHANGED SIGN

"Say, that was a shot!"

"That's what! Just in time, too!"

Thus cried Jack and George. Bert was too surprised to utter a word, and Tom was too anxious to make sure he had bagged the first specimen of real game since coming to camp.

But there was no mistake about it. There lay the slain deer, and a fine specimen it was. The one Bert had photographed with his camera had, on the first alarm, darted into the underbrush, and was now far away, doubtless wondering what had happened to her mate.

"Say, why didn't you fellows tell me what was going on?" asked Bert, as he whirled about and saw what had happened.

"We did," spoke George.

"There came pretty nearly not being time enough to do anything," went on Jack. "It was touch and go, Bert, old man. Tom, here, fired just in time."

"Was it really as close as that?" asked the lad with the camera.

"It certainly was," Jack assured him. "That deer had it in for you. I guess he thought you were trying to pot his mate with a new-fangled gun, and he made up his mind to stop you."

"Well, Tom stopped him all right," spoke George. "Say, it's a fine specimen!" and he gazed admiringly at the head and horns. "It will make a fine trophy for your room, Tom."

"I wasn't thinking so much of that when I fired," was the modest answer. "I was wondering whether I could bowl him over before he reached Bert with those business-looking horns."

"And you did, old man. I shan't forget that!" exclaimed Bert, fervently. "I'll do as much for you some day, only I'm not as good a shot as you, so don't take any chances. If a deer or a bear comes after you, run first, and get in a safe place. Then wait for me to shoot at it."

"It was more luck than anything else that I got him," Tom said. "If I had stopped to think, I'm sure I'd have had a touch of 'buck-fever,' and I wouldn't have been able to hold my gun steady. But I just up and blazed away."

"Well, now we've got it, what are we going to do with it?" asked Jack. "Shall we trail after the one that got away—the one Bert took a picture of?"

"What's the use?" asked Bert. "She's miles away from here now."

"Besides," added Tom, "we've got more meat here now than we can use in a week. No use killing for fun. I've got the head trophy I want, and it will be the turn of you fellows next. I won't shoot any more deer, though I'll bag a bear if I can. We don't want to shoot female deer if we can help it."

"That's right," agreed Jack. "Now let's decide what to do about this fellow. He's a big one, and will take some cutting-up."

The boys were rather dubious about getting the deer's head off, and taking the best part for food. But they were saved what might have been an unpleasant task by the arrival of Sam Wilson.

"Hello!" cried the guide, as he saw his young friends. "Well, you have had some luck, haven't you! Is that your first one?"

"Yes," answered Tom, as he related what had occurred.

"Well, now, that's the way to do!" Sam cried. "He's a fine critter, too; good head and horns. I've got my pung just outside on the road. I'll take him along, dress him for you and send the head to an Indian to be mounted. Old Wombo does pretty good work that way."

"I wish you would have it done," Tom said. "And take some of the venison yourself. There's more than we can use."

"Besides, we're going to get more deer in a few days," added George.

"Oh, you are, eh? Well, nothing like being sure," chuckled the old guide and hunter. "So far, though, you've done as well as the men who come up here, so I wouldn't wonder but what you'd beat 'em. How have you been? Anything happened?"

They told of their experiences in camp, and Tom mentioned Skeel and his cronies.

"Trespassing on these preserves, eh?" exclaimed Sam. "Well, I'll have to look into that. These lands are posted, and only those who get permission can enter on them, and hunt or fish. I'll just put a flea in the ears of those fellows, if they don't look out!"

With the help of the boys, Sam carried the deer out to his waiting pung. He said he had happened to pass near No. 2 Camp, and decided to run in on the chance that the boys might be there.

The deer's legs were tied together, and then a long pole, cut from the woods, was thrust between them, lengthwise. On the shoulders of the boys and the guide the carcass was taken out to the big sled.

"I'll bring the meat over to-morrow," promised Sam, "and the head will be mounted later. It takes a little time."

"Keep plenty of the venison yourself," Tom urged.

"Well, just as you say," was the laughing acceptance. "I haven't had much chance to do any hunting yet. I'm glad you had a good start of luck."

"And I hope my picture of the other deer comes out all right," murmured Bert, his interest, just then, centering in his camera.

"Well, if it hadn't been for Tom, you might not have come out all right," said Jack, more than half seriously.

That was the extent of their luck for that day, however, except that both Bert and George secured some fine snapshots. When Sam had departed with the slain deer, the boys found a good place to stop, and build a fire to make coffee. They ate their lunch with such appetites as come only from life in the open, and, having finished, once more they set out on the trail.

But, though Jack, Bert and George each hoped for a repetition of Tom's luck, in some modified form, it was not to be.

The boy hunters adopted all the suggestions of Sam, in looking for more game, but though they saw signs of it, the game itself had disappeared, at least for the time being.

"But we've got other days ahead of us," suggested Tom. "We don't have to go back for more than two weeks, and that will give us plenty of chances."

They reached Camp No. 2 very tired, but satisfied with their day's trip. And they brought with them appetites that made Jack, who was temporarily doing the cooking, wish his chums had left part of their hunger in the woods.

"What! More beans?" he cried to Bert, who passed his plate for the third time. "Can't you eat anything but beans?"

"Don't need to, when they're cooked as good as this, old man," was the laughing answer. "That molasses you put in just gave 'em the right flavor."

"I'll leave it out next time," grumbled Jack. "I want a chance to get a bite myself."

The meal went merrily on, and then came a delightful evening spent in the flickering blaze of the log fire, talking over the events of the day. Bert had developed his picture of the deer, and found that it would make a good print. Tom was dreaming of the time when he would get back the mounted head to hang on the wall of his den at home, as a memento of the trip.

Tom was destined to have other memories of the trip than his deer-head trophy, but he did not know that yet.

A rather heavy fall of snow the next day prevented the boys from going far from the cabin, for they did not want to take any chances on being lost in the storm.

There was no need to go out for food, as they had plenty, and in the afternoon Sam came over with a generous supply of deer meat, so their larder was well supplied.

"When are we going to take in Camp No. 3?" asked Jack of Tom, when Sam had gone back home in his pung sled.

"Well, we can go over there whenever you fellows want to. I don't believe, from what Sam says, that it's quite as good hunting ground as this, and I thought maybe you'd want to stay here until you each got a deer's head."

"Yes, I guess that would be best," agreed Bert. "This seems to be the most promising location. And there may be bears around. I heard some animal prowling about the cabin last night."

"So did I," confessed George. "Maybe it was Skeel and his crowd," he added.

"Hardly," scoffed Tom. "More like it was a fox looking to pick up something to eat that we had thrown out. But we'll stay around here for a few days longer, and then make a hike for No. 3. We might as well take 'em all in while we're here. No telling when we'll get another chance."

Had the boys known what was in store for them, they would have started for No. 3 Camp at once. But they did not know, and the delay gave the enemies of Tom Fairfield a chance to plan their trick.

For the next day, at some distance from No. 2 Cabin, there might have been seen three men, going along the snow-covered forest trail, in a manner that could only be described as "slinking." A glance would have disclosed their identities—Skeel, Whalen and Murker.

"Think they'll soon be on the move?" asked Professor Skeel. "If they don't take the trail, all our work will be wasted."

"Well, we've got to take some chances," growled Murker. "If this dodge doesn't fool 'em, I'll have to try another. But I think it will. Once we get 'em confused, and off the road, we can separate 'em by some means or other, and deal with Fairfield alone. You leave it to me."

"Very well," assented Professor Skeel.

A little farther walk through the woods brought the three conspirators to a cross-road. It was not much traveled in Winter, but in Summer formed a popular highway. The main road led back to the village, where the boys had left the railroad train, and the cross highway connected two towns—Ramsen and Fayetville.

Reaching this signboard, Murker looked around to make sure he was unobserved. Then, with a few blows from a hammer, he knocked off the two signboards. These he reversed, so that the one marked "Seven miles to

Ramsen" pointed in just the opposite direction—to Fayetville. The other board he also reversed.

"But it's the Ramsen one they'll look at if they come to Camp No. 3," said Murker, "and they're almost sure to come. Then we'll have Fairfield where we want him!"

CHAPTER XIV

THE BEAR'S TRAIL

Bert Wilson was carefully examining his camera, sitting at a table in the cozy quarters of Cabin No. 2, where he and his chums had gathered after the day's hunt. When he had adjusted the shutter, which had stuck several times of late, thereby spoiling some fine pictures, Bert took up his gun, and began taking that apart to clean it.

"I say! What's up?" questioned Tom, who was lying lazily on his back on a blanket-covered couch, staring at the flicker of the flames on the ceiling. "Getting ready for an expedition, Bert?"

"Well, I sort of feel it in my bones that I'll get a bear to-morrow, or a deer anyhow, and I'm taking no chances," was the answer.

"Going to get the game with your gun or your camera?" asked Jack.

"Both," was the quick answer. "I'll snapshot him first and pot him afterward."

"If he lets you," laughed George. "But I'd like to see any healthy bear stand for having Bert poke a camera in his face, and then shoot a slug of lead into him."

"You watch my smoke—that's all," said Bert significantly, as he went on cleaning his gun.

"What's the program for to-morrow?" asked Jack, who, like Tom, was doing nothing, and taking considerable pains at it.

"Well, I thought we'd go off on an all-day hunt again," was the young host's answer, for Tom was really in that position, it being on his invitation, through his father, that the boys had come to the hunting camp.

"That idea suits me," responded Jack. "But take along more grub than we did last time. I was hungry before we got back."

"Why don't we shoot what we want to eat?" suggested George. "I never read of a party of hunters having to depend on canned stuff or the grocery when they were really good shots, as we are!" and he puffed himself up with pretended pride. "What's the use taking a lot of grub along when you can shoot a partridge or two, and broil 'em over the coals of an open fire? Doesn't that sound good?"

"It sounds a great deal better than it really is," spoke Tom. "That sort of thing is all right to read about, but I like my game to stand a little after being killed. And it's hard to dress and get ready anything when you're on a tramp. So I think we'll just take our grub along. We'll have more time for hunting then."

"That's right," assented Jack.

Bert's interest in his gun prompted George to look after his weapon. Jack and Tom declared theirs were already in perfect shape for the morrow's sport, providing they saw any game.

"I do wish we'd spot a bear," said Jack, with an envious sigh.

"Not much chance of that," came from Tom. "I asked Sam about that, and he said while bears were plentiful in this part of the Adirondacks, at certain seasons, this wasn't exactly the time for them. They're probably in their caves, or hollow logs, waiting for Candlemas Day, to come out and look for their shadows."

"Do you really believe in that superstition—that if a bear, or a ground hog, does see his shadow on that day, there'll be six weeks more of Winter, and if he doesn't, there won't?" asked George.

"There you go again—shooting questions at us!" laughed Tom. "No, I don't believe it, but lots of folks do."

"Did Sam say anything about the chances for getting more deer?" Bert wanted to know.

"Well, yes, he admitted there were plenty this year. But I've shot mine, so I'm not interested," Tom said.

"I'm counting on a bear-skin rug to put in front of my bed," remarked Jack. "Then when I have to jump up in the cold, I can warm my feet before I start to dress."

"Nothing like comfort," spoke Bert. "Going to have your bear's skin tanned with the head on, Jack?"

"Yes, I think I will."

"Better get your bear first," said Tom grimly. "Well, let's lay out plans for to-morrow's hunt. What trail shall we take? I rather fancy, from what Sam said, that the old lumber road will be best to start on. Maybe we can make Camp No. 3 in the day's tramp, and do some hunting along the way."

"That's rather too much of a risk, isn't it?" asked Jack. "We could easily make Camp No. 3 in a day's tramp, if we started out from here early enough, and didn't waste any time following game trails. But if we try to do any hunting, we're likely to be delayed. Then we won't be able to start for camp until late. We may not reach it, and not be able to get back here and then——"

"Great Scott!" cried Tom. "Have you any more if and but calamities up your sleeve, old man? If you have, trot 'em out. We can make Camp No. 3 all right, and do some hunting, too. Why, it's a good trail once we get over the mountain and strike the road to Ramsen. That's what Sam said."

Tom spoke of going over the mountain, but what he meant was going over the ridge of the highest range which they were then among. For the mountains were all around them, differing in height and rugged appearance only.

"Well, go ahead and let's try it, then," said Jack, with a shrug of his shoulders. "And if anything happens, don't blame me!"

"We won't, as long as you don't say 'I told you so!'" exclaimed Bert. "That always makes me mad."

"All right—let it go at that," suggested Tom. "Then we'll take as much time as we want for hunting to-morrow, and strike for Camp No. 3 when we feel like it. We'll take along some grub, and make coffee as usual. That sounds good."

"And I do hope I get a bear—or deer," murmured Bert. "If I don't I'm going to——"

"Hark!" suddenly interrupted Tom. He sat up quickly, in a listening attitude on the couch.

"Nothing but the wind," murmured George, as a shutter rattled.

"Hark!" ordered Tom again.

There was some sound outside. All the boys heard it plainly, and a dog they had borrowed that day from Sam, to help them in tracking any game on the trail of which they might get, sat up and growled.

"Someone is out there," said Tom in a whisper.

"Some animal—a skunk, maybe," suggested Bert. "I'm going to stay in. I don't like him—not for a scent!" and he laughed at his own joke.

Tom, however, was softly getting up from the couch. He looked fixedly toward one certain window.

"Jack, turn the light out suddenly!" he ordered in a whisper. "Bert, have your gun ready."

"Do you really think it is—anyone?" asked Bert, as he reached for his gun, which he had finished cleaning, and put together again.

"Someone or—something," went on Tom, and his voice did not rise above a whisper. He moved slowly over toward the window.

"Here goes the glim!" Jack announced, and at once the cabin was darkened. It took but a minute, however, for the boys' eyes to become accustomed to the change, and they saw moonlight streaming through the window toward which Tom was moving. The others followed him, walking softly.

"There he goes—it is someone!" hoarsely whispered Bert, and he pointed to a black figure stealing over the snow. It was plainly in sight, for the ground was deeply covered with snow.

"It's a bear!" George burst out. "It's a bear! Where's my gun? Where do you shoot a bear, anyhow? I don't want to spoil the skin. Say, where's my gun?"

"Dry up!" ordered Tom sharply. "It isn't a bear!"

"It is so!" began George. "Where's my——"

Before anyone could stop him, or object, Bert had slipped to the door, opened it, and had fired his gun at the retreating black object.

"Look out!" Tom cried. "You might kill him! That's a man—not a bear, Bert!"

"I know it," was the calm answer. "I only fired over his head to scare him. Look at him scoot, would you?"

And indeed the black object that George had thought was a bear suddenly straightened up, revealing itself to be a man. He ran with fast strides toward the circle of woods that were all about the hunting cabin. The man reached the shelter of the black trees a little later, and was soon lost to sight.

"A man!" gasped George. "It was a man!"

"That's what it was," added Bert.

"Well, what do you know about that?" demanded Jack. "Was he sneaking around this cabin?"

"That's about it," answered Tom.

"But who was he?"

"That's for us to guess," went on the young hunter. "But I fancy I can come pretty near it."

"You mean Professor Skeel?" asked Bert.

"Him, or one of his two friends."

"But what would he, or they, be doing around our cabin?"

"That," said Tom, and he spoke more soberly than he had for some time, "that is something I'd give a great deal to learn. It's a mystery that's been bothering me for some time."

The chums looked at their friend in silence for a moment, and then Jack remarked:

"I'm going to have a peep around outside."

The others followed, two of them carrying guns. They made a circuit of the cabin in the moonlight, but no other uninvited callers were observed. There were footprints about the shack, however, which showed that the man, whoever he was, had been listening under several of the windows.

"Well, he didn't hear any secrets, for we weren't talking any," Tom said with a laugh, as he and his chums went indoors again.

"Except to say that we were going to Camp No. 3 to-morrow," said Bert.

"That's no secret."

But it was the very information the man, who had been eavesdropping under the window, had come to obtain. He ran off with a smile of satisfaction on his evil face.

"They've got nerve—firing at me!" he muttered, not thinking of his own "nerve" in doing what he had done.

The boys were rather alarmed for a while, and quite indignant. They decided to take some harsh measures, if need be, to keep Skeel and his cronies off the game preserve. And with this resolve they went to bed, for they wanted to make an early start the next morning.

Ten o'clock the next day found our four friends well on their way to Camp No. 3. They had started their hunt in that general direction. It was an hour later, when, after several false alarms, the dog gave tongue to a peculiar cry.

"What's that?" asked Jack.

"It's a bear!" decided Bert. "Sam said the dog would yelp that way when he struck the trail. Come on, fellows!"

They ran forward to rejoin their dog, that had gone on ahead. He was now barking fast and furiously, and had evidently gotten on the track of something.

"Yes, it is a bear!" decided Tom, when he had noted the tracks in the snow. "And they're fresh, too, otherwise the dog couldn't smell 'em! They won't lie long on snow. Go on, old sport!" and thus encouraged the dog bounded forward.

How the bear came to be out at that time of the year, the boys did not stop to think. But they eagerly followed the trail. It led on through the woods, and they hardly noted their direction.

At noon they stopped for a hasty lunch, grudging the time it took, for they were anxious to get sight of the big game. Once more they were on the trail.

"But it seems to be getting dark suddenly," commented Jack. "I wonder if we'd better keep on?"

"Certainly—why not?" asked Bert. "The trail is getting fresher all the while. Come on, we'll have him soon. He's a big one, too!"

Again the boys pressed forward, the dog baying from time to time.

CHAPTER XV

LOST IN A STORM

Either the bear was a better traveler than the boys gave the brute credit for being, or the trail was not as fresh as Bert had supposed. For though they went on and on, they did not see the black ungainly form of Bruin looming up before them.

They were traveling through a rather thin part of the forest then, making good time, for the snow was not so deep here. Occasionally they thought they had glimpses of the animal they sought, but it always proved to be nothing but a shadow, or a movement in the bushes, caused by the passage of some big rabbit.

"There he goes!" suddenly cried George, pointing to the left.

"Yes, that's him!" eagerly agreed Jack.

Tom and Bert also agreed that they saw something more substantial, this time, than a shadow. But a moment later the black object, for such it had been, was lost sight of.

"Come on!" cried Tom, as enthusiastic as any of his chums. "We've got him now."

They raced forward, until they came to the place where they had seen the black object, and then they noticed a curious thing. For there were two sets of marks—human footprints, and the broad-toed tracks of the bear.

"Look at that!" cried Jack. "Was that a man we saw, or the bear?"

No one could say for certain. But this much was sure. The bear's tracks led in one direction, and the man's in another.

Was the bear chasing the man, or was the man hunting the bear, was another phase of the question.

"Look here!" said Tom, who had been carefully examining the two sets of impressions in the snow. "Here's how I size this up. The bear's tracks go in a straight line, or nearly so, as you can easily see. But the man's tracks are in the form of a letter V and we are at the angle right here. The angle comes up right close to the trail of the bear, too.

"Now I think the man was walking through the woods, approaching the bear. He didn't know it until he was almost on the beast and then the man saw it. Of course he turned away at once and ran back. You can tell that the footprints that approach the bear's trail are made more slowly than the others—going away. In the last case the man was running away from the bear. But the bear wasn't afraid, and kept straight on, paying no attention to the man."

"That's good argument," observed Bert.

"Can you tell us who the man was?" demanded George.

"I'm not detective enough for that," Tom confessed. "But I don't believe the man was a hunter with a gun."

"Why not?" Jack wanted to know.

"Because if he had a gun, he would have fired at the bear, and we'd have seen some change in the bear's trail. Bruin would either have run at the shot, or attacked the man, provided the bullet didn't kill at once. And you can see for yourselves that nothing like that happened. So I argue that the man had no gun."

"Then he was Skeel, or one of his two partners," said George.

"What makes you think that?" asked Bert, curiously.

"Because we never saw either of them with a gun."

"That doesn't prove anything," Tom said. "There are lots of men in these woods who haven't guns. It might have been Sam Wilson."

"Can you tell anything by the footprints?" asked Bert.

"No. The star mark isn't there, but that's nothing. Well, whoever he was he got away, and we didn't get close enough to make out who he was."

"I tell you where you're wrong in one thing, though, Tom," spoke Jack.

"How's that?"

"You said the man came up to the bear and ran away, turning off at an angle. I don't believe he saw the bear, because we were watching the man, and we would have seen the bear if he had seen him, too. For it was right here we lost sight of the man."

"Well, maybe I am wrong about that part of it," admitted Tom, "but at least the man didn't cross the bear's trail. Something turned him back when he saw the marks of the paws in the snow."

That seemed reasonable enough.

"Well, let's follow the dog," suggested Bert. "He's after the bear, anyhow."

This was so, for the dog had not even paused at the prints of the man's feet in the snow. He evidently preferred Bruin for game.

But now it was getting so dark that it was difficult for the boys to see, even with the whiteness caused by the covering of snow on the ground.

"I say," Tom spoke, when they had gone on a little farther. "I think we'd better turn back. It will be night before we realize it, and we're a long way from either camp. It's a question in my mind whether we hadn't better start back for Camp No. 2, and let three wait for a day or so. It's going to snow too, soon, if I'm any judge."

"Why, we're probably as near to No. 3 as we are to No. 2," observed Jack. "Why not keep on? We haven't been to Camp No. 3 yet, and I want to see what it's like."

"Well, we'll leave it to a vote," decided Tom, who never tried to "run" things where his chums were concerned. "One place is as good as another to me, but we've got to do something—and that pretty soon."

"We'd better give up the bear, at least for to-night," spoke Bert, and there was regret in his voice. "But we can take up the trail to-morrow."

"Whistle back the dog," suggested George. "And then we'll decide what to do."

But the dog did not want to come back. They could hear him baying in the depths of the now dark forest, but whether he was in sight of the bear, or was giving tongue because the trail was getting fresher, was impossible to say.

At any rate, the dog did not come back in response to the whistles shrilly emitted in his direction.

"Well, let him go," said Bert. "He'll find his way to one camp or another, I guess, if he doesn't go home to Sam. He said the dog often stayed out in the woods all night, and came back in the morning."

"All right—let him go," assented Tom. "And now what shall we do about ourselves? Here comes the snow!" he cried a moment later, for the white flakes began falling in a swirl all about them.

"In for a blizzard!" commented Jack.

"Oh, not as bad as that," murmured Bert.

"Do they have blizzards up here? How long do they last? Does it get very cold? How much snow——"

"That'll do, Why!" exclaimed Tom. "We've got something else to do besides answering questions. Now, fellows, what is it to be—Camp No. 3 or Camp No. 2? We've got to decide."

"I say No. 3," called out Bert.

"Same here," echoed Jack.

"I'm with you," was the remark of George.

"Well, I don't agree with you, but I'll give in," assented Tom. "The majority rules. But I think it would be better to go back to No. 2 Camp."

"Why?" asked Jack.

"Because we know just where it is, and we know we can be sure of a warm place, and plenty to eat."

"Can't we at No. 3?" asked George.

"Maybe, and then again, maybe not. We certainly will have to hunt for it, and it's only a chance that it may have wood and food stored there."

"Sam said it had," observed Bert.

"Yes, I know. But there have been men roaming about these woods that I wouldn't trust not to take grub from an unoccupied cabin," went on Tom. "However, we'll take a chance, but I think it's a mistake."

They turned about, and headed in as straight a line as they could for Camp No. 3. They knew the general direction, and had some landmarks to go by.

The storm grew more and more fierce. The snow was almost as impenetrable as a fog, and there was a cold, biting wind. It stung the faces of the boys and made walking difficult. It was constantly growing darker.

"I say!" called Bert, after a bit. He stopped floundering about in a drift, and went on: "I say, does anyone know where we are?"

"On the road to Ramsen," suggested Tom.

"I don't believe we are," Bert resumed. "I think we're off the trail—lost!"

"Lost!" echoed George.

"Yes, lost, and in a blinding snowstorm," went on Bert.

CHAPTER XVI

THE DESERTED CABIN

Bert's words struck rather a chill to the hearts of his chums. Not that they were cowards, for they were not, and they had faced danger before, and were used to doing things for themselves.

But now they were in a strange, mountain wilderness, following an unknown trail, and night was coming on rapidly. The storm had already burst, and it was growing worse momentarily.

"Do you really think we are lost?" questioned Jack, looking about him as well as he could in the maze of white.

"Don't you?" responded Bert. "I can't make out the least sign of a trail in these woods, and we have to follow one to get to Camp No. 3, you know."

"Yes, that's right," put in George. "We are going it blind."

"We've been going according to compass, since we gave up the hunt for the bear," commented Tom.

"Well, it will be more by good luck than good management if we find either camp now," said Bert. "But come on—we've got to do something."

"Which way shall we go?" asked George. "We don't want to get lost any worse than we are."

"We can't!" spoke Bert, dryly—that is, as "dryly" as he could with snow forcing itself into his mouth. "We're as lost as we'll ever be. The thing now is to start finding ourselves."

"Let's try this way," proposed Tom, indicating the left. "According to my compass Camp No. 3 ought to lie off about there."

"And how far away?" asked Jack.

"Not more than four miles—maybe five. But we can make that in about an hour and a half, if we don't get off the trail."

"That's the trouble," commented Bert. "We can't see any trail. We are going it absolutely blind!"

And going it blind they certainly were. They were all a bit alarmed now, for they had no shelter for the night, and they had eaten most of their food.

Suddenly, as they tramped along over the snow, there came a crash in the underbrush to one side.

"What's that?" cried George, nervously.

"That bear——" began Bert, slinging around his gun.

"Don't shoot!" cried Tom. "It's our dog come back to us!"

And so it was. The intelligent and lonesome brute had abandoned the bear's trail, and had come back to join his human friends. He was exhausted from long, hard running.

"Now he'll lead us to one camp or another," said Tom. "Welcome to our city, Towser!"

"What happened to the bear?" asked Jack, as the dog leaped about caressingly from one to the other.

"Evidently nothing," Tom said. "I don't believe the dog found him. His name isn't Towser though, by the way. I've forgotten what Sam did call him, but it wasn't Towser."

"What makes you think he didn't find the bear?" Bert wanted to know.

"He'd show some evidence of it if he had," was the reply. "He'd have a scratch or two. No, I think he gave up the chase soon after we did, and came after us."

"Well, now he's here, let's make some use of him," suggested George. "Do you really think he'll lead us back to camp, Tom?"

"Well, there's a chance of it," Tom affirmed. "Let's give him a trial. Here, old boy!" he called to the dog, a beautiful specimen. "Home, old fellow!"

The dog barked, wagged his tail, and set off on a run through the driving snow. He barked loudly, turning now and then to see if any of the four young hunters were following.

"That's the idea!" cried Jack. "Come on, boys. He'll lead us, all right!"

"But where, is another question," Tom put in. "My early education was neglected. I never learned dog talk, though I can swim that fashion pretty well."

"Swimming isn't going to do any good—not in this weather," murmured Bert, buttoning his mackinaw tighter about him, and beating his arms at his sides, for they all had been standing still, and were rather chilled.

"I could talk hog-Latin," Jack said with a smile, "but I don't believe that is any good for a dog. Call him back, Tom. You seem to have more influence over him than anyone else, and he's getting too far ahead. I wonder where he's going, anyhow?"

"I don't much care—Camp one, two, or three will suit me just about now," Tom remarked, as he turned his face to avoid a stinging blast of snowflakes. "Surely the dog knows his way to all three of them, and, if they are too far, he may lead us to Sam's farm. That wouldn't be so bad."

"Nothing would be bad where there was a warm fire and plenty of grub," commented Bert. "But call that dog back, Tom, or we'll lose him again. He's off there somewhere, barking to beat the band!"

Tom whistled shrilly. A series of barks came in answer, and, a little later the dog himself came bounding through the snow. His muzzle was all whitened where he had been burrowing, perhaps after some luckless rabbit. But his bright eyes were glowing as the boys could see in the half-darkness that had fallen, and Towser, as they continued to call him, for want of a better name, seemed delighted at something or another. Whether it was the storm, the fun he had had trailing the bear, or whether he was just glad to be with the boys, and happy over the prospect of adventures to come, no one could say.

The dog barked, wagged his tail, ran on a little way, came back, barked some more, ran on again, and then repeated the performance over and over, getting more and more excited all the while.

"He wants us to follow him," decided Tom. "All right, old man, I'm with you," he said. "Come on, boys. We'll see what comes of it."

Together the four hunters set off with the dog in the lead. Truth to tell they did not feel very much like hunters that day, nor had they had any luck. Matters seemed to be going against them. And in the storm and darkness there was a distinct feeling of depression over everyone. The dog was really the only cheerful creature there, and he had spirits enough for all of them, could they but be transferred.

"Whew! This is a storm!" cried Tom, as he bent his head to the blast.

It did seem to be getting worse. The wind had a keener cut and whirled the sharp flakes of snow into one's face with stinging force.

"It's a young blizzard," affirmed Jack.

"Well, if it does this in its youthful days, what will happen when it grows up?" Bert wanted to know, as he paused and turned around to get the wind out of his face while he caught his breath. No one took the trouble to answer him.

The dog seemed impatient at the slow progress of the lads, for he was now well ahead of them. They could only tell where he was by his barks, and by an occasional flurry of snow as he burrowed in some drift and then scrambled out again.

"Better call him back again, Tom," suggested George. "He'll get away beyond us, and soon it will be so dark we can't see our hands before our faces."

"Yes, I guess I will," Tom assented. "I'd put a leash on him if I had a bit of cord, and hold him back."

"Here's some," Jack said, offering a piece. "I had it tied around the package of sandwiches."

"By the way—any of those same sandwiches left?" asked Tom.

"A few—why?"

"Because that may be all we'll get to eat to-night."

"What's that?" cried Bert. "Aren't we going toward camp?"

"That's what I can't say," was Tom's answer, as he whistled for the dog. "We may, and then, again, we may not."

"But where are we heading, then?" George wanted to know, as Tom proceeded to tie the cord on Towser's collar.

"That's more than I can say," Tom made answer. "We're in the hands of fate, as they say in books."

"Well, I'd rather hang to Towser's tail," spoke Jack, with grim humor.

"I'm sorry I got you fellows into this mess," went on Tom, as they advanced again through the storm and darkness, this time keeping the dog closer to them by means of the cord.

"What mess?" asked Bert.

"Getting lost, and all that."

"Forget it!" advised Jack. "It wasn't your fault at all. You wanted to go back to No. 2 Camp, and the rest of us favored this move. I wish, now, we had taken your advice."

"Oh, well, mine was only a guess," Tom said. "We might have been as badly off had we gone the other way. We'll just have to trust to luck. Come on. But what I meant was that coming out to-day to hunt was my proposition. I was afraid there was a storm coming."

"We wouldn't have stayed home on that account," George asserted. "We're all in the same boat together, and we'll have to sink or swim—or skate," he added, as the icy wind smote him.

It was now about six o'clock, but as dark as it would have been at midnight. The moon was hidden behind dark clouds, but of course the white snow made it lighter than otherwise would have been the case. But in the dense woods even this did not add much to the comfort of our friends, and its increasing depth made it harder to walk.

Almost before the boys knew it, they had emerged from the forest to a road. They could tell that at once.

"Hurray!" cried Tom. "Now we'll be all right. A good road to follow."

"And a signpost, too, to tell us which way to go!" added Jack.

He pointed through the storm to where was evidently a crossroad, at the intersection of which was a post with the familiar boards on it.

"What does it say?" asked Bert, as Tom stood at the foot of it.

"Have to get out the electric light," Tom said, producing a pocket flashlight. By its powerful tungsten gleam, he read:

SEVEN MILES TO RAMSEN

"That's the ticket!" he cried. "Ramsen is the way we want to go. Camp No. 3 lies in that direction. Now we're all right, boys!"

"Good old signpost!" murmured Jack.

But, had he only known it, the signpost was a "bad" one, though, as we know, that was not the fault of the post itself.

Trudging along the road was easier now, and the boys made better time. But it was tiresome work at that. And when, a little later, they saw a building looming up at one side of the road, Bert cried:

"There's our camp now!"

For a moment they thought it was, but a closer look showed that it was not. It was an old deserted hut, almost in ruins, and as Tom flashed his light within, a sorry sight was presented to the eyes of the boys.

"Let's go inside," was Tom's proposal, and his chums looked at him in some amazement.

CHAPTER XVII

SPIED UPON

"What do we want to go in there for?" asked Jack, at length.

"Because," was the rather short answer of Tom. Then, feeling perhaps that he might explain a little more at length, he turned from where he stood in the tumbled-down doorway, and added:

"Let's get in out of the storm. This is a good place to rest, away from that cutting wind. Quiet, Towser," he added, for the dog showed signs of not wanting to go in. He growled and hung back. Then he looked in the direction in which they had come, and his hair rose on the back of his neck as though he saw something the boys did not see, and resented the sight—whatever it was.

"I don't like that," commented Bert. "Dogs know more than we do—sometimes."

"Oh, come on in!" repeated Tom, and he spoke to the dog again. This time Towser followed his temporary master inside the hut.

"But what gets me is why are we going in?" objected George. "It will only delay us, and if we've got to make seven miles to Ramsen to-night, we'd better be getting at it."

"That's just it," spoke Tom quickly. "I think we can't get at it."

"What do you mean?" came from Jack.

"I mean that we can't go on in this storm. It's getting worse every minute, and we may stray off the road. We have found this shelter providentially, and we ought to take advantage of it. It will give us a half-decent place to stay, and we won't be buried in the snow which may happen if we keep on.

"Come inside and stay here, that's what I mean," Tom went on. "It might be a heap-sight worse," and he flashed his torch about the bare and crumbling ruin of the cabin.

"What!" cried Bert. "Do you mean to stay here all night?"

"Why not?" asked Tom. "It's better than being out in the storm, isn't it? Hark to that wind!"

As he spoke a blast howled around the corner of the shack, and blew a cloud of flakes in through a glassless window.

"It's a little better than outside—but not much," murmured George. "Look at those windows."

"We can find something to stuff in them," said Tom cheerfully. "There may be some old bags about. And we haven't been upstairs yet. This place may be furnished better than we think. Come on, boys, make up your minds to stay here."

"Well, we might do worse, that's a fact," slowly admitted Jack. "Say, look at that dog, would you!"

His manner, as he said this, was excited, but no less so than that of the dog. The animal brushed past the group of boys, fairly pulling loose the improvised leash from Tom's hand and stood in the doorway with bristling hair, lips drawn back from his teeth and showing every appearance of anger.

"Something ails him," spoke George, in a low voice.

"I should say so," agreed Tom, rubbing his hand where the stout cord had cut into him, even in spite of his heavy mitten.

"It's that bear!" cried Jack.

"What?" questioned Tom.

"That bear we were following," explained Jack. "It's outside now, and the dog has winded him. Where's my gun? I'm going to have a potshot at him!"

He started toward the corner where he had stood up his gun. The interior of the cabin was fairly light, for Tom had snapped on the permanent switch of his little pocket electric light.

"Hold on a minute!" Tom said, placing a hand on his chum's shoulder. "What are you going to do?"

"Don't go out," advised Tom. "I don't believe it's the bear, to begin with, and, in the second place, if it is, you wouldn't stand any chance of hitting him in this storm. And you might get lost. It's a regular blizzard outside."

"What makes you think it isn't the bear?" asked Jack, ignoring Tom's other reasons.

"Well, from the way the dog acts, for one thing," was the answer. "He didn't act that way before, when we had a plain sight of the trail, and Towser may even have come close to Bruin himself."

"If it isn't the bear—who is it—or—what is it?" demanded George.

"I don't know," was Tom's frank reply.

"Let's give a yell," suggested Bert. "Maybe it's Sam Wilson, or someone who could put us on the right road. I don't fancy staying here all night if it can be helped. Let's give a yell."

"All right," Tom agreed. "Here, Towser," he went on to the dog, "come in here and behave yourself."

But the animal did not seem so disposed. He remained in the doorway, looking out into the storm, now and then growling hoarsely in his throat, but showing no disposition to dash out. Certainly he was acting very strangely, but whether it was fear or anger the boys could not decide.

"Well, whoever it is, or whatever, we've got plenty of guns and ammunition," remarked George. "We haven't had a decent shot to-day."

Which was very true. They had had great hopes, but that was all.

"Come on if we're going to yell," suggested Jack. "And if we don't raise someone, we'll prepare to stay here. It's the best we can do, fellows."

They united their voices in a shout, and the dog added to the din by barking. He seemed to feel better when the lads were making as much noise as they could.

But the echoes of the boys' voices, blown back to them by the snow-laden wind, was all the answer they received. They waited, and called again, but no one replied to them. Nor, as at least George half-expected, did they hear the growls of a bear. The wind howled, the snow rattled on the sides and roof of the cabin, for the flakes were almost as hard as sleet. But that was all.

"Guess we'll have to put up at this 'hotel,'" said Bert, after a pause. The dog had quieted down now, as though whatever had aroused him had passed on.

"Let's take a look around and see what we've drawn," suggested Jack. "If there's any wood, we can make a fire, and there must be some of that grub left."

"There is," announced Bert, who had constituted himself a sort of commissary department. "We've got some sandwiches, and I can make coffee."

"That isn't so bad," remarked Tom. "Once we have a little feed, we'll all feel better. And in the morning the storm may have stopped, so we can easily find our road. We're on the right one, I'm sure, for that signboard said seven miles to Ramsen, and that's in the direction of Camp No. 3."

If Tom had only known about that changed signboard!

Each of the lads carried a powerful electric light, with a tungsten bulb. It was operated by a small, dry battery. It was intended only for a flashing light, of a second or so each time, but there was a switch arrangement so that the light could be held steady and permanent, though of course this used up the battery quickly.

"I'll let my light burn," proposed Tom. "It's nearly burned out anyhow, and you fellows can save yours until later."

"If we could have a fire, we wouldn't need a light," Bert said.

"That's right," agreed Tom. "Let's look about a bit."

There was a hearth in the main room of the deserted cabin, and on it were the ashes of a fire, long since dead and cold. But it seemed to show that the chimney would draw. Scattered about the room were pieces of old boxes and barrel staves, and a pile of these was soon set ablaze on the hearth.

"That looks better!" remarked Bert, with satisfaction, as he rubbed his hands in front of the blaze. "Now if we had a way of stopping up some of these broken windows, we wouldn't be so cold."

"Take some of those bags," suggested Tom, indicating a pile in a corner. It looked like the bed of some chance tramp who had accepted the shelter the deserted shack offered.

The boys soon had the broken lights filled in, and when the tumble-down door had been propped up in the entrance, the cabin was not such a bad shelter, with a blazing fire going.

"Now for a look upstairs," suggested Tom, for the cabin was of two stories, though the top one was very low.

"I'd rather eat," suggested George.

"It won't take long to investigate," Tom said.

They went up the rickety stairs, but the trip hardly paid for their pains, for there was less upstairs than there was down. Some few rags, bits of broken bottles, boxes and barrels were seen, and that was all.

"And now for grub!" cried George, when they were once more in the main room downstairs. "Let's get that coffee going, and eat what there is."

The boys carried a coffee-pot with them, and a supply of the ground berries. Some snow was scooped up in the pot, which was set on the coals to provide the necessary water by melting the white crystals. Then the packages of sandwiches, rather depleted, it is true, were set out. A little later the aroma of the boiling beverage filled the room.

"That smells fine!" murmured Jack.

"It surely does," agreed Bert. "Now for a feed."

They all felt better after they had eaten what food was left from lunch. And surely they needed the grateful and stimulating warmth of the coffee, even though it was rather muddy, and was drunk out of tin cups they carried with them. They even had condensed milk and sugar, for these were carried in a case, in which fitted the pot and the ground coffee. This was one of Tom's up-to-date discoveries.

To Towser were tossed the odds and ends of the sandwiches, and he ate them greedily, drinking some snow water which George melted for him in a tin he found in one corner of the cabin.

Then the boys prepared to spend the night in the deserted cabin. They sat about the fire, on improvised seats made from broken boxes, and watched the fire, which certainly was cheerful. They expected to only doze through the night, and hoped to get on the proper road by morning.

Suddenly the dog, which had been peacefully lying in front of the hearth, sprang up with a growl and bark. He startled the boys.

"Quiet!" commanded Tom, but the animal continued to growl.

"That's funny," remarked Jack.

"What is?" asked Tom. "Just because he barks on account of hearing something, or scenting something, that's beyond us?"

"No, not that so much, but it's a funny feeling I have," said Jack. "I feel just as if we were being spied upon."

"Spied upon!" repeated Tom. "Say, you're as nervous as a girl, old man!"

Before Jack could reply, the dog had leaped up and rushed out into the storm through a small opening where the old door was only propped against the frame.

CHAPTER XVIII
LOST AGAIN

"Now what's up?" cried Tom, as he made a rush after the dog. But he was too late. Towser was out in the snow.

"It's that bear again," George said.

"You've got bear on the brain," commented Bert.

The boys looked out and listened, but they could neither see nor hear anything, and soon the dog came back. But, even as he reached the door, he turned and sent a challenging bark toward someone—or something.

"This sure is queer," murmured Bert.

"And it's queer what Jack said," went on Tom. "About being spied upon. What do you mean, old man?"

"Just what I said," was the answer. "Just before the dog gave the alarm, I had a feeling as though someone outside was keeping watch over this shack."

"That sure is a funny feeling," commented George. "Who would it be? There aren't any persons up around here except Sam Wilson, or maybe some of those Indian guides he knows."

"It might be one of the Indians," suggested Bert. "They might be sneaking around, to see what they could pick up."

"A wild animal wouldn't make a fellow feel as I felt," decided Jack. "But maybe I'm only fussy, and——"

"You are—worse than a girl," said Tom, with a laugh that took the sharpness out of the words. "I guess it's only the storm, and the effect of being in a strange place. Now let's settle down and take it easy. There's no one outside."

Once more they disposed themselves before the cheerful blaze, the dog stretching out at full length to dry his shaggy coat that was wet with melting snow.

"I wonder what sort of a place this was?" spoke Jack, at length.

"Must have been a hunter's cabin," suggested Tom.

"It's too big for that. This looks as though people had lived in it once," declared Bert. "Besides, it's too near the road for a hunter to want to use it. I guess the family died off, or moved away, and there isn't enough population up here to make it so crowded that they have to use this shack."

"Well, it comes in handy for us," remarked George. "I could go another sandwich, but——"

"All the going you'll do will be to go without," laughed Bert, grimly. "There isn't a crumb left, but I could manage to squeeze out some more coffee."

"Better save it for morning," advised Tom. "We'll need it worse by then."

The storm still raged, but inside the deserted cabin the boys were fairly comfortable. They had on thick, warm garments, and these, with the glowing fire, made them feel little of the nipping cold that prevailed with the blizzard.

The wind howled down the chimney, scattering the light ashes now and then, and filling the room with the pungent odor of smoke. Around some of the windows, where the rags were stuffed in the broken panes, little piles of sifted snow gathered.

At times the whole frail structure shook with the force of the blast, and at such times the boys would look at each other with a trace of fear on their faces. For the ramshackle structure might fall down on them.

But as it did not, after each recurrent windy outburst, they felt more confident. Perhaps the cabin was built stronger than they thought. The dog showed no uneasiness at these manifestations of Nature. He did not even open his eyes when the wind howled its loudest and blew its strongest. And, too, he seemed to have gotten over the strange fear that caused him to act so oddly.

The other boys had rather laughed at Jack's "notion" of being "spied upon," but had they been able to see through the white veil of snow that was falling all about the cabin, they would have realized that there is sometimes something like telepathy, or second sight. For, in reality, the boys were being observed by a pair of evil eyes.

And the evil eyes were set in an evil face, which, in turn belonged to the body of a man who had constructed for himself a rude shelter against the storm.

It was such a shelter as would be hastily built by a hunter caught in the open for the night—a sort of "lean-to," with the open side away from the direction in which the wind blew. But it could not have been made in this storm, and, consequently, must have been put up before the blizzard began.

The lean-to showed signs of a practiced hand, for it was fairly comfortable, and the man in it chuckled to himself now and then as he looked over toward the deserted cabin.

The man was on the watch, and he had prepared for just this emergency. At times, when he heard the barking of the dog, a frown could have been seen on his face, had there been a light by which to observe it. But the lean-to was in absolute darkness, save what light was reflected by the white snow.

"I thought they'd end up here," was the man's muttered remark to himself, for he was all alone. "Yes, I thought they would. It's the nearest shelter after they left the doctored signboard. Naturally they turned in here. That changed sign did the trick all right. Lucky I thought of it. Now I wonder what the next move will be?"

He did not answer himself for a few seconds, but crouched down, looking in the direction of the cabin, through the chinks of which shone the light of the fire.

"They'll stay there until morning, I reckon," communed the man to himself. "Then they'll light out and try to find Ramsen. But they won't locate it by going the way that sign pointed," and he chuckled. "They'll only get deeper in the woods, and then, if we can cut out that Fairfield from among the others, we'll have him where we want him. If we can't, we'll manage to take him anyhow."

He paused, as though to go over in his mind the details of the evil scheme he was plotting, and resumed:

"Yes, they'll light out in the morning. I'll have to follow 'em until I make sure which trail they take. Then the rest will be easy. It isn't going to be any fun to stay here all night, but it will be worth the money, I guess.

"That is, if Skeel ponies up as he says he will. And if Skeel tries to cut up any funny tricks, and cheat me and Whalen, he'll wish he never had. He'll never try it twice!"

With another look out at the dimly lighted cabin, as if to make sure that none of those he was spying on had left, the man composed himself to pass the night in his somewhat uncomfortable shelter. He curled up in a big blanket and went to sleep. For he was a woodsman born and bred, and he thought nothing of staying out in the open, with only a little shelter, through a long, cold night. He was even comfortable, after his own fashion.

And slowly the night passed for our four friends in the deserted cabin.

They had managed to construct a rude sort of bed by placing old inside doors on some boxes. Their heavy mackinaws were covers, and the nearness of the fire on the hearth kept them warm. Occasionally, through the night, as one or another awoke from a doze, he would toss on more wood, to keep the blaze from going out.

The dog whined uneasily once or twice during the night, but he did not bark or growl. Perhaps he knew that the man in the lean-to was asleep also, and would not walk abroad to plot harm.

"Well, it's still snowing," remarked Tom, as he arose and stretched his cramped muscles.

"How do you know? Is it morning?" asked George, yawning.

"It's an imitation of it," Tom announced. "I looked out. It's still snowing to beat the band."

"Oh, for our cozy camp—any one of them!" sighed Jack. "Let's have what's left of that coffee, Bert, and then we'll hike out and see what we can find."

The coffee was rather weak, but it was hot, and that meant a great deal to the boys who had to venture out in the cold. Every drop was disposed of, and then, looking well to their guns, for though they hardly admitted it to each other, they had faint hopes of game, the boys set out.

As they emerged from the cabin, they were not aware of a pair of sharp, ferret-like eyes watching them from the hidden shelter of the lean-to. As the wind was blowing toward that shack, and not away from it, the dog was not this time apprised by scent of the closeness of an enemy, whatever had happened the night before.

"Well, let's start," proposed Tom. "This is the road to Ramsen," and he pointed to the almost snow-obliterated highway that ran in front of the deserted cabin they were leaving.

Their hearts were lighter with the coming of the new day, though their stomachs were almost empty. But they hoped soon to be at one of their camping cabins, where, they knew, a good supply of food awaited them.

On they tramped through the snow. It was very deep, and the fall seemed to have increased in rapidity, rather than to have diminished. It had snowed all night, and was still keeping up with unabated vigor. In some places there were deep drifts across the road.

"This sure is heavy going," observed Jack, as he plunged tiresomely along.

"That's right," agreed Bert.

"I don't see how Towser keeps it up," spoke George, for the dog was having hard work to get through the drifts.

"He seems to enjoy it," commented Tom. "But it is deep. I think——"

He did not complete the sentence, for, at that moment, he stepped into some unseen hole and went down in a snow pile to his waist.

"Have a hand!" invited Jack, extending a helping arm to his chum, to pull him up. "What were you trying to do, anyhow?"

"I don't know," answered Tom, looking at the hole into which he had fallen. "But I think we're off the road, fellows."

"I do, too," came from Bert. "It seems as though we were going over a field. Yes," he went on, "there's a stump sticking up out of the snow. We're in some sort of a clearing. We're clean off the road!"

It took only a moment for the others to be also convinced of this.

"We'd better go back," George said. "We've probably come the wrong way. I don't believe this is the road to Ramsen at all."

"The signboard said it was," Bert reminded him.

"I can't help that. I believe we're wrong again—lost!"

"Lost—again!" echoed Jack. "Lost in this wilderness!"

"It does begin to look so," admitted Tom slowly. "Where's that dog?"

CHAPTER XIX

THE CAPTURE

Towser had run off again, on one of his attempts to wiggle through a drift. A shrill whistle from Tom brought him back again, however, sneezing because some snow had gotten up his nose and into his mouth.

"Towser, you old rascal!" Tom exclaimed. "Why don't you lead us back to camp?"

"Or to Sam Wilson's," added Bert. "That would be good enough on a pinch, until we get straightened out. Home, old fellow! Wilson's farm! Lead the way!"

The dog barked and leaped about, but he did not show any inclination to take any particular direction through the snow-covered wilderness. He seemed to want to follow, rather than lead.

"I don't believe he knows where Sam Wilson's place is," was Tom's opinion, after watching the animal for a while.

"I guess he's as badly lost as we are," said Bert.

For a few seconds the boys stood there rather at a loss what to do. They had done their best, but they did not seem to be on the way to success. The storm was worse than when it first started. It still snowed hard, and the wind, while not as strong as it had been during the night, was still cold and cutting.

The boys turned their backs to it as they stood there huddled together, hardly knowing what to do next. Towser, finding he was not wanted immediately, to trail a bear or some other game, devoted his energies to burrowing in a snowbank.

"Well, I would like to know where we are," said Tom at length.

"Wouldn't it be a good idea to go back to the deserted cabin?" asked Jack.

"It might not be so bad, if we knew where it was," agreed Tom.

"We could at least take that for a starting point, and try to head for Camp No. 2," Jack went on. "I'd be satisfied with that, as long as we can't locate No. 3."

"Oh, I side with you there, all right, old man," Tom said, "but where does the old cabin lie?"

"Off there!" said Bert, pointing to the right.

"No, it's over there," was the opinion of George, and he indicated the left.

"It's right behind you," insisted Jack.

"And I should say it was in front of us," spoke Tom. "So you see we each have a different opinion, and, as long as we can't agree, what are we going to do about it?"

"That's so," admitted Jack. "But we can't stay here doing nothing. We've got to get somewhere."

"Somewhere is very indefinite," was the remark George made. "It's very easy to say it, but hard to find it. If we could only get back on the road, we could head in either direction, and some time or other we would get somewhere. But now we are in the woods and we may be heading right toward the middle of the forest instead of toward the edge. And these forests are no little picnic groves, either."

"I should say not!" Tom exclaimed. "But where is the road? That's the question."

It was a question no one could answer, and they did not try. Eagerly and anxiously they scanned the expanse of snow for some indication that a road existed—even a rough, lumberman's highway.

But all they could see, here and there, were little mounds of snow that indicated where stumps existed under the white covering. They were in a clearing, with woods all around them. If they advanced, they might be going toward the deeper forest instead of toward the place where civilization, in the shape of man, had begun to cut down the trees to make a town or village.

"Well, we sure have got to do something," Tom said, and it was not the first time, either. "We'll try each direction, fellows, and see where we come out. We may have to go the limit, and tramp a bit in each of four directions, and, again, it may be our luck to do it the first shot. But let's get into action. It's cold standing still."

They had given up all hope of game now. Indeed, the snow was falling so thickly that they could not have seen a deer or bear until they were very close to it—too close it would be, in the case of the bear.

As for smaller game—rabbits, squirrels and partridges, none of those were to be seen. The snow had driven the smaller animals and the birds to cover.

"Bur-r-r-r-r! But this is no fun, on an empty stomach," grumbled George, as he followed the others. The dog, having seen his friends start off, was following them. He seemed to have no sense of responsibility that he was expected to lead his friends in the right direction. "I sure am hungry!" George went on.

"Quit talking about it," urged Tom. "That doesn't do any good, and it makes all of us feel badly. Have a snow sandwich!"

"It makes you too thirsty," interposed Jack. "If you want to drink, we'll stop, make a fire of some fir branches, and melt snow in our tin coffee cups. If you start chewing flakes, you'll get a sore mouth, and other things will happen to you. That's what a fellow wrote in a book on Arctic travel."

"If only we hadn't eaten all the grub!" sighed Bert.

"Too late to think of that now," Tom spoke. "Come on—let's hike!"

Off they started. They decided to make an effort in each of the four cardinal points, first selecting that which one of the boys declared led back to Camp No. 2.

"If we go on for a mile or two, and find we're wrong again, back we come and try the other side," Tom explained. "But I can't see why that sign says seven miles to Ramsen, when the road is so easy to lose yourself on."

"It will take us the rest of the day to do that experimenting," grumbled George.

"Well, suggest a better plan," spoke Tom, quickly. "We're lost, and if we don't find the proper road soon, we'll be more than all day in this pickle."

George had no more to say.

The boys were now a little alarmed at their plight, for they were cold and hungry, and that is no condition in which to fight the wintry blast. But there was nothing they could do except keep moving. In a way, that was their only hope, for the exercise kept them warm, though it made them all the more hungry.

"Keep a lookout for game—even small kinds," advised Tom, as they went on. "A rabbit or a squirrel wouldn't come amiss now. We could manage to broil it over the coals of a fire, though it probably won't be very nice looking."

"Who cares for looks when you're hungry?" demanded Bert.

But game did not show itself as the boys tramped on through the snow. They went on for some distance in the direction first decided on, but could see no familiar landmarks. Nor did they reach anything that looked like a road.

"Better go back," Tom decided, and they did manage to find the little clearing again.

"Say!" cried Bert, as they stood irresolute as to which of the three remaining directions to select next, "aren't we silly, though?"

"Why?" asked Tom.

"Why, because all we had to do was to follow our trail back in the snow. That would have led us to the old cabin."

Tom shook his head.

"What's the matter?" asked Bert.

"Our footprints are blown or drifted over three minutes after we make them, in this wind and shifting snow," Tom said. "Look!"

He pointed over the route they had just come. Their earlier footprints were altogether gone. The expanse of snow was white and unbroken.

"Well, we go this way next," said Jack. "I remember because I saw that broken white birch tree. Head straight for that."

They did so, but again were doomed to disappointment. That way led to a low, swampy place, though there was no water in it at present, it having been frozen and covered with snow.

"No road here," Tom said. "Let's try some other route."

"Say!" cried Jack. "What's the sense of all four of us going in the same direction all the while? Why not try four ways at once? The one who finds the road can fire two shots in quick succession. The rest of us will then come to where we hear the shots."

"A good idea!" commented Tom. "We'll try it. Scatter now, and don't go too far. Oh, you're coming with me, are you, Towser?" for the dog followed him, evidently considering Tom his master.

The four boys now set off in different directions, and soon were lost to sight of one another in the storm. Tom was sure he was going the route that would take him to the road. He pressed on eagerly.

The dog ran on ahead, and disappeared.

"He's fond of taking a lot of exercise," was Tom's mental comment. Then he saw some bushes, just ahead of him, being agitated and he went on: "No, he's coming back. Maybe he's found something."

Suddenly the bushes back of Tom parted with a crackling of the dry twigs. The lad thought perhaps it was some animal stirred up by the dog, and he was advancing his gun, to be in readiness, when he felt, all at once, something cover his head. He was in blackness, but he could tell by the smell that a bag had been thrust over his eyes.

"Here. Quit that! Stop!" yelled Tom, and then his voice ended in a smothered groan. Something like a gag had been thrust between his lips and he was thrown heavily.

For a moment Tom's senses seemed to leave him. He could see nothing, but he felt that he was being mauled. He had a momentary fear that it might be a bear. But, he reflected, bears do not throw sacks over one's head, nor gag one. It must be men—but what men?

Vainly Tom struggled. He felt his hands being tied—his feet entangled in ropes. He fought, but was overpowered. Then he heard a voice saying:

"Well, we've captured him, anyhow."

"Yes," agreed another voice, and Tom vainly wondered where he had heard it before. "Yes, we have him, and now the question is, what to do with him."

CHAPTER XX

A PRISONER

Tom was in sort of a daze for the first few moments following the unexpected and violent attack on him, an attack culminating in his being bound so that he could hardly move.

Dimly, and almost uncomprehendingly, he heard voices murmuring about him—he could hear the voices of men above the howl of the gale that seemed to continue with unabated fury.

Gradually Tom's senses cleared. The haze that seemed to envelope his mind passed away and he began to realize that he must not submit dumbly to this indignity. He first strained lightly at his bonds, as if to test them. The sack was still over his head, so he could not see, and there was a horribly stuffy and suffocating feeling about it.

Tom's effort to loosen his bonds, slight as it was, had the effect of starting his blood up in a better circulation, and this helped him to think better and more quickly.

"I've got to get out of this!" he told himself energetically. "This won't do at all! I wonder who the scoundrels are who have caught me this way?"

But Tom did not stop then to argue out that question. He wanted to devote all his time to getting himself loose. With that in view, he put forth all his strength. He was lying on his back, in a bank of snow, he judged, and he now strained his arms and legs with all his might.

But he might just as well have saved his strength. Those who had tied the bonds about him knew their evil business well, and poor Tom was like a roped steer. Not only was he unable to loosen the bonds on his arms and legs, but he found the effort hurt him, and made him almost suffocate, because of the gag and the closeness of the bag over his head.

Then he heard voices speaking again.

"He's coming to," said someone—a vaguely familiar voice.

"Yes, but he'll have to come a great deal harder than that to get away," was the answer, and someone chuckled. Tom wished he could hit that person, whoever he was. His gun had either fallen or been knocked from his hand at the first attack.

"Well, what are we going to do with him?" asked the voice that had first spoken.

"Wait until——" but the rest of the sentence Tom did not hear, for the wind set up a louder howling at that point, and the words were borne away with it. Then, too, Tom was at a disadvantage because of the bag over his ears.

He felt himself being lifted up, and placed in a more comfortable position, and he was glad of that, for he felt weak and sick. It must be remembered that aside from a little coffee that morning, he had had no breakfast, and that he had had little or no sleep the night before. With a scant supper, a battle with the storm, the anxiety about being lost, and having led his friends, unconsciously enough, into a scrape, it was no great wonder that Tom was not altogether himself.

"But who in the world has captured me, and what do they want of me?" Tom asked himself. He had an idea it might, perhaps, be some of the half-breed Indians who had caught him for the sake of his gun and clothing. Or perhaps some trapper or guide was guilty.

But if they were after his gun, or what money he carried, or even the fine mackinaw he wore, why did they not take those things and make off into the woods? That would at least leave Tom free.

But the men remained on guard over the bound figure of the boy, now sitting upright on a bank of snow. Tom could dimly hear them movingabout. They were evidently waiting for someone.

"But if they wait long enough, the fellows may come to look after me," Tom reasoned. "Jack, George, and Bert will know how to deal with these scoundrels."

Then he reflected that the other lads would not know where he was unless he fired his gun, and he could not do that. If one of the others—Bert, Jack or George—found the road, they would not know where Tom was.

"Unless the dog could lead me to them, or them to me," he mused. "I wonder where Towser is, anyhow?"

Tom's last view of the animal had been when it darted into a bush, after some rabbit, perhaps. Then had come the sudden attack. If the dog had returned, Tom did not know of it. He only hoped the animal would "raise some sort of row," as he put it.

But there was no evidence of Towser. Tom could hear only the now low-voiced talk of two men, and the rush of the wind. That it was still snowing he was quite sure, and he wondered what his companions were doing.

Suddenly he became aware of some new element that entered into his predicament. One of the men exclaimed:

"Here he comes now!"

"That's good!" responded the other, and there seemed to be relief in his tones.

"I didn't see anything of him," called the newcomer. "I saw the others—they've separated, all right, but Fairfield——"

"He's here! We've got him!" was the triumphant rejoinder of one of the men near Tom. "Got him good and proper!"

"You have! That's the ticket. Now we'll see what the old man has to say. I guess he'll pony up all right."

Tom felt a shock as though someone had thrown cold water over him.

That voice!

Tom knew now. It was Professor Skeel.

He began to understand. He saw the meaning of many things that had hitherto puzzled him. The vagueness was clearing away. The plot was beginning to be revealed.

Was this why Skeel had come to the wilderness of the Adirondacks? Was this why he and his cronies had been sneaking around the camp cabins? It seemed so.

"And yet, what in the world can he want of me?" Tom asked himself. "If it's revenge for what I did to him, this is a queer way of showing it. I didn't think he'd have spunk enough to plot a thing like this, though he certainly has meanness enough."

Tom was thinking fast. He was putting together in his mind many matters that had seemed strange to him. Certain it was that at Skeel's instigation he had been made a prisoner, and probably with the help of Murker and Whalen, though Tom had not seen their faces clearly and could not be sure of their identity.

"But what's it all about?" poor Tom asked himself over and over again. "Why should he make a prisoner of me?"

"Can we carry him?" asked Skeel's voice. "We've got to take him to the old shack, you know. Can't leave him here. Besides, there's some business to attend to in connection with him. Can you carry him through the snow?"

"Sure," was the answer. "He isn't so heavy. Up on your shoulders with him, Whalen, and we'll follow the professor. I'm all turned about in this storm!"

Tom was sure, then, of the identity of his three captors. He was as sure as though he had seen them.

A moment later he found himself being lifted up, and he could feel that the men were adjusting him to their shoulders. It was no easy task, for Tom was rather heavy, and his clothing, for he was dressed warmly for the cold, made an additional burden. But the men were strong, it seemed.

"Shall we take that off?" asked one of the men. Tom had an idea he referred to the head-covering bag.

"No, better leave it on until we get farther off. Some of the others might see him," was Skeel's answer. Tom felt sure he referred to the bag.

"I wish they'd take this gag out of my mouth," Tom mused. "I don't care so much for the bag. But my tongue will feel like a piece of leather in a little while."

On through the storm Tom was carried, on the shoulders of the two men. In fancy he could see the former instructor leading the way.

"He spoke of the old shack," mused Tom. "I wonder if he means the deserted cabin where we were? If he takes me there, the boys will have a better chance of finding me if they look."

But Tom was soon to know that it was not to the deserted hut he was being carried. For the journey soon came to an abrupt termination. The young prisoner felt himself being carried into some building, for he was lowered from the men's shoulders.

"They never could have reached the old cabin in this time," Tom decided to himself. "They must have brought me to some new place. I wonder what will happen now?"

Tom felt himself laid on some sort of bed or bunk. Then he heard a door closed and locked.

"Well, we've got him just where we want him," said Skeel. "Now we'll go ahead with our plans."

And the prisoner wondered what those plans were.

CHAPTER XXI

SKEEL REVEALS HIMSELF

"Shall we loosen him up now?" asked the voice of one of the men. Tom could still see nothing, as the bag remained over his head.

"Yes, take off the headgear, and ungag him," answered Skeel. "It won't matter if he does holler up here. No one will hear him. But keep his hands tied, except when we feed him."

Tom felt a sudden sense of elation in spite of his most uncomfortable position. At least he was going to get something to eat, and he needed it, for he felt nearly famished.

"Is the door locked?" asked one of the men.

"I attended to that," was Skeel's answer. "He can't get away from here."

"We'll see about that," mused Tom. "I'll have a good try, at any rate, the first chance I get."

He felt the fastenings of the bag being loosed, and when it was taken off, he looked about him quickly. The first glance was enough to tell him, if he had not already been sure of it, that he was in some shack where he had never been before. This was not the deserted cabin where he and his chums had spent the night. Tom glanced toward the windows, hoping to get a glimpse outside so he might determine his position, but there were dirty curtains over the casements.

His next glances were directed toward the men themselves, though he was already sure, in his own mind, who they were. Nor was his judgment reversed.

There stood Skeel, a grin of triumph in his ugly face, and there were the two other men, of evil countenance, whom Tom had seen with the erstwhile professor.

"We're going to take the gag out of your mouth," said Skeel to his prisoner. "We don't want to hurt you any more than we have to, but we're going to have you do as we say, and not as you want to. You can yell, if you like, but you'll only be wasting your breath. This is a good way from nowhere, up here, and you won't be heard. You can't get away, because one of us will be on guard all the while. I tell you this to save you trouble, for I know you, and I know that you'll make a row if you possibly can," and Skeel stuck out his jaw pugnaciously. He and Tom Fairfield had been in more than one "row" before.

"Take it off, Murker," the former instructor said to the worse-looking of his two helpers. "Let's see if he'll yelp now."

It was a relief to Tom to have the bunch of not overly-clean rags taken from his mouth. His tongue and jaws ached from the pressure and now he sighed in relief.

Tom Fairfield was not foolish. He had already made up his mind to do all he could to circumvent the plans of the plotters, and he was going to begin as soon as possible. He did not altogether believe Skeel when the latter said that shouting would do no good, but Tom did not intend to try, at once, that method of getting help.

He wanted to rest his throat from the strain, and he wanted to see how best to direct his voice in case he did feel like shouting. He had no doubt but what if he cried out for help now, the gag would be put back in his mouth. And that he did not want. He wanted to eat, and oh! how he did long for a drink of cold water.

"Guess he isn't going to yap," murmured the man known as Murker.

"So much the better," said Skeel. "Now you can loosen those ropes on his legs. He can't get away."

Tom wished, with all his heart, that they would loosen the bonds on his hands and arms, but he stubbornly resolved to stand the pain those cordsgave him, rather than ask a favor of any of the trio of scoundrels.

He simply could not endure his thirst and hunger any longer. He tried to speak—to ask at least for a glass of water, for the men could not be so altogether heartless as to refuse what they would give to a dumb beast. But Tom's throat was so parched and dry that only a husky sound came forth.

"Guess he wants to wet his whistle," suggested Whalen.

"Well, get him a drink then," half-growled Skeel. "Then we'll talk business."

Tom thought nothing ever tasted so good as that draught of water from the cracked teacup one of the men brought in from another room, and held up to his lips. It was better than nectar ever could be, he was sure.

"How about a little grub?" asked Murker.

"Oh, he could have it, I guess," Skeel replied. "Guess they didn't any of 'em have much. They were away from their camp all night, you say, and there wasn't anything in the old shanty."

"That's right," assented Whalen.

Then Tom realized that he and his companions had been spied upon, just as Jack had so strangely suspected. They had also been followed, it was evident, for the men knew of the movements of himself and his chums.

"I meant grub for all of us," went on Murker. "I'm a bit hungry myself, and it's about time for dinner."

"All right—get what you want," assented Skeel. "And give him some. One of you can sit by him, and take off the ropes while he eats. But watch him—he's like a cat—quick!"

Tom felt like smiling at this tribute to his prowess, but he refrained. It was no time for laughter.

"I've got a bit of writing to do," Skeel went on. "You fellows can eat if you like. I'll take mine later."

"All right," assented Whalen. "But what about—well, you know what I mean," and he rubbed his fingers together to indicate money.

"I'll attend to that," said Skeel, a bit stiffly. "You mind your own affairs!"

"Oh, no offense!" said Whalen, quickly. "I only wanted to know."

"You'll know soon enough," was the retort, as the former teacher moved toward another room.

"Well, I'm in on this too. Don't forget that!" exclaimed Murker, and there seemed to be menace in his tones.

"Oh, don't bother me!" answered Skeel, apparently a bit irritated.

Evidently the feeling among the conspirators was not as friendly as it might have been. It was very like a dissention, and Tom wondered if the truth of the old adage was to be proved, "When thieves fall out, honest men get their dues."

"I hope it proves so in my case," Tom reflected. "But first I would like something to eat. And I wish the others had some, too. I wonder where they are now, and what they think of me?" Professor Skeel went into another room, and closed the door after him. Murker also went into another apartment—there seemed to be three rooms, at least, on the first floor of the cabin—and presently the evil-faced man came back with a platter on which were some chunks of cold meat and bread. It looked better to Tom, half famished as he was, than a banquet would have seemed—even a surreptitious midnight school-feed.

"Help yourself," growled Murker, as he set the platter down in front of Tom, on a rough table, and loosed the bonds of our hero's arms.

"Guess I'll have a bit myself," murmured Whalen.

"Go on," mumbled Murker, his mouth half full. "The boss will eat later, I reckon."

Tom reflected that by the "boss" they must mean Skeel.

As for the young hunter, he eagerly took some of the bread and meat. It was cold, but it was good and nourishing, and seemed to have been well cooked.

It put new life into Tom at once. He would have liked a cup of coffee, but there seemed to be none. Perhaps the men would make some later. Tom certainly hoped that they would do so.

The men ate fast—almost ravenously, and Tom was not at all slow himself. He did not realize what an appetite he had until he saw the victuals disappearing.

Then, when the edge of his hunger had been a little dulled and blunted, to say the least, Tom once more began wondering why he had been caught and brought as a prisoner to the lonely hut.

"What's the game?" he asked himself.

He was soon to know.

"Well, if you fellows have had enough, and he's been fed, tie up his hands again," said Skeel, coming from the room just then. "I want to have a talk with him. You can wait outside," he added, when the ropes had once more been put on Tom's hands and arms.

Skeel waited until the men had left the hut. Then, locking the door after them, the former teacher confronted Tom. Up to now our hero had said nothing. He believed in a policy of silence for the time being.

"Well, what do you think of yourself now?" sneered Skeel, folding his arms. "You're not so smart as you thought you were, are you?"

"I haven't begun to think yet," said Tom, coolly. "But I would like to know why you have brought me here—by what right?"

"By the right of—might!" was the answer. "I've got you here, and here I'm going to keep you until your father pays me a ransom of ten thousand dollars. That will square accounts a little, and make up for some of the things you did to me. It's you against ten thousand dollars, and I guess your father would rather pay up than see you suffer. Now I'll get down to business," and he drew up a chair and sat down in front of Tom.

CHAPTER XXII

AN ANXIOUS SEARCH

George Abbot had the luck of finding the road for which he and his chums had all vainly sought so long in the storm. It will be remembered that the four boys had started in different directions, corresponding to the different points of the compass, to search for a route, either back to the hut where they had spent the night, or to one of the three camps.

And it was George who found the road.

True he did not know which road it was at the time, but when he had stumbled on through the drifting snow, fighting his way against the storm for some time, he fairly tumbled down a little embankment, rolling over and over.

"Well, what's this?" George asked himself, rather dazed, as he rose to his feet.

He had his answer in a moment.

"It's a road—I hope it's the road," he went on, as he saw that the little declivity down which he had fallen was where the road had been cut through a hill, leaving a slope on either side of the highway.

"I must signal to the others at once," George decided. His gun had slipped from his grasp when he fell, but he now picked up the weapon, and fired two shots in quick succession. It was the signal agreed upon.

The wind was blowing hard, and George was not sure that the sound of the shots would carry to his chums. He did not know just how far they were from him. So, after waiting a bit, he strolled down the snow-covered road a bit, and fired again. He repeated this three times, at intervals, before he heard an answering shot. Then he raised his voice in a yell, and soon was relieved to be joined by Jack.

"What is it?" Jack asked.

"The road—I've found it," George answered.

"Where's Bert—and Tom?"

"Haven't seen either of them."

"Well, they're probably looking yet. We'll fire some more shots and bring 'em up."

George and Jack fired at intervals, the signal each time being two rapid shots, but it was some time before they had an answer. It finally came in the shape of another shot, followed quickly by a shout.

"It's Bert," said George.

"Sounded more like Tom," was his chum's guess. While they waited, they exchanged experiences. Jack told of vainly floundering about in the drifts, while George had better news to impart.

"I fairly stumbled on the road," he said.

"Any way at all, as long as you found it," said Jack. "Here comes someone now."

It proved to be Bert, who staggered up through the storm, himself almost a living snowball.

"Found anything?" he gasped, for he was quite "winded."

"The road," answered George.

"Where's Tom?" asked Jack.

"Why, isn't he with you?" asked Bert, in some surprise. "I haven't seen anything of him."

"He's probably off searching for a highway," said George, hopefully. "We'll fire a few more shots."

They fired more than a few, but received no response from Tom, and we well know the reason why, though his chums did not at the time.

"Well, what had we better do?" asked Jack, at length. "I'm about all in, and I guess you fellows feel about the same."

"I would like something to eat," admitted Bert.

"And I'm terribly cold," confessed George, who was shivering.

"Well, let's look about a bit on either side of this road, then go up and down it a ways, and keep firing and shouting," suggested Jack. "We may find Tom. If we don't—well, I think we'd better see where this road goes."

They adopted that plan, but though they shouted vigorously, and fired many shots, there came no answer from Tom.

The exercise and the shouting, however, had one good result. It warmed George so he was no longer in danger of coming down with pneumonia.

"Well, it's six of one and a half dozen of the other," said Bert, at length. "What shall we do, and which way shall we go on this road to get to camp?"

"We'd better try to find one of the cabins," said Jack. "And I think this direction seems to be the most likely," and he pointed to the left.

"Go ahead; I'm with you," said Bert, and George nodded assent.

"What about Tom, though?" asked George, anxiously.

"Well, we can't find him. He may have gone on ahead, or he may still be searching for a road. In either case he's too far off for us to make him hear—that's evident. And we may find him just as well by trying to make our way back to camp as staying here," said Jack.

So it was decided to do this, and off they started. The storm did not seem quite so fierce now. In fact, there were indications that the fall of snowwas lessening. But a great deal had fallen, making walking difficult. The cold was intense, but it was a dry cold, not like the damp, penetrating air of New Jersey, and the boys stood it much better.

They had not gone far before Jack uttered a cry.

"Here he comes! There's Tom!" he shouted, pointing at a figure advancing toward them through the mist of flakes that were still falling, but more lazily now.

"It's someone, but how do you know it's Tom?" asked Bert.

"Who else would it be?" Jack wanted to know.

"It might be—Skeel," suggested George.

"Or that—bear!" and, as he said this, Bert advanced his gun.

"Nonsense—that's no bear!" exclaimed Jack. "It isn't Tom though, either," he added, as the figure came nearer.

A moment later they all saw at once who it was.

"Sam Wilson!" exclaimed Bert. "That's good! Now he can tell us what to do, and where Tom is. Hello, Sam!" he called, for that was how everyone addressed the genial guide—even those who had met him only once or twice.

"Hello yourselves!" Sam answered in greeting. "What are you fellows doing here?"

"We've been lost, and we've just found ourselves," explained Jack. "We're on our way to Camp No. 3."

"Oh, no, you're not!" exclaimed Sam, smiling.

"Why not?" Bert wanted to know.

"For the simple reason that you're on your way to Camp No. 2," answered Sam. "You're going the wrong way for Camp No. 3."

"Well, maybe we are twisted," admitted Jack, "but as long as we're headed for some camp, I don't care what it is.

"We've been out all night," he added, "or at least sheltered in only an old cabin. We haven't had anything to-day but some coffee, and we're about done out. Isn't this storm fierce?"

"Oh, we're used to these up here in the Adirondacks," spoke Sam.

Then the boys told how they had been out hunting and had seen the signpost that informed them it was seven miles to Ramsen.

"But you went the wrong way!" exclaimed Sam, when he had heard the details. "Ramsen was in just the opposite direction."

"Then the signboard was wrong!" declared Jack.

"That's funny," Sam spoke, musingly. "Signboards don't change themselves that way. There's something wrong here."

"Well, never mind that," went on Bert. "Have you seen anything of Tom Fairfield?"

"Tom Fairfield! Why, I thought he was with you!" exclaimed Sam, quickly looking around.

"He was, but we separated to find the road," explained George, "and now we can't locate Tom."

"Well, this won't do," Sam spoke, and his voice was serious. "We will have to hunt for him right away. He hasn't had anything to eat, you say?"

"None of us have," said Jack. "That's why we were so glad to find some sort of road."

"Well, I've got my pung back there a piece," said the guide. "I have some grub in it that I was taking over to your Camp No. 2. I can give you a snack from that, and then we'll do some searching for the boy. I like Tom Fairfield!"

"So do I!" exclaimed Jack, and the others nodded emphatic agreements, with a chorus of:

"That's what!"

Never did food taste so good as that which Sam brought up from his pung. He explained that he had walked on ahead while his horses were eating their dinners from nose-bags.

"And it's lucky for you fellows I did," he said, "though of course you might have stumbled on the camp yourselves. But now for a search."

And with anxious hearts the boys took it up. Where could Tom Fairfield be? That was a question each one asked himself.

CHAPTER XXIII
DEFIANCE

Tom, a bound prisoner, watched the insolent professor who sat facing him. The latter had on his face a sneer of triumph, but mingled with it, as Tom could note, was a look that had in it not a little fear. For the desperate man had planned a desperate game, and he was not altogether sure how it would work out.

Tom steeled himself to meet what was coming. He did not know what it was, but that it was something that would concern himself, vitally, he was sure. And he was better prepared to meet what was coming than he had been an hour or so previous.

For now, though he was a prisoner, and bound, he was warm, and he had eaten. These things go far toward making courage in a man, or boy either, for that matter.

"Now," said Professor Skeel, and the sneer on his face grew more pronounced, "we'll talk business!"

"Oh, no, we won't!" exclaimed Tom, quickly.

"We won't?" and there was a sharp note in the man's voice.

"I'll have nothing to do with you," went on Tom. "You brought me here against my will, and you are liable to severe penalties for what you did. As soon as I can get to an officer, I intend to cause your arrest, and the arrest of those two miserable tools of yours.

"I'm not at all afraid—don't think it. You can't keep me here for very long. Sooner or later I'll get out, and then I'll make it hot for you! That's just what I'll do—I'll make it hot for you!"

During this little outburst on the part of Tom, Professor Skeel sat staring at his prisoner. He did not seem at all frightened by what Tom said, though the young man put all the force he could into his words. But Tom was observant. He noticed that the little look of worry did not leave the man's face.

"I'll make it so hot for you," went on Tom, "that you'll have to leave this part of the country. You'll have to leave if you get the chance, and perhaps you won't. My father and I will push this case to the end. I don't know what your game is, but I can guess."

"Well, since you can guess, perhaps you can guess what I'm going to do with you!" angrily interrupted the professor.

"No, I can't, exactly," spoke Tom, slowly, "but if it's anything mean or low-down, you'll do it. I know you of old. I've had dealing with you before."

"Yes, and you're going to have more!" the professor fairly shouted. "I'm going to get even with you for what you did for me. You caused me to lose my place at Elmwood Hall——"

"You deserved to lose it!" said Tom, cuttingly.

"And you mistreated me when we were out in that open boat——"

"Mistreated you!" fairly gasped Tom, amazed at the man's hardness of mind. "Mistreated you, when you tried to steal the little water and food we had left!"

He could say no more. His mind went back vividly to the days of the wreck of the Silver Star, when he and others had been in great peril at sea. He had indeed prevented the professor from carrying out his evil designs, though Tom was not more harsh than needful. But now he was to suffer for that.

"I've got you where I want you," went on Skeel, when Tom had become silent. "I've laid my plans well, and you fell into the trap. I won't deny that the storm helped a lot, but I've got you now, and you're going to do as I say, or it will be the worse for you. You'll do as I say——"

"Don't be too sure!" interrupted Tom.

"That's enough!" snapped the angry man. "You may not realize that you are in my power, and that you're up here in a lonely part of the woods, away from your friends. They don't know where you are, and you don't know where they are. They can't help you. Those two men of mine will do as I say, and——"

"Oh, I've no doubt but that you've trained them well in your own class of scoundrelism," said Tom, coolly.

"Silence!" fairly shouted the infuriated man. Tom ceased his talk because he chose, not because he was afraid.

Professor Skeel hesitated a moment, and then drew from his pocket some papers. Tom was at a loss to guess what they might be. In fact, he had but a dim idea why he had been captured and brought to the hut in the wilderness.

Some things the two men—Murker and Whalen—let fall, however, gave him an inkling of what was to come. So he did not show any great surprise when Professor Skeel, handing him a paper, said:

"That's a copy of a letter I want you to write to your father. Copy it, sign it in your natural hand, without any changes whatever, or without making any secret signs on the paper, and give it back to me. When I get the right kind of an answer back, I'll let you go—not before. Write that letter to your father!"

There was a veiled threat implied in the insolent command.

Professor Skeel held the letter out in front of Tom. The latter could not take it, of course, for his hands were tied.

"Oh!" exclaimed the plotter, as though he had just wakened to this fact. "Well, I'll loosen your hands for you, but you must promise not to fight. Not that I'm afraid of you, for I can master you, but I don't want to hurt you, physically, if I can help it."

Tom did not altogether agree with the professor that he would be the master if it came to an encounter. For our hero was a vigorous lad, he played football and baseball, and his muscles were ready for instant call. True, he was tired from lack of rest and the hardships he had gone through, but he was not at all afraid of a "scrap," as he afterward put it.

So, then, when Professor Skeel made the remark about the bonds, Tom was ready for what came next.

"I'll loosen those ropes, so you can copy this letter, if you'll promise not to attack me," went on Skeel.

"I'll promise nothing!" exclaimed Tom, defiantly.

"All right. Then I'll have to call in my helpers to stand by," grimly went on the former instructor. "They'll take care of you if you cut up rough."

He went to the door, and called out:

"Murker—Whalen! Come in. We may need you," he added significantly.

Tom steeled himself for what was to come.

"Take off those ropes," went on the professor, when his two mean men had come in. "Then, if he starts a row—let him have it!"

The words were coarse and rough, and the man's manner and tone even more so.

"Are we to take off these ropes?" asked Murker.

"Yes, and then stand by. I'm going to make him write this letter. That will bring the cash."

"That's what we want!" exclaimed Whalen, with an unctious smile. "It's the cash I'm after."

"You'll get none from my father!" cried Tom, beginning to understand the course of the plot.

"We'll see about that," muttered the professor. "Loose his bonds, but look out! He's a tricky customer."

"Not any more so than you are," Tom said, promptly. "And I want to tell you here and now, when you have your witnesses present—mean and low as they are—I want to tell you that you'll suffer for this when I get out. I'll make it my business, and my father will also, to prosecute you to the full extent of the law!"

"Words—mere words!" sneered Skeel.

"You won't get out until you do as the boss wants," said Whalen.

"Don't be so rough. Better give in, it will be easier," spoke Murker, who seemed a little alarmed by what Tom said.

"I'll attend to him," said Skeel curtly. "Take off the ropes. Then you read this letter and copy and sign it!" he ordered.

A moment later Tom's hands were free. He did not see any chance for making an escape then, so he waited, merely stretching his arms so that the bound muscles were more free. True, he might have made a rush on his captors, but the door had been locked, after the entrance of Murker and Whalen, and Tom did not see what opportunity he would have with three against him. He might be seriously hurt and that would spoil his chances for a future escape.

"Read that," ordered Skeel, thrusting the paper into Tom's hands. A glance showed that it was addressed to his father. It recited that Tom was in trouble, that he had been made a prisoner by a band of men who would release him only on payment of ten thousand dollars. Details were given as to how the money, in cash, must be sent, and Mr. Fairfield was urged to make no effort to trace Tom, or it would result seriously for the prisoner.

"Sign that and we'll send it," ordered Skeel.

Tom dropped the letter to the floor, disdaining to hand it back.

"What's this?" fairly roared the professor. "Do you mean you won't do as I say?"

"That's just what I mean," said Tom, coolly. "You may keep me here as long as you like, and you can do as you please, but I'll never sign that letter. Go ahead! I'm not afraid of you!" and he faced his enemies defiantly.

CHAPTER XXIV

THE ESCAPE

Professor Skeel retained control of himself with an obvious effort. Clearly he had expected more of a spirit of agreement on the part of Tom, though he might have known, from his previous experiences with our hero, that compliance would not be given. But Tom did not even take the trouble to hand back the letter. It had fluttered to the floor of the cabin.

"You—you——" began Whalen, angrily spluttering the words.

"Silence!" commanded Skeel. "I'm attending to this." His face and his tone showed his anger, but he managed to keep it under control. He picked up the letter—something of a condescension on his part, and said to Tom:

"Then you refuse to do as I ask?"

"I most certainly do! The idea is positively—silly!" and Tom had the nerve to laugh in the faces of his enemies.

"We'll make you sweat for this!" declared Whalen. "We'll——"

"Better let the boss work the game," suggested Murker. In spite of his evil face, and the fact that he was just as guilty in the matter as the others, he seemed of a more conciliatory spirit.

"Yes, you keep out of this," commanded the professor to the former employee of the school. "I know what I'm doing."

Tom wondered what the next move would be. He did not have to wait long to find out.

"Well, if you won't sign this now, you will later," said Skeel, as he folded the letter and put it into his pocket. "Take him to the dark room," he ordered. "Maybe he'll come to his senses there. And don't give him too much bread and water," and the man laughed as he gave this order. "A little starving will bring some results, perhaps. Lock him up, and bring me the key."

"All right, you're the boss," assented Murker. "I'm in this thing now, and I'm going to stick it out, but I wish——"

"You're right; you're going to stick!" interrupted Skeel. "You're in it as deep as I am, and you can't get out!"

Murker did not finish what he started to say. He shrugged his shoulders and seemed resigned to what was to come. Tom disliked him the least of the three, though the man's face was not in his favor.

"Shall we tie him up again?" asked Whalen.

"Yes, and tie him good and tight, too. Don't mind how you draw those cords. The more trouble we make now, the less we'll have to make later. Tie him up and put him away where he can cool off," and Professor Skeel laughed mockingly.

For an instant a desperate resolve came into Tom's mind to make a rush and a break for liberty. But the idea was dismissed almost as soon as it was formed.

What chance would he stand with three full-grown men to oppose him? The door was locked, and Tom's feet were still bound. He had a knife in his pocket, but to reach it, and cut the ropes on his ankles would take time, and in that time he would easily be overpowered by his captors. It was out of the question now.

"But I'm going to escape, if it's at all possible," Tom declared to himself. "And when I do get out of here——"

But he could not finish his thought. His gun and mackinaw had been taken away from him, and now when Whalen roughly seized him, and put the ropes on his wrists, Skeel said:

"Search his pockets. Take what money he has and any sort of weapons. Then lock him up!"

Tom did have considerable money on him, and this was soon out of his pockets, and in that of the professor. Tom's knife and other possessionswere also removed. Then he was lifted up, carried to another room, and roughly thrust into sort of a closet that was very dark. Tom fell heavily to the floor. His mackinaw was tossed in to him.

"He can use that for a blanket—we're short of covering," he heard Skeel say. "We don't want him to be too comfortable, anyhow."

Tom was anything but at his ease just then, but he did not falter in his determination not to give in. He shut his teeth grimly.

The door was closed and locked, and our hero was left to his not very pleasant reflections. He managed to struggle to a sitting position, and to edge over until he was leaning back against the wall. He drew his heavy mackinaw to him. It would be warm during the cold night, for that he would be kept a prisoner at least that length of time, he could not doubt.

Tom's thoughts were many and various. So this was why Skeel had followed him and his chums. This was why he had reappeared at Elmwood Hall, and had caused Whalen to ask questions about the hunting trip.

So this was Skeel's plan for enriching his purse and at the same time getting revenge. So far, fate had played into the hands of the unscrupulous man and his confederates.

"But I'll get away!" Tom told himself. He sat there in the gloomy darkness, trying to think of a plan.

Meanwhile his chums, with Sam Wilson, were frantically searching for him in the storm. Sam's idea was not to leave the neighborhood where Tom had last been seen, until they had exhausted every effort to locate their missing chum.

But it was difficult to search in the storm, and the whirl of flakes made a long view impossible. Then, too, they were in a dense part of the wilderness. Sam Wilson's farm was perhaps the largest cleared part of it, though here and there were patches where trees had been cut down.

Up and down the road, and on either side of it, the search went on. Sam Wilson was a born woodsman, as well as a hunter and farmer, and he brought his efficiency to the task.

"But it seems to be no go, boys," he said, at length.

"But what has become of him?" asked George with a look of worriment on his face.

"That's what we can't say except that he's lost," spoke Jack.

"Yes, but lost in this wilderness—in this storm," added Bert. "It's dangerous."

"Yes, that's what it is, provided he is still lost," Sam said.

"Still lost! What do you mean?" asked Jack.

"I mean he may have gone so far that he found his way back to one of the camps."

"Really?" hopefully cried Bert, who thought Sam might be saying that simply to cheer them up.

"Why, of course it's possible," the caretaker went on. "He may have gone on beyond the sound of your guns. And, unexpectedly, he may have hit the trail to one of the camps. For there are trails that lead through the woods. They're not easy to find, or follow, but Tom might have had luck."

"Then what shall we do?" asked Jack.

"Go back to Camp No. 2," answered Sam. "Tom may be there. If he isn't, we'll go to the others in turn. Let's go back. We'll drive."

So, abandoning the search for the time being, they started back for camp in the pung, drawn by the powerful horses. They were hoping against hope that Tom would be there, or that they would find him at one of the other cabins.

But Tom was still a prisoner in the dark closet of the lonely shack. What his thoughts were you can well imagine, but, above everything else stood out the determination not to give in and sign the letter asking for the ransom money.

Hours passed. Tom again felt the pangs of hunger. He had an idea the men might try to starve him, but after an interval, which he imaginedbrought the time to noon, Murker came in with some bread and water.

"Boss's orders," he growled. "I'll untie your hands while you eat, and don't try any tricks."

Tom did not answer. The bread was welcome, but the water more so. Murker left him a glass full after he had once emptied the tumbler. Then the ropes were again put on his hands, and he was left alone in the darkness.

Whether it was the same day or not, Tom could hardly tell. He must have dozed, for he awoke with a start, and he knew at once that some noise had caused it.

He listened intently, and heard a scratching, sniffing sound back of him. He could feel the board side of the shack, against which he was leaning, vibrate.

"Can it be that the boys are trying to release me?" Tom asked himself. But in another moment he knew this could not be true. His chums would come boldly up and not try to get him out in this secret fashion. The scratching and sniffing increased.

"It's some animal!" Tom decided. He edged away from the side of the closet-room, and waited. The sound increased. Then came a splintering, rending sound as of wood breaking. Tom fancied he could feel a board move.

An instant later a streak of light came suddenly into his prison. It was from the moon which was shining brightly on the snow outside, and by the light through the crack Tom could see a big hairy paw thrust in where the board had been torn off.

"It's a bear!" cried the lad. "He must smell something to eat, and he's trying to get after it. He's standing outside and has pulled off a loose board, and—by Jove! I can get out that way!" he said aloud. As he spoke the board was pulled farther loose, leaving a large opening. A sniffing snout was thrust in. Tom had no intention of sharing his prison with a bear, and, raising his two bound feet Tom kicked the animal on its most tender place—the nose. With a growl Bruin withdrew, and Tom could hear him sniffing indignantly as he scampered over the snow. But the bear had made for Tom a way of escape.

"If I could only get my arms and legs free, I could squeeze out through that opening," Tom decided. Then like a flash the plan came to him.

The tumbler of water had been left within reach. Tom kicked it over with sufficient force to break the glass. He had to make a noise, but after waiting a while, he felt sure his captors had not been aroused. They did not seem to be on guard, or they would have heard the bear when he pulled loose the outside board.

Tom's muscles were in good control, but he had to strain himself unmercifully to bend over and get a piece of the broken glass between his hands. Then he put it between his two boots, and held it there, with a sharp edge up, by pressing his feet tightly together.

You have doubtless guessed his plan. He was going to use the glass as a knife and saw the rope of his wrists upon it. This he proceeded to do. The moonlight outside, streaming in, gave him enough illumination to work by.

He cut himself several times before he succeeded in fraying the rope enough so it could be broken. Then, rubbing his arms to restore the interrupted circulation, Tom used the glass on the rope that bound his ankles. This he cut through quickly enough, and, was able to stand up. His legs were weak, and he waited a few minutes until he could use them to better advantage. Then, forcing farther off the dangling board, Tom crawled out in the snow, putting on his mackinaw when he was outside.

The storm had ceased. It was night—a night with a dazzling moon, and Tom was free. But where his chums were, or in what direction the camp lay, he could not tell.

CHAPTER XXV

THE SHOT

For a moment, after getting outside the cabin, Tom hardly knew what to do. He was at a loss in which direction to start, but he realized the necessity of getting away from that vicinity as soon as possible.

Though his escape did not seem to have aroused his captors, there was no telling when they would take the alarm and start after him. Tom looked for the bear. The animal was not in sight, though he could see by marks in the snow, where it had approached the cabin from the woods, and where it had run off into the forest again.

"Too bad I haven't my gun!" mused Tom. "But I don't dare try to get it."

Then began for Tom a time he never forgot. He set off toward the woods, wishing to gain their friendly shelter as soon as he could, but once there he was at a loss how farther to proceed.

"But there's no need to wait for morning," he reasoned. "I can see almost as well now, as long as the moon is up. I'll try to find some sort of a trail."

He staggered on, yes, staggered, for he was weak from his experience, and he had not had proper food in some time. It seemed almost a week, but of course it was not as long as that.

Scarcely able to walk, but grimly determined not to give up, Tom urged himself on. Whither he was going, he knew not, but any way to leave that hateful shack, and the more hateful men behind, was good enough for the time being.

All night long Tom kept on going. He fancied he was on some sort of trail or road, but he could not be sure. Certainly the trees seemed cut down in a line, though it was a twisting and turning one.

Then the moon went down, leaving the scene pretty dark, but the white snow made objects plain. Tom kept on until at last he was fairly staggering from side to side. He was very weak.

"I—I've got to give up," he panted. "I—I've got to—to rest."

He looked about and saw sort of a nook under some bushes. On top was a matting of snow, like a roof. Tom crawled into this like some hunted animal, and sank down wearily. He pulled his mackinaw about him, thankful that he had it with him. He must have frozen without its protection.

Again Tom was unaware of the passage of time. He must have dozed or fainted, perhaps, but when he opened his eyes the sun was shining. The day was a brilliant one, and warm, for that time of year. Tom took heart. He crawled out, and once more started on his wearying tramp. He was very weak and exhausted, and there was a "gone" feeling to his stomach.

"Or the place where it used to be," Tom said, with grim humor. "I don't believe I have a stomach left."

But he forced himself onward. It seemed that he had been staggering over the snow for a week. Time had lost its meaning for him.

"Oh, if I only had something to eat! If I only could find the camp!" murmured poor Tom.

He reached a stump, and sat down on it to rest. He closed his eyes but suddenly opened them again.

Was that fancy, or had he heard a shot? He leaped up, electrified, and then hesitated. Perhaps it was Skeel and the others after him. But a quick look across the snow showed him no one was in sight. Tom reasoned quickly.

"Skeel and his crowd wouldn't shoot unless they saw me, and then it would be to scare me. It can't have been those men who fired. It must be the boys. But where are they?" Tom looked eagerly about.

Again came the shot. There was no mistake this time. Then Tom heard a shout. He tried to answer it, but his voice was too weak. Another shot cracked on the frosty air, and then came a series of confused calls.

"There he is!"

"We've found him!"

"Hurry up!"

A mist dimmed Tom's vision. He cleared his eyes with a quick motion of his hand, and then he saw his three chums and Sam Wilson rushing toward him. They came out of the woods, and, a moment later, had surrounded him.

"Where were you?"

"What happened?"

"Where's your gun?"

"You look all in!"

Fast came the questions.

"I—I am all in," Tom faltered. "It's that rascal Skeel. I—I——"

He could not go on for a moment. Then he pulled himself together.

"Here! Drink this!" exclaimed Jack, producing a small vacuum bottle. "It's coffee and it's hot yet." He poured some out into a tin cup and Tom drank it. It revived him at once. Then, with a little more of the beverage, and a hasty swallowing of a sandwich which formed part of the emergency lunch the boys had brought with them, Tom was able to tell his story.

Hot indignation was expressed by all, and then Jack related how they had found the road, but lost Tom, and how they had met with Sam. Their trip to Camp No. 2 had been fruitless, as we know, nor were they any more successful when they came to Camp No. 3. Tom was not there. Then they started for Camp No. 1, and were on their way thither when they came upon the object of their search. On the way they shouted and fired signal guns at intervals. The dog had found his way to Camp No. 1, after leaving Tom, but the animal could not lead Tom's friends to him.

"And now to make it hot for those scoundrels!" exclaimed Sam. "We'll prosecute them not only for kidnapping and robbing you, for that's what they did when they took your gun and money, but we'll bring an action in trespass against them. That shack where they kept you belongs to the hunting club."

"And to think Tom was there all the while and we never knew it," said Bert.

"Oh, I intended to have a look there, if we hadn't found him at Cabin No. 1," declared Sam. "But now let's get busy! Can you walk, Tom, or will you wait here until I can go get a horse?"

"Oh, I'll be all right soon. I was just weak from hunger."

Soon Tom was able to proceed. They were about half way between Camp No. 1 and the shack where our hero had been kept a prisoner, and it was decided to go to the latter place and make an endeavor to capture Skeel and his cronies.

But our friends were too late. The kidnappers had fled, but Tom's gun and all his possessions, save his money, were found in the cabin. Doubtless the personal belongings were too conclusive evidence against the plotters, to risk taking, but someone had succumbed to the temptation of the cash.

"Well, I'm glad to get this back," Tom said, taking up his gun.

"Yes, and we'll get those rascals yet!" declared Sam. "I'll rouse the whole country after them!"

They went on to Camp No. 1 and there Tom had a good rest. It did not take long to pull himself together, and he was as eager as the others to start out on the trail of the scoundrels. For the time being hunting and the taking of photographs was forgotten. Sam sent word to the authorities, and a sheriff's posse was organized. It was done so quickly that Skeel and the others, who had taken the alarm and fled when they discovered Tom's escape, were apprehended before they could leave the neighborhood. The heavy storms had blocked the railroad and there were no trains. The men could not hire a sled and team and so were forced to walk, which put them at a disadvantage. They left a trail easy for the woodsmen, hunters and trappers to follow.

"Well, you got us, and you got us good!" said Murker, when they were arrested and confronted by Tom and the others. "I was afraid something like this would happen."

"Why didn't you say so, then, and keep me out of it?" asked Whalen, sullenly.

Professor Skeel said nothing, but he scowled at Tom. The plotter's plans had fallen through, and he faced a long prison term, which, in due course he received, as did his confederates. The letter Skeel had tried to force Tom to write was found on the man and made conclusive evidence against him and the others. So the scoundrel-professor was cheated of his revenge and the money he hoped to get from Mr. Fairfield.

It became known that Professor Skeel had various experiences after Tom had last seen him. The man was in desperate circumstances when he formed a plan of kidnapping Tom, and holding him for ransom. It was a foolish and risky plan, but Skeel talked it over with his two cronies anddecided to try it. They knew Mr. Fairfield was rich.

Then came Skeel's trip to Elmwood Hall. The snowball was an accident he had not counted on, and it made him more angry than ever against Tom.

Professor Skeel's injured ear, which looked, as Sam said, "like it had been chawed by some critter," was the result of a fight he had with a man before this story opened, and with which we have nothing to do. Sufficient to say that it served to identify the man, and put our friends on their guard, so that justice was finally meted out.

The trial and conviction of the men came later. After the trio were safely locked in jail, Tom and his chums returned to the woods where they had been lost. But they were better acquainted with the forest now.

"And we'll have some fine hunting!" cried Tom, now himself again.

"And get some photographs!" added Bert. "I want a view of that hut where the bear pulled the board off so you could get out."

"That was queer," said Tom, smiling. "I don't believe I'll like to shoot a bear now, after that one did me such a good turn."

"You won't have much chance," Sam said. "I guess even the oldest and toughest bear is 'holed-up' by now. Better be content with deer!"

And the boys had to be, rather against their wills. But they were made happy when each one got a specimen, though none was as fine as was

Tom's antlered head. Moreover, Bert and the others secured all the photographs they wanted.

But deer was not the only game they shot.

Rabbits, partridges and squirrels were plentiful, and the boys had more than enough for their meals. They enjoyed to the utmost the holiday time spent in the hunting camps, and Tom paid his first visit to Camp No. 3.

"Well, take it all in all, how did you enjoy it, fellows?" asked Tom, when, after a last successful hunt they were preparing to go back to home and Elmwood Hall.

"Couldn't have been better!" was the enthusiastic answer from all.

"But it was rather tough on you, Tom," said Jack.

"Oh, I didn't mind it so much, except the 'hunger-strike' I had to go on, after I escaped," was the reply. "And I had the satisfaction of besting Skeel."

"He'll hate you worse than ever," commented Bert.

"He'll be a long while getting out," Tom said. "That's one consolation. Well, here comes Sam with the pung. I suppose we've got to go back!"

And with sighs of regret at what they were leaving, real regret in spite of the hardships, the boys prepared to return to civilization, at which point we will take leave of them.

THE END

TOM FAIRFIELD'S HUNTING TRIP

CHAPTER I

THE BIG SNOWBALL

"Well, Tom, it sure is a dandy plan!"

"That's right! A hunting trip to the Adirondacks will just suit me!"

"And we couldn't have better weather than this, nor a better time than the coming holiday season."

Three lads, who had made the above remarks, came to a whirling stop on their shining, nickeled skates and gathered in a small ring about the fourth member of the little party, Tom Fairfield by name. Tom listened to what was said, and remarked:

"Well, fellows, I'm glad you like my plan. Now I think——"

"Like it! I should say we did!" cried the smallest of the three lads grouped about the one in the centre. "Why, it's the best ever!" and he did a spread eagle on his skates, so full of life did he feel that crisp December day.

"Do you really think we can get any game?" asked Jack Fitch, as he loosed his mackinaw at the throat, for he had warmed himself by a vigorous burst of skating just before the little halt that had ended in the impromptu vote of thanks to Tom.

"Get game? Well, I should say we could!" cried another of the lads.

"What do you know about it, Bert Wilson?" demanded Jack. "Were you ever up there?"

"No, but I'm sure Tom Fairfield wouldn't ask us up to a hunter's camp unless he was reasonably sure that we could get some kind of game. I'm not very particular what kind," Bert went on, "as long as it's game—a bear, a mountain lion, a lynx—I'm not hard to suit," he added magnanimously.

"Well, I should say not!" laughed Tom.

"But say!" exclaimed the youngest member of the quartette—George Abbot by name. "Do you really think we can bag a bear? Or a lynx, maybe? Or even a fox? Are there really any big animals up there, Tom? What sort of a gun had I better take? And what about an outfit? Do you think——"

Tom reached out and gently placed a gloved hand over the mouth of the questioner, thereby cutting off, for the time being, the flow of interrogations.

"Just a moment, Why, if you please," he said, giving George the nickname his fellow students at Elmwood Hall had fastened on the lad who seemed to be a human question mark.

"Well, I—er—Buu—er—gurg——"

But that was the nearest semblance to speaking that George could accomplish. His companions laughed at him. He finally made a sign that he would desist if Tom removed the hand-gag, and when this had been done, Jack proposed a little sprint down to one end of the small lake on which they were skating.

"No, we've had enough racing to-day," declared Bert Wilson. "I vote Tom tells us more about this hunters' camp, and what we expect to do there."

"All right, I'm agreeable," Jack said.

"Are they——?" began Why, but a look from Bert warned him, and he stopped midway in his question. His chums well knew that if George once got started it was hard to stop him.

"Well, there isn't so much to tell that you fellows don't know already," began Tom slowly. "In the first place, there are three hunters' camps, not one."

"Three!" exclaimed Jack and Bert, while George looked the questions he dared not ask.

"Yes. You see they belong to a party of gentlemen, a sort of camping club. The camps are about five miles apart, in the wildest part of the Adirondacks."

"Why—three?" came at last from George. Really he could not keep it back any longer. Tom did not seem to mind.

"Oh, I suppose they wanted to change their hunting ground," he answered, "and they found it easier to make three camps, or headquarters, than to come all the way back to the first one. And the club is pretty well off, so it didn't mind the expense."

"But you don't mean to say we can use all three of 'em?" cried Jack, incredulously.

"That's the idea," Tom said. "We're just as welcome to use all three camps as one. They're all about alike, each with a log cabin, nicely fitted up, set in the midst of the big woods."

"That's jolly!" cried Bert.

"And aren't the men themselves going to use them?" George wanted to know. Again he went unrebuked.

"Not this season," Tom Fairfield explained. "The club is sort of broken up for the time being. Some of the men want to go, but they can't get enough together to make a party, so they had to give up their annual holiday outing this year.

"A business friend of my father's belongs to the club, and he mentioned to Dad that there was a chance for someone to use the camps. Dad happened to speak of it to me, and I—well, you can imagine what I did! I jumped at the chance, and now you know almost as much as I do about it.

"I'll tell you later just where the camps are, and how we are to get to them. We want to get together and have a talk about what we'll take with us. School closes here day after to-morrow, and then we'll be free for nearly a month."

"And won't we have some ripping old times, though!" cried Jack.

"Well, I should say yes!" chimed in Bert.

"Tell you what let's do, fellows!" broke in George. "Let's go up to the top of that hill and have a coast. Some of our lads from Elmwood are there with the bobs, and they'll give us a ride. I've had enough of skating."

"So have I," chimed in Jack.

"I'm with you," agreed Bert, stooping to loosen his skates, an example followed by Tom Fairfield.

"I hope this snowy weather holds," spoke Jack. "But are you allowed to shoot game when there is tracking snow?"

"I don't just know all the rules," said Tom, "but of course we will do what is right. I guess we'll have plenty of snow in the mountains, and cold weather, too."

"It's getting warm here," observed Bert. "Too warm," for the variable New Jersey climate had changed from freezing almost to thawing in the night, and the boys were really taking advantage of the last bit of skating they were likely to have in some time.

There were not many besides themselves on the ice of the lake when they started from it, heading for the big hill not far away—a hill whereon the youth of Elmwood Hall, a boarding school near the Jersey state capital, had many jolly times.

When Tom Fairfield and his chums, talking about the camping and hunting trip in prospect, reached the hill, they found it deserted—that is, by all save a few small town boys with their little sleds.

"No coasting to-day," observed Jack, ruefully.

"No, it's getting too soft," added Bert, digging his foot into the snowy surface of the hill. But the small boys did not mind that. With the big lads out of the way, smaller fry had a chance.

George Abbot picked up a handful of snow and rolled it into a ball. As he noticed how well it packed, he exclaimed:

"Say, fellows, another idea!"

"Ha! He's full of 'em to-day!" laughed Jack.

"Get rid of it, Why," advised Tom. "Don't keep ideas in your system."

"Let's roll a whopping big snowball," proposed George, "and send it down hill. It will roll all the way to the bottom, and pick up snow all the way down."

"It will be some snowball when it gets to the bottom," observed Tom. "This snow does pack wonderfully well," he added, testing it.

"Come on!" cried George, and he started to roll the ball. In a few minutes he had one so large that it needed two to shove it about, and as it gathered layer after layer of snow, it accumulated in size until the strength of the four lads was barely sufficient to send it slowly along.

"Now to the top of the hill with it!" cried Tom, and it was placed on the brink. The boys held it at a point where it would not interfere with the small coasters. It was poised on the brink a moment.

"Let her go!" cried Tom.

"There she goes!" echoed Jack Fitch.

They shoved the ball down the slope. On and on it rolled, gaining in momentum and size with every bound.

"Look at it!" cried George. "Say, it sure is going!"

"And it's getting as big as a house!" excitedly shouted Bert.

"It will roll all the way across the lake," said Tom, for the frozen body of water was at the foot of the hill, and it did seem as though the snowball had momentum enough to carry it over the ice.

A moment later the ball was at the foot of the hill, and rolling along with increasing speed. And then, so suddenly that the boys were startled with fear, something happened.

Out on the ice drove a horse and a cutter, containing a man. He had left the road and taken a short cut across the ice. And now he was directly in the path of the immense, rolling snowball.

"Stop! Stop!" cried Tom Fairfield. "Look out!"

But it was too late to stop, even if the man in the cutter had heard him.

On rushed the great ball directly toward the horse and vehicle.

CHAPTER II

A SURPRISE

"Say, it's going to hit him, sure as fate!" cried Tom.

"No help for it," half-groaned Jack.

"And there will be some smash!" murmured Bert. "Oh, what did you do it for, George?"

"Me do it? Why, say, you fellows had as much to do with it as I did! I didn't do it all!" and the smaller lad looked indignantly at his companions.

"Come on!" cried Tom, as he started on a run down the snowy side of the hill.

The others followed.

"We can't do anything!" shouted Jack.

"Of course not," agreed Bert. "By the time we get there——"

He did not finish the sentence. All this while the big snowball had been rushing on. The man in the cutter had seen it, but too late. He tried to whip up the horse and get out of the way, but even as Bert spoke the mass of snow struck fairly between the horse and cutter.

In an instant the vehicle was overturned.

The boys, running to the rescue, had a confused vision of a man flying out to one side, head first, toward a snowbank. They also saw the horse rear up on his hind legs, struggle desperately to retain his balance and then, with a fierce leap, break loose from the cutter and run on, free, across the ice.

As the boys hastened on, they saw the man slowly pick himself up out of the snowbank, and gaze wonderingly about him, as if trying to fathom what had happened, whether it had been an earthquake or an avalanche. Indeed, so large was the snowball, and so strong was the force of it, for it had gained speed by the rush down the steep hill, that it really was a small avalanche.

The ball had split into several pieces on hitting the cutter, the shafts of which were broken and splintered, showing how the horse had been able to free himself.

"We'll have to—to apologize," murmured Tom, as he and his companions kept on toward the man who was now gazing down disconsolately at the ruin wrought.

"Yes, I guess we will," agreed Jack. "We—why, Cæsar's corn-plasters!" he cried. "Look who it is—Professor Skeel!"

"The old tyrant of Elmwood Hall!" murmured Bert. "Who'd have thought it?"

"Now we are in for it," added Tom, grimly.

"Burton Skeel!" said George in a whisper as he caught sight of the angry-looking man, gazing at his smashed cutter and staring off over the ice in the direction taken by the runaway horse. "Skeel, the man who made so much trouble for Tom Fairfield. And we upset him! Oh—good-night!"

Those of you who have read the first volume of this series, entitled "Tom Fairfield's Schooldays," do not need to be introduced to Professor Skeel. The unpopular instructor of Elmwood Hall, where Tom and his chums attended, had been the cause of a rebellion, in which Tom was a sort of leader, and, later, a pacifier. Tom Fairfield, the son of Mr. and Mrs. Brokaw Fairfield, of Briartown, N. J., had made himself popular soon after coming to Elmwood, where he had been sent to board while his parents went to Australia about some property matters.

And now to find that the man upset from his cutter was this same unpopular teacher, Professor Skeel, was enough to give pause to any set of lads.

But Tom Fairfield was no coward. He proved that when the Silver Star was wrecked, an account of which you may read of in my second volume, called "Tom Fairfield at Sea," for the days that followed the foundering of that vessel were trying ones indeed, and the dreary days spent in an open boat, when Mr. Skeel proved himself not only a coward, but almost a scoundrel, showed Tom fully what sort of a man the professor was.

Tom finally reached Australia, and set out on another voyage in time to rescue his parents from some savages on one of the Pacific islands. So it was such qualities as these, and those developed when Tom had other adventures, set forth in the third book, "Tom Fairfield in Camp," that made our hero keep on instead of turning back when he found what had happened to Mr. Skeel.

In camp Tom and his chums succeeded in clearing up the mystery of the old mill, though for a time it seemed that they were doomed to failure. But Tom was not one to give up easily, and this, I think, was more fully shown, perhaps, in the volume immediately preceding this, called "Tom Fairfield's Pluck and Luck."

True, Tom did have "luck," but, after all, what is luck but hard work turned to the best advantage? Almost any chap can have luck if he works hard, and takes advantage of every opportunity.

And now, after many weeks of tribulations, Tom found himself at the beginning of the Christmas holidays, and he and his chums had in prospect a very enjoyable time.

But just at the present moment they would have given up part of anticipated pleasures, I believe, not to have had the snowball accident happen.

"It is Skeel," murmured Tom, as though at first he had doubted the evidence of his own eyes.

"Of course it is," said Jack.

"And we're in for trouble, or I miss my guess," added Bert.

"I wonder what in the world he is doing in these parts?" came from George. "You thought you'd seen the last of him, didn't you, Tom, after the wreck of the Silver Star?"

"I certainly did."

"And yet he bobs up again," went on George. "What does he want? Is he trying to get back on the faculty of Elmwood Hall?"

No one answered his questions, nor did Tom, or any of the others, rebuke Why for his queries. They had too much else to think about.

"Well, young men, well!" began Professor Skeel in his pompous voice. "Well, are you responsible for this?"

"I—I'm afraid we are," said Tom. He did not add "sir," as once he would have done. He had lost the little respect he had for the former teacher, and when a man loses the respect of a manly youth, it is not good for that man.

"Humph! Yes, you certainly have done mischief enough," went on Mr. Skeel, in snarling tones. "My cutter is broken, I am thrown out, and may have sustained there are no telling what injuries, my horse has run away and may be killed, and you stand there like—like blithering idiots!" he cried, with something of his old, objectionable, schoolroom manner.

"We—we didn't mean to," said Tom.

"We just made a big snowball and rolled it down," George said, determined to take his share of the blame.

"Hum! Yes, so I see—and so I felt, young men!" cried the irate man, as he brushed the snow off his garments.

The boys had not yet gotten over the surprise of identifying Professor Skeel. They could not understand it.

"We will do anything we can to make amends," Tom said, slinging his skates over his shoulder with a jangling of steel. "We will try to catch your horse, and we can get you another cutter. We are——"

Something in Tom's voice caused the man to look up quickly. As he did so Tom noticed that his right ear appeared as though it had been recently injured. The lower part was torn and hung down below the other lobe.

"Ha! So it's you, is it!" fairly snarled Mr. Skeel. "It's you, Tom Fairfield?"

"Yes, Mr. Skeel. And I can only say how sorry I am——"

"Don't tell me how sorry you are!" interrupted the former teacher, in a voice filled with passion. "I don't want to listen to you. I've had enough of you. Don't you dare to address me!

"This was done on purpose. It was a deliberate attempt to injure me, perhaps kill me, for all I know. But I will not submit. I will at once go to town and cause your arrest, Tom Fairfield. The arrest of yourself, and those rascals with you. I'll have you all arrested."

George turned pale under his ruddy cheeks. He was not afraid, but he was thinking of the disgrace. But Tom Fairfield was master of the situation.

"Oh, I wouldn't have anyone arrested if I were you, Mr. Skeel," he said, in easy tones.

"Yes, I shall, too!" blustered the man. "I'll have you all arrested! The idea of rolling a snowball on me and almost killing me. I'll have everyone of you arrested."

"Oh, I wouldn't," Tom said. "You forget that little matter of the forgery, Mr. Skeel. That indictment is still hanging over you, I believe. And if you were to go to the authorities, it might come out, and there would be some other arrests than ours. So if I were you——"

He did not need to finish. Mr. Skeel turned pale and uttered an exclamation under his breath.

At that moment George created a diversion by crying:

"Here comes your horse back."

CHAPTER III
THE PLOT

George Abbot was not exactly correct in saying that the runaway horse was coming back. The animal was being brought back, and he seemed quiet and docile enough. Perhaps he had lost his fright in the run he had taken after being freed from the cutter.

"Who's leading the horse?" asked Bert Wilson, while Tom turned to look, after having faced the angry professor until the latter turned aside his head. Well he knew that Tom spoke the truth. A shady transaction, while a member of the Elmwood faculty, had placed Professor Skeel under the ban of the law, and he realized that he could not appeal to it without bringing himself into its clutches.

"That's Morse Denton with the animal," said Jack.

"Morse must have caught him before he went very far, or he wouldn't be back so soon," spoke Bert, waving his hand toward the former Freshman football captain.

"Does that horse belong there?" Morse called across the ice.

"Yes, bring him over here," said Tom. "Perhaps we can patch up the shafts and send you on your way again, Professor Skeel," Tom went on, for he did not hold enmity, and he was willing to let bygones be bygones, if the professor did not push matters too far.

"Um!" was all the answer the former teacher vouchsafed. He was arranging his garments, which had been rather twisted, to say the least, by his sudden exit from the cutter.

"What happened?" asked Morse, when he led the horse up to the little group standing partly on the ice of the lake and partly on the shore, for the accident had happened close to the edge.

"It was a big snowball," volunteered George. "We rolled it down the hill, and Professor Skeel ran into it."

"Be correct, young man. Be correct!" growled the former instructor. "The snowball ran into me, but I'll have satisfaction. I'll——"

He caught Tom's eye on him, and fairly quailed.

"Why, it's Professor Skeel!" cried Morse. "Where did you——"

But Tom gave Morse a quick and secret sign to cease questioning, and the newcomer, still holding the captured horse, acquiesced.

"Is the animal hurt?" demanded the former teacher.

"Doesn't seem to be," Morse replied. "I saw him coming at a slow canter across the ice, and I had no trouble in stopping him. I guessed it was a runaway and I started him back in just the opposite direction to that he was going. Then I saw you fellows," he added to his chums.

"I have told Professor Skeel how sorry I am that the accident occurred," went on Tom, "and I have assured him that we will do all that we can to repair the damage." He was speaking slowly and with reserve, and choosing his words carefully.

"Repair the damage!" snapped the man.

"The shafts are all that seem to be broken," proceeded Tom. "I know a farmer near here, and I'm sure he will lend you another pair of shafts for your cutter. The harness is not damaged, the cutter itself is all right, and the horse is not hurt. There is no reason why you should not continue your journey, Professor Skeel."

"Well, do something then, don't stand there talking about it!" burst out the irritated man.

Tom did not answer, and his chums rather marveled, for Tom was not the youth to take abuse quietly. But Tom realized that, through no fault of his own, Professor Skeel had been put to serious inconvenience, and it was no more than just that the lads should make good the damage they had unwittingly done.

"Let's set up the cutter, fellows," proposed Tom, after a pause, "and then we'll see about getting another pair of shafts. We can't use these, that's certain." They were splintered beyond repair.

The boys of Elmwood Hall were used to doing things quickly, especially under Tom's leadership. In a trice the cutter was righted, and the robes and the scattered possessions of Professor Skeel were picked up and put into it. Then while Morse, George and Bert remained to adjust the harness on the now quieted horse, Tom and Jack went to a farmhouse near the lake to borrow a spare pair of shafts.

Tom knew the farmer, of whom he had often hired a team in the summer, and the man readily agreed not only to loan the shafts, but to adjust them to the cutter.

He made a quick and neat job of it, and soon the horse was once more hitched to the righted vehicle.

"There you are, Professor Skeel," said Tom. "Not quite as good as before, but almost. You can keep on, and once more I wish to tell you how sorry I am that it happened."

"Um!" sneered Mr. Skeel.

"You may not believe it," Tom went on. "We did not see you coming until we had started the ball down hill, and then it was too late to stop it. We never thought anyone would cross the lake on the ice at this point, as no one ever does so."

"I had a right to, didn't I?" demanded the irate professor.

"A right, certainly," agreed Tom. "But it is unusual. Teams go down on the lake about a mile farther on, and you would have been perfectly safe there."

"Humph! I guess I can cross this lake where I please! And the next time you roll a snowball on me, I'll——"

"I told you," said Tom, and his voice was cuttingly cool, "that we did not roll the ball on you. It was unintentional, but if you persist in thinking we did it purposely, we can't help that. Now, is there anything more we can do for you?" and he looked about the snow to make sure all the contents of the cutter had been picked up and returned to it.

The professor did not answer, but busied himself getting into the vehicle, and taking the reins from Morse Denton.

"You can send them spare shafts back any time," said the farmer who had kindly loaned them.

"We'll pay for 'em if he doesn't," said Jack in a low voice, anxious to preserve peace. "It's getting off cheap as it is," he added.

"That's right," agreed Bert. "I thought he'd raise no end of a row."

"So he would have—only for Tom. Tom closed him up in great shape, didn't he?"

"He sure did."

Without a word of thanks, Professor Skeel drove off over the ice. He never looked back, but the boys could hear him muttering angrily to himself, probably giving vent to threats he dared not utter aloud.

"I wonder what he is doing in this neighborhood?" ventured Bert.

"It's certainly a puzzle," admitted Tom Fairfield. "He's up to no good, I'll wager."

"That's right," agreed Jack. "Well, I'm glad he's gone, anyhow. That sure was some upset!"

"Say, did you notice his ear?" asked George. "It wasn't that way when he was teaching school here. Looks as if a knife had cut him."

"Was his ear like that when he was shipwrecked with you, Tom?" asked Bert.

"No. That's a new injury," was the answer. "Rather a queer one, too. He might have been in a fight."

The lads remained standing together, for a little while, gazing at the now fast-disappearing cutter and its surly occupant.

"Well, let's get back to school," proposed Jack. "It will soon be grub-time."

"And Tom can tell us more about that hunting trip," suggested Bert.

"All right," agreed our hero, but as he walked along he was puzzling his brain, trying to think what Professor Skeel's object was in coming back to Elmwood Hall.

Perhaps if Tom could have seen Mr. Skeel a little later, as the cutter drew up at a road-house some miles away—a road-house that did not have a very enviable reputation in the neighborhood—Tom would have wondered still more over his former teacher's return.

For, as the cutter drew up in the drive, there peered from a window two men, one with a more evil-looking face than the other, which was his only claim to distinction.

"There he comes," murmured the man with the less-evil countenance.

"Yes, but he's late," agreed the other. "Wonder what kept him?"

"He looks mad—too," commented his companion.

A few moments later Professor Skeel entered the rear room of the road-house. The two men arose from the table at which they had been sitting.

"Well, you kept your word, I see," muttered Skeel to the man with the evil face. "You're here, Whalen. And you too, Murker."

"Yes. We're here, but you didn't say what you wanted of us," spoke the one addressed as Whalen.

"You'll know soon enough," was the rejoinder. "We sha'n't want anything—at least not for a while," Mr. Skeel went on to the landlord, who had followed him into the room. "You can leave us alone. We'll ring when we want you. And close the door when you go out," he added, significantly.

The landlord grunted.

"Well, now, what's the game?" asked Whalen, when Mr. Skeel had seated himself at the table.

"Revenge! That's the game!" was the fierce answer, and a fist was banged down on the table. "I want revenge, and I'm going to have it!"

"Who's the party?" demanded Murker.

"Someone you don't know, but whom you may soon. Tom Fairfield! I owe him a long score, but I'm going to begin to pay it now. I want you to help me, Whalen."

"Oh, I'll help you quick enough," was the ready answer.

"He was instrumental in having you discharged from Elmwood Hall, wasn't he?" went on the former instructor.

"That's what he was."

"Something about beating one of the smaller boys, was it not?" and Skeel smiled in a suggestive way, as though he rather relished, than otherwise, the plight of Whalen.

"Naw, I only gave the kid a few taps 'cause he threw a snowball at me," the discharged employee went on, "but that whelp, Fairfield, saw me, and complained to Doc. Meredith. Then I was fired."

"And you'd like a chance to get even, wouldn't you?"

"That's what I would!" was the harsh answer.

"Well, I want to square accounts with him also, and, at the same time, make a little money out of it. I thought you and Murker could help me, and that's why I asked you to meet me here. I'm a bit late, and that's some more of Fairfield's doings. Now to business. This is the game!"

And the three plotters drew their chairs closer together and began to talk in low, mumbling voices.

CHAPTER IV
HOLIDAY FUN

"Jolly times to-night, fellows!" exclaimed Jack Fitch as he, with Tom and the other chums, walked along the snowy road on their way back to Elmwood Hall. "No boning to do, and we can slip away with some eats on the side and have a grub-fest."

"That's right," chimed in Bert Wilson. "Maybe you'd better put off telling us about the hunting trip, Tom, until we all get together. Suppose we meet in my room—it's bigger."

"All right," agreed Tom. "Anything suits me as long as you fellows don't grab all the crackers and cheese before I get there."

"We'll save you a share," promised Morse Denton.

"I've got part of a box of oranges my folks sent me," volunteered George Abbot.

"Bring 'em along," advised Jack. "They'll come in handy to throw at the fellows if any of 'em try to break in on us."

"What! Throw my oranges!" cried George. "Say, they're the finest Indian Rivers, and——"

"All right. If they're rivers, we'll let 'em swim instead of throwing 'em," conceded Bert. "Anything to be agreeable."

"Oh, say now!" protested George, who did not always know how, or when, to take a joke.

"It's all right, don't let 'em fuss you," advised Tom in a low voice. "But, fellows, we'd better hustle if we're going to have doings to-night."

"That's right!" chorused the others, and they set off at a rapid pace toward Elmwood Hall, which could be seen in the distance, the red setting sun of the December day lighting up its tower and belfry. The skates of the students jangled and clanked as they hurried on, making a musical sound in the frosty air, for it was getting colder with the approach of night.

"Seasonable weather," murmured Jack. "It'll be a lot colder than this up in the Adirondacks, when we start hunting deer and bear."

"What's all this?" asked Morse, with a sudden show of interest.

"Some of Tom's schemes," answered Jack. "We're going on a hunting trip."

Morse looked to Tom for confirmation.

"That's the idea," Tom said, briefly sketching his plan. "Bert, Jack and George are going with me. Like to have you come along."

"I'd like to, first rate, old man," was the answer, given with a shake of the head, "but the governor has planned a trip to Palm Beach for the whole family, over Christmas, and I have to go along to keep order."

"I'm sorry," voiced Tom, but his words were lost in a gale of laughter from his chums as they sensed the final words of Morse.

"You keep order! You're a fine one for that!"

"The fellow who tied the cow to Merry's back stoop!"

"Yes, and the lad who put the smoke bomb in the furnace room! A fine chap to keep things straight!"

"Oh, well, you don't have to believe me!" said Morse, with an air of injured innocence that ill became him.

"They evidently don't," commented Tom dryly.

"Say, what was the row about just before I came back with that horse?" asked Morse, as though he wanted to change the subject.

"Snowball and old Skeel," explained Tom briefly. "It was sort of a case of a perfectly irresistible force coming in contact with a perfectly immovable body—but not quite," and he went more into the details of the accident on the ice.

"Humph! He must have been pretty mad," commented Morse.

"He was. Threatened arrest and all that. But Tom calmed him down," said Jack with a chuckle. "I guess Skeel didn't want to see the police very badly."

"What gets me, though," spoke George, in his perpetually questioning voice, "was what Skeel was doing around here."

"I'd like to know that myself," voiced Tom. But he was not to know until later, and then to his sorrow.

As the group of lads progressed, they were joined, from time to time, by other students from Elmwood, who had been out enjoying the day either by skating, coasting or sledding, and it was a merry party that approached the gate, or main entrance to the grounds, passing through the quadrangle of main buildings, and scattering to their various dormitories.

The holiday spirit was abroad. It was in the air—everywhere—the glorious spirit of Christmas, the day of which was not far distant. The boys seemed to know that the school discipline would be somewhat relaxed, though they did not take too much advantage of it.

Various engagements were made for surreptitious parties to meet here and there, to enjoy forbidden, and, therefore, all the more delightful, midnight lunches. The lads had been saving part of their allowances for some time, just for this occasion, and some had even arranged to bring away with them, from the refectory, some of their supper that night.

In due time a merry little party had gathered in the room of Bert Wilson in one of the larger and newer dormitories. The boys slid in, one by one, taking reasonable care not to meet with any prowling professor or monitor. But they knew that unless the rules were flagrantly violated, little punishment would be meted out. Each lad who came brought with him a more or less bulky package, until Bert's room looked like the headquarters of some war, earthquake or flood-relief society, as Tom said.

"And are these the oranges George boasted of?" asked Jack, taking up one and sampling it.

"Aren't they dandies?" demanded George.

"Whew! Oh, my! Who put orange skins on these lemons?" demanded Jack, making a wry face.

"Lemons?" faltered George, a look of alarm spreading over his expressive countenance.

"Lemons?" cried Tom. "Let me taste. Whew! I should say so," he added. "They're as sour as citric acid."

"And he said they came from Indian River," mocked Morse.

"Let's throw 'em out the window," proposed Joe Rooney.

"And him after them!" added Lew Bentfield.

"No, let's save them to fire at Merry in chapel in the morning," was another suggestion.

"I say, you fellows," began the badgered one, "those oranges——"

"They're all right—the boys are only stringing you," whispered Tom. "Don't get on your ear."

The advice came in good time. The arrival of other revelers turned the topic of conversation.

"Oh, here's Hen Watson. What you got, Hen?"

"A cocoanut cake!" cried someone who looked in the box Hen carried. "Where'd you get that?"

"Bought it—where'd you s'pose?" asked Hen. "Here, keep your fingers out of that!" he cried, as Jack took a sample "punch" out of the top of the pastry.

"I wanted to see if it was real," was the justifying answer.

"Oh, it's real all right."

"Here's Sam Black. What you got, Sam?"

"Why, he's all swelled up as though he had the mumps."

Sam did indeed bulge on every side. He did not speak, but, entering the room, began to unload himself of bottled soda and root beer. From every pocket he took a bottle—two from some—and others from various nooks and corners of his clothes, until the bed was half covered with bottled delight.

"Say, that's goin' some!" murmured Jack enviously.

"It sure is," agreed Tom. "We won't die of thirst from my olives now," for Tom had brought a generous supply of those among other things.

Someone leaned against the bed, and the bottles rolled together with many a clatter and clash.

"Easy there!" cautioned Bert. "Do you want to bring the whole building up here? Remember this isn't the dining-hall. Go easy!"

"I didn't mean to," spoke George, the offending one.

Gradually the room filled, until it was a task to move about in it, but this was no detriment at all to the lads. Then in the dim light of a few shaded candles, for they did not want the glimmer of the electrics to disclose the affair to some watching monitor, the feast began.

It was eminently successful, and the viands disappeared as if by magic. The empty bottles were set aside so their accidental fall would not make too much noise.

Gradually jaws began to move more slowly up and down in the process of mastication, and tongues began to wag more freely, though in guarded tones.

"This sure is one great, little Christmas feed!" commented Jack.

"All to the horse-radish," agreed Tom. "But it's nothing to what we'll have when we get up in the Adirondack camp, fellows. I wish you were all coming."

"So do we!" chorused those who were not going, for various reasons.

"Hark! What's that?" suddenly cried George. Instantly there was silence.

"Nothing but the wind," said Tom. "Say, fellows," he went on, "I have an idea."

"Chain it!" advised Jack. "They're rare birds these days."

"Let's hear what it is," suggested Bert. "If it's any good, we'll do it."

CHAPTER V

OFF TO CAMP

Tom Fairfield disposed himself comfortably on the bed before replying. There was room there, now, for the food and drink had been disposed of. Tom stretched out, finished a half-consumed sardine sandwich, and went on.

"You know old Efficiency, don't you?" began Tom, with tantalizing slowness.

"I should say we did!" came in a whispered chorus.

"The prof who's always lecturing on improving your opportunities, isn't he?" asked a student who had not been at Elmwood very long.

"That's the one," resumed Tom. "You know he claims we all eat and drink too much. He holds that a person should find the minimum amount of food on which he can live, and take no more than that."

"I've had more than my share to-night, all right," comfortably murmured Jack.

"And Efficiency, as we call him," went on Tom, "is a hater of feasting of any sort, unless it be a feast of reason. I think he lives on half a cracker and a gill of milk a day, or something like that."

"Well, what's the idea?" asked Bert, impatiently.

"This," answered Tom, calmly. "We will take the remains of our herewith feast, the broken victuals, the things in which they were contained, the empty tins, the depleted bottles, and deposit them on the doorstep of the domicile of Professor Hazeltine, otherwise known as Old Efficiency. When they are seen there it will show to the world that he does not practice what he preaches."

There was silence for a moment following Tom's announcement, and then came chuckles and smothered laughter.

"Say, that's a good one all right!"

"It sure is!"

"Ha! Ha! Ha! It takes Tom Fairfield to think 'em out!"

"Easy there!" Bert cautioned them. "You'll give the whole snap away, if you're not careful."

"Well, shall we do it?" asked Tom.

"I should say we will!" declared Jack.

"Then gather up the stuff and come along, a few at a time," advised the ringleader. "We don't want to make too much noise."

A little later dark and silent figures might have been observed stealing across the school campus, carrying various objects. The front stoop of the professor, who was such a stickler for efficiency and the maximum of effect with the minimum of effort, was in the shadow, and soon it was piled high with many things.

Emptied sardine tins, olive bottles which contained only the appetizing odor, pasteboard cartons of crackers or other cakes, ginger-ale bottles with only a few drops of the beverage in the bottom, papers and paper bags, the pasteboard circlets from Charlotte russes—these and many more things from the forbidden midnight feast were piled on the steps. Then the conspirators stole away, one by one, as they had come.

Tom Fairfield lingered last to make a more artistic arrangement of the empty bottles; then he, too, joined his chums.

"I rather guess that'll make 'em lie down and close their eyes," he said, in distinction to the process of "sitting up and taking notice."

"It sure will," agreed Jack, with a chuckle.

There were whispered good-nights, pre-holiday greetings and then the students sought their rooms, for there was a limit beyond which they did not want to stretch matters.

In the morning they were sufficiently rewarded for their efforts—if rewarded be the proper word.

Professor Hazeltine, going to his front door to get his early morning paper, saw the array of bottles and debris. At first he could not believe the evidence of his eyesight, but a second look convinced him that he could not be mistaken.

"The shame of it!" he murmured. "The shame of that disgraceful gorging of food. They must be made an example of—no matter who they are. The shame of it! I shall report them! Oh, the waste here represented! The shameful waste of food! I suppose all that is here represented was consumed in a single night. It might have lasted a month. I shall see that they are punished, not only for their disgraceful action in thus littering my stoop, but for gorging themselves like beasts!"

But the professor forgot one thing, namely, that to punish a culprit one must first know who he is, and how to catch him. It was the old application of first get your rabbit, though doubtless the professor would have changed the proverb to some milder form of food.

However, he took up his paper, ordered the servant to remove the debris, and then proceeded to his simple breakfast of a certain bran-like food mingled with milk, a bit of dry toast and a cup of corn-coffee. After which, bristling with as much indignation as he could summon on such cold and clammy food, he went to Dr. Meredith and complained.

The Head smiled tolerantly.

"You must remember that it is the holiday season," he said. "Boys will be boys."

"But, Doctor, I do not so much object to the disgraceful exhibition they made of me. I can stand that. No one who knows me, or my principles, would think for a moment that I could consume the amount of food represented there."

"No, I think you would be held guiltless of that," agreed the President.

"But it is the fact that the young men—our students—could so demean themselves like beasts as to partake of so much gross food," went on Professor Hazeltine. "After all my talks, showing the amount of work that can be done, mental and physical, on a simple preparation of whole wheat, to think of them having eaten sardines, smoked beef, canned tongue, potted ham, canned chicken—for I found tins representing all those things on my steps, Dr. Meredith. It was awful!"

"Yes, the boys must have had a bountiful feast," agreed the President with a sigh.

Was it a sigh of regret that his days for enjoying such forbidden midnight "feeds" were over? For he was human.

"I want those boys punished, not so much for what they did to me as for their own sakes," demanded Professor Hazeltine. "They must learn that the brain works best on lighter foods, and that to clog the body with gross meat is but to stop the delicate machinery of the——"

"Yes, yes, I know," said Dr. Meredith, a bit wearily. He had heard all that before. "Well, I suppose the boys did do wrong, and if you will bring me their names, I will speak to them. Bring me their names, Professor Hazeltine."

But that was easier said than done. Not that "Efficiency" did not make the effort, but it was a hopeless task. Of course none of the boys would "peach," and no one else knew who had been involved.

Professor Hazeltine came in for some fun, mildly poked at him by other members of the faculty.

"I understand you had quite a banquet over at your house last night," remarked Professor Wirt.

"It was—disgraceful!" exploded the aggrieved one, and he went on to point out how the human body could live for weeks on a purely cereal diet, with cold water only for drinking purposes.

So the boys had their fun; at least, it was fun for them, and no great harm was done. Nor did Professor Hazeltine discover who were the culprits.

The school was about to close for the long holiday vacation. Already some of the students, living at a distance, had departed. There were the final days, when discipline was more than ever relaxed. Few lectures were given, and fewer attended.

Then came the last day, when farewells echoed over the campus.

"Good-bye! Good-bye!"

"Merry Christmas!"

"Happy New Year!"

"See you after the holidays!"

"Get together now, fellows, a last cheer for old Elmwood Hall! We won't see her again until next year!"

Tom Fairfield led in the cheering, and then, gathering his particular chums about him, gave a farewell song. Then followed cheers for Dr. Meredith, and someone called:

"Three cheers for Professor Hazeltine! May his digestion never grow worse!"

The cheers were given with a will, ending with a burst of laughter, for the professor in question was observed to be shaking his fist at the students out of his window. He had not forgiven the midnight feast and its ending.

"Well, we'll soon be on our way," said Tom to Bert, Jack and George, as they sat together in the railroad train, for they all lived in the same part of New Jersey, and were on their way home.

"What's the plan?" asked George.

"We'll all meet at my house," proposed Tom, "and go to New York City from there. Then we can take the express for the Adirondacks. We go to a small station called Hemlock Junction, and travel the rest of the distance in a sleigh. We'll go to No. 1 Camp first, and see how we like it. If we can't get enough game there, we'll go on to the other camps. As I told you, we'll have the use of all three. None of the members of the club will be up there this season."

"But will whoever is in charge let us in?" asked Jack.

"Yes, all arrangements have been made," Tom said. "There is grub up there, bedclothes, and everything. All we'll take is our clothes, guns and cameras."

"Yes, don't forget the cameras," urged Bert. "I expect to get some fine snapshots up there."

"And I hope we get some good gun-shots," put in Tom. "We're going on a hunting trip, please remember."

The time of preparation passed quickly, and a few days later, and shortly after Christmas, the boys found themselves in the Grand Central Station, New York, ready to take the train for camp.

They piled their belongings about them in the parlor car, and then proceeded to talk of the delights ahead of them, delights in which their fellow passengers shared, for they listened with evident pleasure to the conversation of our friends.

CHAPTER VI

DISQUIETING NEWS

Three men sat in the back room of the road-house, talking in whispers, a much-stained table forming the nucleus of the group. Two of the men were of evil faces, one not so much, perhaps, as the other, while the third man's countenance showed some little refinement, though it was overlaid with grossness, and the light in the eyes was baleful.

The men were the same three who foregathered as Tom Fairfield and his chums left the scene of the snowball accident, and it was the same day as that occurrence. It must not be supposed that the men had been there during all the time I have taken to describe the holiday scenes at Elmwood Hall.

But I left the three men there, plotting, and now it is time to return to them, since Tom and his chums are well on their way to the winter camps in the Adirondacks.

"Well, what do you think of that plan?" asked Professor Skeel, for he was one of the three men in the back room.

"It sounds all right," half-growled, rather than spoke, the man called Murker.

"If it can be done," added the other—Whalen.

"Why can't it be done?" demanded the former instructor. "You did your part, didn't you? You found out where they were going, and all that?"

"Oh, yes, I attended to that," was the answer. "But I don't want to get into trouble over this thing, and it sounds to me like trouble. It's a serious business to take——"

"Never mind. You needn't go into details," said Professor Skeel, quickly, stopping his henchman with a warning look, as he glanced toward the door through which the landlord had made his egress.

"But I don't want to be arrested on a charge of——" the other insisted.

"There'll be no danger at all!" broke in the rascally teacher. "I'll do the actual work myself. I'll take all the blame. All I want is your help. I had to have someone get the information for me, and you did that very well, Whalen. No one else could have done it."

"Yes, I guess I pumped him dry enough," was the chuckling comment.

"It's a pity you had to go and get yourself discharged, though," went on Mr. Skeel. "You would be much more useful to me at Elmwood Hall than out of it. But it can't be helped, I suppose."

"I didn't go and get myself discharged!" whined he who was called Whalen. "It was that whelp, Tom Fairfield, who was to blame."

The man did not seem to count his own disgraceful conduct at all.

"Well, if Tom Fairfield was to blame, so much the better. We can kill two birds with one stone in his case," chuckled the professor. "Now I think we understand each other. We needn't meet again until we are up—well, we'll say up North. That's indefinite enough in case anyone hears us talking, and I don't altogether like the looks of this landlord here."

"No, he's too nosey," agreed Murker. "Well, if that's settled, I guess we're ready for the next move," and he looked significantly at Mr. Skeel.

"Eh? What's that?" came the query.

"We could use a little money," suggested the evil-faced man.

"Money. Oh, yes. I did promise to bring you some. Well, here it is," and the former instructor divided some bills between his followers and fellow plotters.

"Now I'll leave here alone," he went on. "I don't want to be seen in your company outside."

"Not good enough for you, I reckon," sneered Whalen.

"Well, it might lead to—er—complications," was the retort. "So give me half an hour's start. I'm going to drive back where I hired this cutter, and then take a train. You follow me in two days and I rather guess Tom Fairfield will wish he'd kept his fingers out of my pie!" cried Mr. Skeel, with a burst of anger.

The three whispered together a few minutes longer, and then the former instructor came out of the road-house alone and drove off.

"What do you think of him?" asked Murker of Whalen.

"Not an awful lot," was the answer. "But he'll pay us well, and it will give me a chance to get square with that Fairfield pup. I owe him something."

"Well, I don't care anything about him, one way or the other," was the rejoinder. "I went into this thing because you asked me to, and to make a bit of money. If I do that, I'm satisfied. Now let's get cigars and slide out of here at once."

And thus the plotters separated.

Meanwhile, Tom and his friends were a merry party. They talked, laughed and joked, now and then casting glances at their pile of baggage, which included gun cases and cameras. For they were to do both kinds of hunting in the mountain camps, and they were particularly interested in camera work, since they were taking up something of nature study in their school course.

The railroad trip was without incident of moment, if we except one little matter. It was when George Abbot mentioned casually the name of Whalen, one of the men employed at Elmwood Hall.

"I wonder why he left so suddenly?" George said, as they were speaking of some happening at school.

"I guess I was to blame for that," Tom explained, as he related the incident of the cruel treatment on the part of Whalen.

"I thought he looked rather sour," went on George.

"Why, were you talking to him lately?" asked Tom, a sudden look of interest on his face.

"Yes, the day before we left the Hall. He met me in town and borrowed a quarter from me. Said he wanted to send a telegram to friends who would give him work. Then he and I got talking, and I happened to mention that we fellows were going camping."

"You did!" exclaimed Tom.

"This Whalen was quite interested," resumed George. "He asked me a lot of questions about the location of the camps, and what route we were going to take."

"Did you tell him?" demanded Tom.

"Why, yes, I told him some things. Any harm?"

"No, I don't know that there was," spoke Tom more slowly and thoughtfully. "But did Whalen say why he wanted to know all that?"

"No, not definitely. He did mention, though, that he might look for a job somewhere up North, and I suppose that was why he asked so many questions."

"Maybe," said Tom, in a low voice. Then he did some hard thinking.

In due time Hemlock Junction was reached. This was the end of the train journey, and the boys piled out with their baggage, their guns and cameras. It was cold and snowing.

"I guess that's our man over there," remarked Tom, indicating a person in a big overcoat with a fur cap and a red scarf around his neck. "Does he look as though his name was Sam Wilson?" asked our hero of his chums.

"Why Sam Wilson?" asked Jack.

"Because that's the name of the man who was to meet us and drive us over to camp," Tom said.

The man, with a smile illuminating his red face, approached.

"Looks to be plenty of room in the pung," remarked Tom.

"What's a pung?" asked George.

"That big sled, sort of two bobs made into one, with only a single set of runners," explained Tom, indicating the sled to which were hitched four horses, whose every movement jingled a chime of musical bells.

"Be you the Fairfield crowd?" asked the man.

"That's us," Tom said. "Are you Sam Wilson?"

"Yes."

"Then, we are discovered, as the Indians said to Columbus," Jack murmured, in a low voice.

"Pile in," invited Sam Wilson, indicating the pung. "I'll get your traps. Ain't this fine weather, though?"

"It's a bit cold," Bert remarked.

"That's what a party said that I drove over to your camp the other day," spoke Sam. "He was from down Jersey way, too. You fellers must be sort of cold-blooded down thar! This chap complained of the cold. But pshaw! This is mild to what we have sometimes. Yes, this feller I drove over kept rubbin' his ears all the while. One ear was terrible red, and it wasn't all from the cold either. It had some sort of a scar on it, like it had been chawed by some wild critter. It sure was a funny ear!"

Tom looked at his chums with startled gaze. This was disquieting news indeed.

CHAPTER VII

AT CAMP

Seemingly by common consent on the part of Tom's chums, it was left for him to further question Sam Wilson and learn more about the man the caretaker had driven over to the hunting camp. And Tom was not slow to follow up the matter. He had his own suspicions, but he wanted to verify them.

"You say you drove someone over to our camp yesterday?" Tom asked.

"Not yesterday, the day before," was the answer. "And it wasn't exactly to your camp, but near it. Your camp is a private one, you know—that is, it belongs to an association, and I understand you boys are to have full run of all three places."

"Yes, the gentlemen who make up the organization very kindly gave us that privilege," assented Tom.

"Then you're the only ones allowed to use the camps," went on Sam. "I'll see to that, being the official keeper. I'm in charge the year around, and sometimes I am pretty hard put to keep people out that have no business in. So, naturally, I wouldn't drive no stranger over to one of my camps—I call 'em mine," he added with a smile, "but of course I'm only the keeper."

"We understand," spoke Tom, and his tone was grave.

"Well, then you understand I wouldn't let anyone in at the camps unless they came introduced, same as you boys did."

"Well, where did you drive this man then—this man with——" began George, but Jack silenced him with a look, nodding as much as to say that it was Tom's privilege to do the questioning.

"I drove this man over to Hounson's place," resumed the camp-keeper, as he saw that all the baggage was piled in the pung. "This man Hounson keeps what he calls a hunters' camp, but shucks! It's nothing more than a sort of hotel in the woods. Some hunters do put up there, but none of the better sort.

"The gentlemen who own the three camps you're going to tried to buy up Hounson's place, as they didn't like him and his crowd around here, but he wouldn't sell. That's where I took this Jersey man who complained of the cold. Kept rubbing his ears, and one of 'em was chawed, just as if some wild critter had him down and chawed him. 'Course I didn't say anything about it, as I thought maybe it might be a tender subject with him. But I left him at Hounson's."

"Did he say what his name was?" asked Tom, but he only asked to gain time to think over what he had heard, for he was sure he knew who the man with the "chawed" ear was.

"No, he didn't tell me his name, and I didn't ask him," Sam said. "Whoa there!" he called to his horses, for they showed an impatience to be off.

"Some folks are sort of delicate about giving out their names," went on the guide when the steeds were quieted, "and as I'm a sort of public character, being the stage driver, when there's one to drive, I didn't feel like going into details. So I just asked him where he wanted to go, and he told me. Outside of that, and a little talk about the weather, him remarking that he come from Jersey, that's all the talk we had.

"But maybe you boys know him," he went on, as a thought came to him. "He was from Jersey, and so are you. Do you happen to know who he is?" he asked.

"We couldn't say—for sure," spoke Tom, which was true enough.

"Well, maybe you'll get a chance to see him," went on Sam Wilson. "Hounson's isn't far from your first camp, where we're going to head for in a minute or so. You could go over there. You probably will have to, anyhow, if you want your mail, for the only postoffice for these parts is located there. And you'll probably see your man.

"To tell you the truth, I didn't take much of a notion to the feller. He was too sullen and glum-like to suit me. I like a man to take some interest in life."

"Didn't this man do that?" asked Tom, as he stowed his gun away on the straw-covered bottom of the pung.

"Not a cent's worth!" cried Sam, who was hearty and bluff enough to suit anyone, and jolly in the bargain. "This chap sort of wrapped himself up in one of my fur robes, like one of them blanket Indians I read about out West, and he hardly spoke the whole trip. But you'll probably see him over at Hounson's. Well, are you boys all ready?"

"I guess so," assented Bert, as he slung his camera over his shoulder by a strap. He hoped to get a chance at a snapshot.

"Well, then we'll start," went on Sam. "Pile in boys, and wrap them fur robes and blankets well around your legs. It's colder riding than it is walking. So bundle up. It'll be colder, too, when we get out of town a ways. We're in sort of a holler here, and that cuts off the wind."

"What about grub?" asked Jack. "Do we need to take anything with us? I see a store over there," and he indicated one near the small depot.

"Don't need to buy a thing," said Sam. "Every one of the three camps is well stocked. There's bacon, ham, eggs, besides lots of canned stuff, and I make a trip in to town twice a week. As for fresh meat, why, you'll probably shoot all that you want, I reckon," and he seemed to take that as a matter of course.

"Say, look here!" exclaimed Tom, determined not to sail under false colors, nor have his companions in the same boat. "We aren't regular hunters, you know. This is about the first time we ever came on a big hunting trip like this, and maybe——"

"Don't say another word!" exclaimed Sam, good-naturedly. "I understand just how it is. I'm glad you owned up to it, though," he went on, with a twinkle in his blue eyes. "Some fellers would have tried to bluff it out, but I guess me and some of the other natives around here, would have spotted you soon enough.

"But as long as you say you haven't had much experience, and as long as you ain't ashamed of it, I'll see that you get plenty of game. I'll take you to the best places, and show you how to shoot."

"Of course we know how to use guns, and we've hunted a little," Tom said, not wanting it to appear that they were absolute novices. And he added: "We're pretty good shots in a rifle gallery, too. But it's different out in the woods."

"I know!" cried Sam. "I understand. You don't need to worry. You won't starve, if that's what's troubling you. Now I guess we'll get along," and the horses stepped proudly out over the snowy road. Bells made a merry jingle as the party of boy hunters started for their first camp.

"Say, Tom," spoke Jack in a low voice to his chum, "do you think that was Skeel, the man with the 'chawed' ear, who was driven over to Hounson's?"

"I'm almost sure of it," was the answer.

"Well, what in the world is his object in coming away up here and at the same time we're due?"

"Give it up. We'll have to look for the answer later," was Tom's reply.

Out on the open road the horses increased their speed, and soon the pung, under the powerful pull of the animals, was sliding along at a fast clip. Much sooner than the boys had expected, they saw, down in a little valley clearing, a comfortable looking log-cabin, and at the sight of it Sam Wilson called out:

"There she is, boys! That's your first camp!"

CHAPTER VIII
THE FIRST HUNT

The pung came to a stop at the head of a driveway that led up to the log cabin, which was situated in a little clearing in the dense woods all about it. Tom and his chums gave one look at the structure which was to be their home, or one of them for several weeks, and were about to leap out of the sled, when Sam stopped them by a sudden exclamation.

"Hold on a minute, boys!" he said. "I want to take a look there before you step out in the snow."

"What's the matter? Are there traps set under the drifts?" asked Bert.

"No, but it looks to me like someone had been tramping around that cabin. I never made them footprints," and he pointed to some in the snow.

The snow on the driveway, leading from the main road through the woods, up to the hunting cabin itself, was not disturbed or broken by the marks of any sled runners or horses' hoofs. There were, however, several lines of human footprints leading in both directions.

"Just a moment now, boys," cautioned Sam, who was following a certain line of footprints, at the same time stepping in a former line, that he had evidently made himself, for his boots just fitted in them.

"What in the world is he doing?" asked George. "Has anything happened? Has a crime been committed? Is he looking for evidence? Why doesn't he go right up to the cabin?"

"Any more questions?" asked Jack, as the other paused for breath. "It seems like old times, Why, to hear you rattle on in that fashion."

"Aw——" began George, but that was as far as he got. Sam was ready now, to make an announcement.

"I thought so!" exclaimed the guide. "There has been someone else up here since I left this morning. Someone has been snooping around here, and they hadn't any right to, as this is private property."

"Did he get in?" asked Bert, thinking perhaps all the "grub" might have been taken.

"Don't seem to have gone in," replied Sam. "Whoever it was made a complete circle around the cabin, though, as if he was looking for something. You can see the tracks real plain," he went on. "Here is where I came up this morning, to see that everything was all right, for I expected you boys this afternoon," he went on. "And here is where I came back," and he pointed out his second line of footprints. "And here is where Mr. Stranger started up, went around the cabin, and came out on the main road again," the guide resumed. "No, he didn't get in, but he looked in the windows all right."

This the boys could see for themselves, for they were now out of the pung, there being no further need of not obliterating the strange footprints.

Tom and his chums noticed where the intruder had paused beneath several of the low cabin windows, as though trying to peer inside. And another thing Tom noticed; in the broad sole-impression of each boot-mark of the stranger's feet was the outline of a star, made in hob nails with which the soles were studded.

"I'll know that footprint if I see it again," thought Tom. "But I wonder who it was that was spying around this cabin?"

Sam, however, did not seem to be unduly alarmed over his discovery. George asked him:

"Who do you s'pose it was that made those marks?"

"Oh, some stray hunter," was the answer. "They often get curious, just like a deer, and come up to see what's going on. No use getting mad about it, as long as no harm's done, and they didn't try to get in. Of course, in case of a blizzard, I wouldn't find fault if a man took shelter in one of the cabins, even if he had to break in. A man's got a right to save his life."

"Do you have bad storms up here?" Bert wanted to know.

"I should say we did!" Sam exclaimed, "and from now on you can count on a storm or a blizzard 'most any day. So watch out for yourselves and carry a compass with you. But here I am chinning away when you want to get in and warm up and tackle the grub. Come on!"

He unlocked the door with a key he carried, and the boys gazed with interest at the interior of the shack. It suited them to perfection.

The cabin contained three rather large rooms. One was the kitchen and dining-room combined, another was sort of a sitting or living-room, made comfortable with rugs on the floor, and a fireplace in which big logs could be burned, while in the middle of the room was a table covered with books and magazines. The third room, opening from the living apartment, was where several bunks were arranged, and the momentary glimpse the boys had of them seemed to promise a fine place to rest at night.

A second glance into the kitchen showed a goodly stock of food. There was a stove, with a fire laid ready for lighting; and a pile of kindling and logs on the hearth was also prepared for ignition. In short, the place was as comfortable as could be desired, and with a blazing fire on the hearth, the knowledge that there was plenty of "grub" in the pantry, and with a blizzard raging outside, there was little more that could be desired—at least, the boys thought that would be perfect.

"Can you fellows cook?" demanded Sam.

"Well, we can make a stab at it," answered Jack.

"We've done some camping," spoke Tom, modestly enough. "I guess we can get up some sort of a meal."

"All right. Then I'll leave you, for I've got to get back to my farm," the guide explained. "Of course there isn't much to do in the Winter, but attend to the chores and feed the stock, but they have to be looked after. I live about seven miles from here," he explained, as he brought in the baggage, guns and cameras. "Now the two other camps, that go with this one, are several miles from here, almost in a straight line. There's a map showing just how to get to 'em," he said, indicating a blueprint drawing on the cabin wall. "Study that and you won't get lost. But if you can't find the other camps when you want to, I'll come and show you."

"Oh, I guess we can manage," said Tom, who was getting off his coat preparatory to helping start the fires and cooking.

"I'll stop and see you about once in four days, in case you need anything," Sam went on. "Just pin a note to the door of the cabin you last leave, saying where you're going, or whether you're coming back, so's I'll know where to look for you. My farm is located about half way between Camp No. 1, that's this one, and Camp No. 3, which is the farthest off.

"Well, now if you think you can manage, I'll leave you. It's getting on toward night, and my folks will be looking for me," and Sam prepared to start for home.

"We can get along all right," Tom assured him. "And may we begin hunting whenever we want to?"

"Start in now if you like, but I'd advise waiting until to-morrow," the guide said, with a chuckle.

"Yes, we'll wait," agreed Jack.

Though the four chums had never been to a real hunters' camp before, they had often shifted for themselves in the woods, or at some lake, and though they were perhaps not as expert housekeepers as girls, or women, they managed to get up a good meal in comparatively short time.

The fire was started in the kitchen stove, and another blaze was soon roaring up the big chimney in the living-room. This would take the chill off the bunk-room, for it was very cold in there, the windows being covered with a coating of ice.

"Baked beans—from a can—bacon and eggs—coffee and canned peaches, with bread and butter. How does that strike you for the first meal?" asked Tom, who had been looking through the cupboard.

"Fine!" cried Jack. "But what about bread? If there's any here, it will be as stale as a rock."

"Sam had some in the sled. His wife baked it, I guess," said Tom, indicating a bundle on the table. "I found some butter in a jar here."

"Then start the meal!" cried Bert. "I'm hungry."

They all were, and they did ample justice to the viands that were soon set forth. The cabin was filled with the appetizing odor of bacon and coffee, and wagging tongues were momentarily stilled, for jaws were busy chewing.

Rough and ready, yet sufficiently effective, was the dish-washing, and then came a comfortable evening, sitting before the crackling blaze on the hearth, while they talked over the experiences of the closing day.

They were all rather sleepy, from the cold wind they had faced on the sled ride, and soon were ready to turn in. Just before banking the fire for the night, Tom paused, and stood in a listening attitude near one of the windows.

"What's the matter?" asked Jack.

"I thought I heard something," was the reply.

"He's worried about the man whose footprints Sam saw in the snow," said George.

"Or the man with the 'chawed' ear," added Bert.

"No, it was the wind, I guess," Tom spoke. "But say, fellows, what do you think Skeel is doing up here?"

"Is he here?" questioned Jack.

"Well, that 'chawed' ear makes it sound so."

They discussed the matter for some time longer and then sought the comfortable bunks. Nothing disturbed them during the night, or if there were unusual noises the boys did not hear them, for they all slept soundly.

They awoke to find the sun shining gloriously, and after breakfast Tom got down his gun, an example followed by the others.

"Now for a hunt!" he cried. "Some rabbit stew, or fried squirrel, wouldn't go half bad."

"Or a bit of venison or a plump partridge," added Jack. "On with the hunt!"

CHAPTER IX

AN UNEXPECTED MEETING

Tom and his chums had no false notions about their hunting trip. They did not expect much in the way of big game, though they had been told that at some seasons bear and deer were plentiful. But while they had hopes that they might bag one of those large animals, they were not too sanguine.

"We'll stand better chances on deer than bears," said Tom. "For the bears are likely to be 'holed up' by now, though there may be one or two stray ones out that haven't fatted up enough to insure a comfortable sleep all Winter. Of course the deer aren't like that. They don't hibernate."

"What!" laughed Bert. "Say it again, and say it slow."

"Get out!" cried Tom. "You know what I mean."

"Well, we might get a brace of fat partridges, or a couple of rabbits," Jack said. "I'll be satisfied with them for a starter."

"Well, I know one thing I'm going to get right now!" exclaimed Bert, with a sudden motion.

"Do you see anything?" demanded Jack, bringing forward his rifle.

"I'm going to snapshot that view! It's a dandy!" Bert went on, as he opened his camera.

"Oh! Only a picture! I thought it was a bear at least!" cried Tom.

But Bert calmly proceeded to get the view he wanted. He was perhaps more enthusiastic over camera work than the others, though they all liked to dabble in the pastime, and each one had some fine pictures to his credit.

"Well, if you're done making snapshots, let's go on and do some real shooting," proposed Jack.

He and Tom each had a rifle, while Bert and George had shotguns, so they were equipped for any sort of game they were likely to meet. For an hour or more they tramped on through the snow-covered woods, taking care to note their direction by means of a compass, for they were on strange ground, and did not want to get lost on their first hunting trip.

As they came out of a dense patch of scrubby woods, into a little semi-cleared place, a whirr of wings startled all of them.

"There they go—partridges!" yelled Bert, bringing up his gun and firing quickly.

"Missed!" he groaned a moment later as he saw the brace of plump birds whirr on without so much as a feather ruffled.

"You don't know how to shoot!" grunted Jack. "You're not quick enough."

"Well, I'd like to see you shoot anything when it jumps up right from under your feet, and almost knocks you over," was Bert's defence of himself.

"That's right," chimed in George. "I couldn't get my gun ready, either, before they were out of sight."

"You've got to be always on the lookout," said Tom. "Well, the first miss isn't so bad. None of us is in proper shape yet. We'll get there after a while."

A little disappointed at their first failure, the boys went on again, watching eagerly from side to side as they advanced. No more did Bert use his camera. He wanted to make good on a real shot.

"Well, there's game here, that's certain," said Tom. "If we can only get it!"

Almost as he spoke there was a whirr at his very feet. He started back, and half raised his rifle, not thinking, for the moment, that it was not a shotgun. Then he cried:

"Bert! George! Quick, wing 'em!"

George was quicker than his companion. Up to his shoulder went his weapon and the woods echoed to the shot that followed.

"You got him!" cried Bert, as he saw a bird flutter to the snow. Bert himself fired at the second partridge, and had the satisfaction of knocking off a few feathers, but that was all. But George, who had not thought to fire his second barrel, ran forward and picked up the bird he had bagged. It was a plump partridge.

"That will make part of our meal to-morrow," he said, proudly, as he put it in the game bag Tom carried.

"Say, we've struck a good spot all right!" exclaimed Jack. "It's up to us now, Tom, to do something."

"That's what it is," agreed his chum.

But if they expected to have a succession and continuation of that good luck they were disappointed, for they tramped on for about three miles more without seeing anything.

"Better not go too far," advised Tom. "Remember that we've got to walk back again, and it gets dark early at this season."

"Let's eat grub here and then bear off to the left," suggested Jack.

They had brought some sandwiches with them, and also a coffee pot and tin cups. They found a sheltered spot, and made a fire, boiling the coffee which they drank as they munched their sandwiches.

"This is something like!" murmured Bert, his mouth half full.

"That's what," agreed George. "You wouldn't know from looking around here that there was such a place as Elmwood Hall."

The meal over, they again took up the march, and they had not gone far before Tom, who was a little in advance, started a big white rabbit. He saw the bunny, and then almost lost sight of it again, so well did its white coat of fur blend with the snow. But in another instant Tom's keen eye saw it turning at an angle.

He raised his rifle.

"You can't hit it with that!" cried Jack.

But Tom was a better shot than his chum gave him credit for being. As the gun cracked, the rabbit gave a convulsive leap and came down in a heap on the snow.

"By Jove! You did bag him!" cried Jack, admiringly.

"Of course," answered Tom coolly, as though he had intended doing that all along, whereas he well knew, as did his chums, that the shot was pure luck, for it takes a mighty good hunter to get a rabbit with a rifle bullet.

However, the bunny was added to the game bag, and then, for some time, the boys had no further luck. A little later, when they were well on their way back, Jack saw a plump gray squirrel on a tree. Bert was near him, but on the wrong side, and Jack, taking his chum's gun, brought down the animal, which further increased their luck that day.

"Well, we've got all we want to eat for a while. What do you say we quit?" suggested Tom. "No use killing just for fun."

"That's right," agreed his chums.

"We won't fire at anything unless it's a deer or a bear," went on Bert, laughing.

As they neared their cabin they were all startled by a movement in the bush ahead of them. It sounded as though some heavy body was forcing its way along.

"There's a deer—or bear!" whispered Jack, raising his rifle.

"Don't shoot at anything you can't see," was Tom's good advice. And the next moment there stepped into view of the boys the figure of Professor Skeel. He was almost as startled on seeing the four chums as they were at beholding him.

CHAPTER X

AT CAMP NO. 2

Professor Skeel might well have shrunk back at the sight which confronted him, for Jack stood poised, with raised weapon, as though he had it pointed at the former instructor. But Professor Skeel did not shrink back. He gazed at the boys, though there was evidence of surprise on his face.

"I—I beg your pardon," said Jack, for he could not forget the time when the crabbed man had been in authority over him. "I—I—didn't see you there," Jack went on.

"Evidently not," said the man, dryly. "You had better be careful what you do with a gun."

"I am careful," answered Jack, a trifle nettled at the words and manner of Mr. Skeel. "I wasn't going to fire until I saw you."

"Oh," said Mr. Skeel.

"I—I didn't mean just that," Jack went on. "I meant I was going to see what it was before I shot."

That was decidedly the better way of putting it.

"You—you are quite a ways from—from Elmwood Hall," said Tom, changing from his first intention of saying "home," for he recollected he did not know where Professor Skeel lived.

"Yes, I am up here on—business," went on the unpopular man. "And I trust there aren't any hills where you can roll down big snowballs," he added significantly.

"You seem to forget that was an accident," Tom said. He did not altogether like Professor Skeel's tone.

"Well, I don't want any accidents like that to happen up here," went on the former teacher. "And now another matter. Are you boys following me? If you are, I warn you that I will not tolerate it. You must leave me alone. I have business to do up here, and——"

"We most decidedly are not following you!" exclaimed Tom, with emphasis. "Besides, we are on private grounds, the use of which we were granted for this holiday season, and——"

"Is that a polite request for me to—get off?" asked Mr. Skeel.

"Well, no, not exactly," Tom answered. "We are not the owners, but we have the privilege of hunting here. It is possible that the caretaker may order you off. But you have no right to say that we are following you. We have a right here."

"I didn't say you were—I only asked if you were," said Mr. Skeel, who seemed to "come down off his high horse a bit," as Jack said afterward.

"Then I'll say that you are entirely mistaken," went on Tom. "We were out hunting, and we came upon you unexpectedly. We were as much surprised as you were, though we guessed you were in the neighborhood."

"You did?" cried Professor Skeel, with sudden energy. He seemed both startled and angry. "Who told you?" he demanded.

"Sam Wilson, the man who drove you over from the depot to Hounson's place," replied Tom, who had no reason for concealment, and who also wanted to show that he knew the whereabouts of Mr. Skeel.

"I never told him my name!" declared the former instructor.

Tom did not care to state that they had guessed the identity of the man by the description of his injured ear. The member was in plain sight as Tom looked—a ragged, torn lobe, of angry-red color, and it did look, as Sam had said, as though it had been "chawed by some critter."

"You seem to know considerable of my affairs," went on Mr. Skeel. "But I want to warn you that I will tolerate no spying on my movements, and if you try any of your foolish schoolboy tricks, I shall inform the authorities." He glared at Tom as he said this, as though challenging him to make a threat. Doubtless the professor knew that any charges which might lie against him in New Jersey would be ineffective in the Adirondacks. But Tom did not care to press that matter now.

"You need not fear that we will spy on you," said the leader of the young hunters. "And as for playing tricks, we have something else to do, Mr. Skeel."

"Very well; see that you keep to it."

He turned as though to go away, and, as he did so the boys saw two other men advancing up a woodland path toward the professor.

Mr. Skeel made a quick motion toward the men, exactly, as Bert said afterward, as though he wanted to warn them back. But either they did not see, or understand, the warning gestures, or else they chose to ignore them, for they came up the inclined snowy path, until they stood in full view of the four boys. At the sight of one of the men, Tom uttered an exclamation, that was echoed by his chums.

"Whalen!" he murmured, recognizing the discharged employee, for whose dismissal he was, in a great measure, responsible, since he had made a report of the man's cruelty to a young student at Elmwood Hall.

"We were looking——" began Whalen, speaking to the professor, when he happened to recognize the four young hunters, whom he had evidently failed to notice, as they stood somewhat in the shadow of a big pine tree, and were well wrapped up from the cold.

"Never mind now," said Mr. Skeel, quickly, as though to keep the man silent. "I was just going back to you. It seems we are on private grounds."

"Well, what of that?" jeered the other man, who had not yet spoken. He had a brutal, evil face.

"Lots of it, if you're not careful," snapped Tom, who did not like the fellow's tone, or manner.

"Oh, is that so, young feller? Well, I'd have you know——"

The man stopped suddenly, for Whalen had administered a quiet kick, and whispered something in his ear. What he said the boys could not hear, but they saw the warning and quieting chastisement.

"Oh," and the other man, who had been addressed as Murker, seemed to swallow the rest of his words.

"Come on," said Professor Skeel, and without a further look at the four chums he turned away, followed by the two men with evil faces.

"Whew! This is going some!" gasped Jack, when the trio was out of sight. "Who'd think of meeting Skeel and those two worthies up here in the wilderness?"

"Well, we practically knew Skeel was here," said Bert, "though we aren't any nearer than we were in guessing at what his object is. But it is a surprise to see Whalen and that other man, whoever he is. They must be trailing in with Skeel. What's the game, Tom?"

Tom Fairfield did not answer for a moment. He was busy looking at some tracks in the snow.

"Yes, they are just the same," he murmured, slowly.

"What is it? A bear?" asked George, eagerly.

"No, but look," and Tom pointed to some footprints. In the middle of the sole of each one was a star made in hob nails.

"Why—why, that's the same mark that was near our cabin," cried Jack.

"Exactly," Tom agreed coolly. "I thought it would prove so."

"But what does it all mean?" asked Bert. "What are they doing up here, and around our cabin?"

"Give it up," spoke Tom. "Maybe they're hunting, as we are."

"But they had no guns," Jack said.

"No. Well, we'll just have to wait and see what turns up," Tom went on. "I think we gave 'em rather a surprise, though."

"We sure did," agreed George. "But that Whalen surprised me, too. I wonder how he got here?"

"Didn't you say you told him where we were coming?" Tom asked.

"Yes, I did, after he pumped me with a lot of questions. I didn't realize what I was doing. I say, Tom, I hope I haven't done any harm!"

"Oh, no. There wasn't any secret about where we were going to spend the Christmas holidays," Tom said. "But it is rather odd to find those three so close after us. But maybe it will be all right. They know they are on private preserves—our private grounds—for the time being, and I guess they won't trouble us."

"Then it was those three, sneaking around the cabin?" asked Jack.

"Professor Skeel, at least," Tom went on, "though it may have been only ordinary curiosity that took him there. We'll take a little trip over to Hounson's some day, and see what we can pick up there."

It was getting late, so the young hunters made haste back to their cabin. They had supper, and then once more sat about the fire and talked through the long Winter evening. The next day they dressed their game and cooked it, finding it a welcome relief from the canned meats and bacon on which they had been living.

The rest of that week they remained in the vicinity of Cabin No. 1, having fair luck, but getting no big game. They saw one deer, but missed him. In this time they saw no more of Skeel or his cronies.

"What do you say we go over to Camp No. 2 for a change?" asked Tom, one night.

"We're with you," his chums agreed, and they made an early start, through the woods, locking up the place they left behind, for they might not be back for several days. They managed to bag several rabbits and squirrels on their march, but saw no signs of deer. Sam had told them they might not have much luck in this direction.

In due time, by following a copy of the blue print map they had made, they came to Camp No. 2. There had been a light fall of snow in the night, and as Tom approached the cabin, he cried out:

"Boys, they've been here ahead of us!" He pointed to footprints in the white blanket—footprints, one of which had a star in the middle of the sole.

CHAPTER XI

MORE PLOTTING

Impetuous George Abbot was about to rush forward when Tom, stretching out a hand, held him back.

"Hold on a minute," he said, and there was some strange quality in Tom's voice that made his chum obey.

"What's up?" he asked, glancing from Tom to the cabin.

"Nothing yet, but there may be," was the cool answer.

"You mean there may be someone in that cabin—Skeel or those other men?"

"That's about the size of it," Tom said.

"That's right—best to be on the safe side," put in Bert. "Those men, or Skeel, especially, have been here lately."

"But they haven't any right in our cabin—at least the cabin your friends gave us the use of, Tom," objected George.

"I know they haven't, and that's just where the trouble might come in. Those two men with Skeel look like ugly customers. If we cornered them in a cabin they had no right to enter, they might turn ugly. It's best to go a bit slowly until we find out whether or not they are in there."

"That's what I say," chimed in Jack. "Not that I'm afraid, but I don't want to run into trouble so early on our vacation. Of course it's possible," he went on, "that someone else besides Skeel and his cronies may have been here, or may still be here, for boots, with nail-marks like those on the sole, can't be so very rare. But I'm inclined to think Skeel wore those," and he nodded toward the marks in the snow.

"I agree with you," Tom said, "and we'll soon find out. Let's look about a bit before we rush up to the cabin," he went on.

Slowly the boys circled about it, gradually coming closer, to give those within, if such unwarranted visitors there might be, a chance to either make their presence known in a friendly manner, or take their departure.

But there was no sign from the cabin of Camp No. 2, and, after waiting a little while, Tom and his chums moved forward. As they came nearer, they could see that some two or three persons had made a complete circle about the cabin, and had even advanced up on the rough steps that led to the front door. Whether they had entered or not was something that could not be stated with positiveness.

"Well, the door's locked, anyhow," Tom said, as he looked at the padlock. "But of course they might have a duplicate key." He drew from his pocket the one Sam Wilson had given him, and a moment later Tom and his chums stood inside the cabin. They breathed a sigh of relief. No one opposed them.

Nor, as far as could be learned by a glance around the interior, had any uninvited guests been present. The place was in order, not as complete, perhaps as that of the first camp, but enough to show that it had been "slicked up," after its last occupancy by the hunting party of gentlemen to whom Tom and his friends were indebted for the use of the camps.

"Skeel and his cronies may have been here all the same, looking for us," said Jack, as he stood his gun in a corner.

"Why should they be looking for us?" inquired George.

"Now don't start that list of questions," objected Jack. "Ask Tom."

George turned a gaze on his other chum.

"Of course Skeel may have been here," admitted our hero. "We were never in this cabin before, and we don't know how it looked, or how it was arranged. But if they were here, they don't seem to have done much damage, and if they had a meal, they washed the dishes up after them."

A look in the kitchen showed that it was in order. This cabin was built just the same as was No. 1, and the arrangements and furnishings were practically similar.

"Well, Skeel or no Skeel, I'm going to have something to eat!" cried Tom. "Come on, fellows, make yourselves at home."

This they proceeded to do, making arrangements to get a meal, for there was plenty of wood for the stove as well as a pile of dry logs for the fireplace. A blaze was not unwelcome, for it was growing colder, and there were signs of a storm.

As our friends sat about the cozy, crackling blaze on the hearth they were unaware of three men, on the edge of the little clearing in which the cabin stood—three men who were gazing at the smoke curling up from the chimney.

"Yes, there they are!" grumbled the one known as Whalen. "There they are in their cabin, nice and warm, and with plenty to eat, and we're out in the cold. I don't like it, I say! I don't like it!"

"Now, don't get rash!" observed Professor Skeel, for he was of the trio. "What is a little discomfort now compared to the satisfaction we'll have later?"

"I wouldn't mind so much, if I was sure of that," said Whalen sullenly. "But it ain't noways sure."

"I'll make it sure," said the hoarse voice of the other plotter.

"Have you decided on a way to get him into our hands?" asked the former teacher eagerly. "Have you a plan, Murker?"

"Yes, and a good one, too!" was the answer. "It's come to me since we've been fiddling around here."

"And can we get him—get Tom Fairfield—where we want him?" asked Professor Skeel eagerly. "That's what I want to know."

"Yes, I think we can," answered Murker, an unpleasant grin spreading over his evil face. "I haven't all the details worked out yet, but when I get through, I think we'll have him just where we want him. Not that I want him particularly," he went on. "I never knew him before you fellows got me into this," and when he classed Professor Skeel as a "fellow," the latter did not object.

It showed to what depths the really talented man had fallen. For Professor Skeel was a brilliant scholar, and would have made his mark in educational circles, had he chosen to be honest. But he took the easiest way, which ends by being the hardest.

"I don't ask you to take any interest in Tom Fairfield, once you help me get him in my power," went on the former instructor. "I'll attend to the rest. But I want him alone. I don't want to have to handle any of the others."

"I should say not!" exclaimed Whalen. "We'll have our hands full, if we try to take care of all four of 'em."

"Oh, I wouldn't be afraid," was the sneering comment of Murker. "I guess we could persuade 'em to be good," and he leered at his companions.

"Four are too many to handle," decided Professor Skeel. "I want Tom Fairfield alone."

"And I'll get him for you," promised Murker. "But you've got to give me a share of the ransom money."

"Oh, I'll do that," readily agreed the former teacher. "I'm doing this as much to square accounts with him as for anything else."

"Well, I'm not working for love—or revenge," chuckled Murker. "I want the cold cash."

"So do I," chimed in Whalen, "but I want revenge, too. It's going to be a regular kidnapping, isn't it?" and he looked at Professor Skeel.

"It will be if he can carry it out," was the answer, with a nod at Murker.

"Oh, I'll do my part," was the assurance given.

"But won't it be risky—dangerous?" asked Whalen. "I don't want to get in trouble," and he looked rather anxiously about him, as though already he feared officers of the law might be after him.

"There's no more risk for you than for us," spoke Professor Skeel.

"There won't be any risk—not up in this lonesome place," Murker said.

"But how are you going to make sure of getting Tom into our hands alone?" asked the rascally professor.

"Leave that to me," was the chuckling answer. "I used to live in this region when I was a young fellow. Folks have forgotten me, but I haven't forgotten them."

"I say!" exclaimed Professor Skeel, "I hope you're not going to bring any more into this. The more there are the more risk there is, and the money I expect to get from Mr. Fairfield, for giving Tom back to him, won't go so far if we have to split it up——"

"Oh, don't worry! No one else but us three will be in it. I should have said I hadn't forgotten the country up around here—not so much the people. I don't care anything about them. But I know every cross-road and bridle-path through the woods, and it will be funny if I can't get this lad where I want him. They're strangers up here, and they have to depend on signposts, and what that guide tells them."

"But they are smart fellows," said Professor Skeel. "I know, for I taught them in school. If they have a signboard to go by, it will be as good to them as a printed book would be to most people."

"That may all be very true," chuckled Murker. "But tell me this. A wrong signboard isn't much use to anyone, is it? Not even to a smart lad."

"A wrong signboard? What do you mean?" asked the professor.

"I mean just what I said—'a wrong signboard'—one that gives the wrong direction. It's worse than none at all, isn't it?"

"Well, I should say it was," was the slow answer of the former teacher. "But are you going to get Tom Fairfield——"

"Now, don't ask too many questions," was the advice of his evil-faced crony. "When you don't know a thing, you can say so with a clear conscience in case the detectives get asking too many personal questions of you."

"That's so," agreed Professor Skeel, readily understanding what was meant.

"Detectives!" exclaimed Whalen. "Did you say detectives?

"But—er—I—they—I don't want to see any detectives," stammered the former employee of Elmwood Hall.

"I don't either," chuckled Murker. "But it's best to be on the safe side, and to prepare for emergencies. So what you and the professor don't know, you can't tell. Leave the details to me, and I'll fix 'em. Now I think we've been here long enough. We know what we came over to this cabin to find out—that they hadn't been here before until just now. And we're pretty certain they'll go next—to No. 3 Camp."

"What makes you think so?" asked Whalen.

"Because boys are like deer at times—mighty curious. They won't rest satisfied until they've tried all three camps. They'll go over to the last one in a few days, and then, Skeel, we may have Tom Fairfield just where we want him!"

"I hope so!" was the fervent exclamation, as the three plotters made their way off through the dense woods.

CHAPTER XII

A LUCKY SHOT

"Well, we're not going to stay in all the rest of the day, are we?" asked Jack Fitch, pushing back his chair from the table.

"I should say not!" exclaimed Bert. "There's plenty of time yet to go out and bag a deer or two."

"Nothing small about you," chuckled Tom, as he looked to his ammunition. "But I agree that there's no use wasting time indoors. It does look like a storm, so we won't go too far away from the cabin."

"Are we going to stay here to-night?" asked George.

"Sure," remarked Tom. "It's too far to tramp back to No. 1 Camp. This is just as well stocked up, and as there are plenty of bedclothes here, and lots of wood, we don't care how cold it gets outside."

They had finished their meal, and it was now early in the afternoon. It would soon be dark, however, for in December the days are very short. But, as Jack had said, the few remaining hours of daylight need not be wasted, and as yet the boys had not bagged any big game.

"It's too dark for photographs," suggested George, as he saw Bert getting out his camera.

"Not if I make a few as soon as I get out," was the answer. "I want to get some views around this camp."

A close search through the cabin had not revealed that Skeel and his companions had entered. The boys felt sure it was those men who had made the tracks in the snow about the little building. But, if they had entered, nothing had been unduly disturbed.

"I wish I knew what their game was," spoke Jack, as he shouldered his gun and followed Tom and the others outside.

"It is sort of a puzzle," our hero agreed. "We'll have to take a walk over to Hounson's some day this week, and see what we can learn. If those fellows think they can trespass all over these camps it's time we told Sam Wilson. He'll send them flying, I'll wager!"

"That's right!" declared Bert.

The boys followed a trail through the woods. Their friend, the guide and caretaker of the camps, had told them about it, advising them to follow it, as they might see some game along it. This they were now hoping for, keeping a bright lookout in every direction.

As they tramped along, the sudden rattle of a dried bush on the right of Tom attracted his attention. He looked in time to see a white streak darting along.

"A rabbit!" he cried and fired on the instant.

"Missed!" yelled Bert, as the echoes of the shot died away.

"No, I didn't!" cried Tom. "You'll find him behind that stump."

And, surely enough, when the other boys looked, there was the rabbit neatly bagged. He was needed for food, too, for they had no fresh meat at this camp, and already they were beginning to tire of the canned variety.

Except for the determination to each bring back a deer's head, and the pelt of a bear, our four boy hunters had made up their minds not to be wanton shots. They wanted to get enough game for food, and the head and skin for relics, after using such of the meat as they needed of the bear and deer.

"Of course we four can't eat all that meat in the short while we'll be in the woods," Tom said, "but we can give it to Sam, so it won't be wasted."

Tom and his chums had the right idea of hunting, and had no desire to slaughter for the mere savage joy of killing.

"Another rabbit and a few partridges and we'll have enough to keep the kitchen going the rest of the week," Bert said, as Tom put the bunny in his bag. "Then all we'll have to look for will be a bear or a deer."

But even small game was scarce, it seemed, and though several shots were tried at rabbits at a distance, and though some partridges were flushed, no further luck resulted.

It was growing dusk when Tom suggested that they had better return to camp, and they retraced their steps. However, the rabbit was a large one, and, made into either a stew or potpie, would provide the main dish for their next day's dinner.

Early in the morning the boys were on the move again. They hunted around the cabin, planning to come back to it at noon for the hot rabbit dinner, and this they did.

The only luck they had was that Bert and George got some fine photographs. But not a rabbit nor a bird fell to their guns that day. Tom scared up a fox, and took several shots at it, hoping he might carry home the skin. But if Reynard were hit he showed no signs of it, and went bounding on through the woods.

"We'll make a regular hunt of it to-morrow," decided Tom, as they sat about the cheerful fire in the cabin that night. "We'll get an early start, take our lunch, a pot to make some coffee over an open fire, and we won't come back until dark."

"That's the talk!" cried Bert.

"This is the best hunting ground, according to what Sam said," Tom went on, "and we want to put in our best licks here. So we'll take a whole day to it, and go as far as we can, working north, I think, as the woods seem to be thicker there."

This met with the approval of the others, and they started out the next morning, equipped for staying several hours in the open. They set out on a new trail, one they had not traveled before, but they had not gone far on it before Tom, who was in the lead, came to a sudden halt, and uttered an exclamation of surprise.

"What's the matter?" called Jack, who was directly behind him. "See some bear tracks?"

"No, these are Skeel tracks, I should say. Those fellows must be just ahead of us, for the marks seem quite fresh."

Tom pointed to some impressions in the snow. Among them were footprints showing that same star mark in hob nails.

"I wonder why they're trailing and following us?" remarked Bert. "It can't be just for fun."

"Maybe they don't know where to look for game, and are depending on us," suggested George.

"That might be so," agreed Tom. "But I wish they'd show their hands, and not keep us guessing all the while. It's getting on my nerves."

"Well, we'll keep a lookout for 'em now," suggested Bert, "and if we see 'em, we'll give 'em a bit of our minds."

"Yes, and I'm going to ask Sam Wilson to tell 'em to go," added Tom. "They haven't any right here. They may be scaring all the game away, and besides, it's risky. They may get in the way of our guns, or we come too close to theirs, though I haven't seen them with either a rifle or a shotgun yet."

"No they don't seem to be hunting, but if they aren't, what in the world are they up here for?" asked Bert.

"That's what gets me," remarked Jack. "Well, come on. Time's too valuable to waste in chinning."

Once more they took up the trail. The footsteps of the three men, on their mysterious errand, crossed the path of our friends at an angle, and they did not think it wise to follow the marks of the hob nails.

Luck seemed to be better to-day, from the very start, for, before they had gone three miles, they had bagged two rabbits, three squirrels and Jack had a partridge to his credit.

"Enough to keep us from starving," he said. "Now for bigger game—a deer, at least."

"I'd like to get a good deer picture," announced Bert, looking to see that his camera was in working order.

A little later the four boys stood in a small clearing in the woods, wondering which way to go next, for, so far, they had seen no signs of either bear or deer. They hoped it was not so late in the season that all the bears would be enjoying their winter sleep.

Suddenly there was a slight noise over in the underbrush to the left of the clearing.

"I'm going to see what that is!" cried Bert, starting forward with his camera.

"Probably nothing but a rabbit," said Jack. "And we've got enough of the bunnies."

"Then I'll take a snapshot; that won't hurt," Bert responded.

The others, not much interested, watched him. Softly he went forward, hoping he might get a picture of a rabbit in its native woodland. The sun was just right for a picture.

But, as Bert looked, a deer suddenly came out of the brush, and stood on the edge of the clearing, seemingly unconscious of the presence of the boys. They had seen the beautiful creature, however, and for the moment none of them raised his rifle. Bert's, indeed, was slung on his back out of the way while he used his camera.

Without speaking, Bert motioned to his chums not to shoot until he had a chance to make a picture. Tom and the others signified that they would hold their fire.

Bert crept up, the deer still unconscious of the presence of its enemies, and the youth soon had the animal in focus. It looked as though it would be a fine photograph.

Suddenly there was another crashing sound in the bushes, and as the boys, startled, turned, they saw a larger deer, with sharp, branching antlers, step from cover just behind Bert. The latter was so intent on getting the photograph that he did not turn to see how he was menaced from the rear.

The male deer, with a snort and a stamping of hoofs, and with lowered head, leaped toward Bert. The animal, evidently thinking its mate in danger, was going to her defense.

"Look out, Bert!" cried Jack, but the warning would have come too late. Bert did not even turn around, for he was on the point of pressing the shutter release of his camera. He had noticed a slight movement on the part of the female deer that indicated she was about to leap into the bushes.

"There, I've got you!" cried Bert, as he pressed the bulb.

The next instant he was startled by a snort behind him. He heard a rattle of hoofs, and the voices of his chums crying a warning.

Bert turned to run, but he would not have been in time, except for what happened. A lucky shot on the part of Tom probably saved his friend from severe injury, if not death.

With a sudden motion Tom threw his rifle to his shoulder, took quick aim, and fired.

The male deer went down in a heap, actually turning a somersault, so great was its speed. And it came to rest, breathing its last, almost at Bert's feet.

CHAPTER XIII

THE CHANGED SIGN

"Say, that was a shot!"

"That's what! Just in time, too!"

Thus cried Jack and George. Bert was too surprised to utter a word, and Tom was too anxious to make sure he had bagged the first specimen of real game since coming to camp.

But there was no mistake about it. There lay the slain deer, and a fine specimen it was. The one Bert had photographed with his camera had, on the first alarm, darted into the underbrush, and was now far away, doubtless wondering what had happened to her mate.

"Say, why didn't you fellows tell me what was going on?" asked Bert, as he whirled about and saw what had happened.

"We did," spoke George.

"There came pretty nearly not being time enough to do anything," went on Jack. "It was touch and go, Bert, old man. Tom, here, fired just in time."

"Was it really as close as that?" asked the lad with the camera.

"It certainly was," Jack assured him. "That deer had it in for you. I guess he thought you were trying to pot his mate with a new-fangled gun, and he made up his mind to stop you."

"Well, Tom stopped him all right," spoke George. "Say, it's a fine specimen!" and he gazed admiringly at the head and horns. "It will make a fine trophy for your room, Tom."

"I wasn't thinking so much of that when I fired," was the modest answer. "I was wondering whether I could bowl him over before he reached Bert with those business-looking horns."

"And you did, old man. I shan't forget that!" exclaimed Bert, fervently. "I'll do as much for you some day, only I'm not as good a shot as you, so don't take any chances. If a deer or a bear comes after you, run first, and get in a safe place. Then wait for me to shoot at it."

"It was more luck than anything else that I got him," Tom said. "If I had stopped to think, I'm sure I'd have had a touch of 'buck-fever,' and I wouldn't have been able to hold my gun steady. But I just up and blazed away."

"Well, now we've got it, what are we going to do with it?" asked Jack. "Shall we trail after the one that got away—the one Bert took a picture of?"

"What's the use?" asked Bert. "She's miles away from here now."

"Besides," added Tom, "we've got more meat here now than we can use in a week. No use killing for fun. I've got the head trophy I want, and it will be the turn of you fellows next. I won't shoot any more deer, though I'll bag a bear if I can. We don't want to shoot female deer if we can help it."

"That's right," agreed Jack. "Now let's decide what to do about this fellow. He's a big one, and will take some cutting-up."

The boys were rather dubious about getting the deer's head off, and taking the best part for food. But they were saved what might have been an unpleasant task by the arrival of Sam Wilson.

"Hello!" cried the guide, as he saw his young friends. "Well, you have had some luck, haven't you! Is that your first one?"

"Yes," answered Tom, as he related what had occurred.

"Well, now, that's the way to do!" Sam cried. "He's a fine critter, too; good head and horns. I've got my pung just outside on the road. I'll take him along, dress him for you and send the head to an Indian to be mounted. Old Wombo does pretty good work that way."

"I wish you would have it done," Tom said. "And take some of the venison yourself. There's more than we can use."

"Besides, we're going to get more deer in a few days," added George.

"Oh, you are, eh? Well, nothing like being sure," chuckled the old guide and hunter. "So far, though, you've done as well as the men who come up here, so I wouldn't wonder but what you'd beat 'em. How have you been? Anything happened?"

They told of their experiences in camp, and Tom mentioned Skeel and his cronies.

"Trespassing on these preserves, eh?" exclaimed Sam. "Well, I'll have to look into that. These lands are posted, and only those who get permission can enter on them, and hunt or fish. I'll just put a flea in the ears of those fellows, if they don't look out!"

With the help of the boys, Sam carried the deer out to his waiting pung. He said he had happened to pass near No. 2 Camp, and decided to run in on the chance that the boys might be there.

The deer's legs were tied together, and then a long pole, cut from the woods, was thrust between them, lengthwise. On the shoulders of the boys and the guide the carcass was taken out to the big sled.

"I'll bring the meat over to-morrow," promised Sam, "and the head will be mounted later. It takes a little time."

"Keep plenty of the venison yourself," Tom urged.

"Well, just as you say," was the laughing acceptance. "I haven't had much chance to do any hunting yet. I'm glad you had a good start of luck."

"And I hope my picture of the other deer comes out all right," murmured Bert, his interest, just then, centering in his camera.

"Well, if it hadn't been for Tom, you might not have come out all right," said Jack, more than half seriously.

That was the extent of their luck for that day, however, except that both Bert and George secured some fine snapshots. When Sam had departed with the slain deer, the boys found a good place to stop, and build a fire to make coffee. They ate their lunch with such appetites as come only from life in the open, and, having finished, once more they set out on the trail.

But, though Jack, Bert and George each hoped for a repetition of Tom's luck, in some modified form, it was not to be.

The boy hunters adopted all the suggestions of Sam, in looking for more game, but though they saw signs of it, the game itself had disappeared, at least for the time being.

"But we've got other days ahead of us," suggested Tom. "We don't have to go back for more than two weeks, and that will give us plenty of chances."

They reached Camp No. 2 very tired, but satisfied with their day's trip. And they brought with them appetites that made Jack, who was temporarily doing the cooking, wish his chums had left part of their hunger in the woods.

"What! More beans?" he cried to Bert, who passed his plate for the third time. "Can't you eat anything but beans?"

"Don't need to, when they're cooked as good as this, old man," was the laughing answer. "That molasses you put in just gave 'em the right flavor."

"I'll leave it out next time," grumbled Jack. "I want a chance to get a bite myself."

The meal went merrily on, and then came a delightful evening spent in the flickering blaze of the log fire, talking over the events of the day. Bert had developed his picture of the deer, and found that it would make a good print. Tom was dreaming of the time when he would get back the mounted head to hang on the wall of his den at home, as a memento of the trip.

Tom was destined to have other memories of the trip than his deer-head trophy, but he did not know that yet.

A rather heavy fall of snow the next day prevented the boys from going far from the cabin, for they did not want to take any chances on being lost in the storm.

There was no need to go out for food, as they had plenty, and in the afternoon Sam came over with a generous supply of deer meat, so their larder was well supplied.

"When are we going to take in Camp No. 3?" asked Jack of Tom, when Sam had gone back home in his pung sled.

"Well, we can go over there whenever you fellows want to. I don't believe, from what Sam says, that it's quite as good hunting ground as this, and I thought maybe you'd want to stay here until you each got a deer's head."

"Yes, I guess that would be best," agreed Bert. "This seems to be the most promising location. And there may be bears around. I heard some animal prowling about the cabin last night."

"So did I," confessed George. "Maybe it was Skeel and his crowd," he added.

"Hardly," scoffed Tom. "More like it was a fox looking to pick up something to eat that we had thrown out. But we'll stay around here for a few days longer, and then make a hike for No. 3. We might as well take 'em all in while we're here. No telling when we'll get another chance."

Had the boys known what was in store for them, they would have started for No. 3 Camp at once. But they did not know, and the delay gave the enemies of Tom Fairfield a chance to plan their trick.

For the next day, at some distance from No. 2 Cabin, there might have been seen three men, going along the snow-covered forest trail, in a manner that could only be described as "slinking." A glance would have disclosed their identities—Skeel, Whalen and Murker.

"Think they'll soon be on the move?" asked Professor Skeel. "If they don't take the trail, all our work will be wasted."

"Well, we've got to take some chances," growled Murker. "If this dodge doesn't fool 'em, I'll have to try another. But I think it will. Once we get 'em confused, and off the road, we can separate 'em by some means or other, and deal with Fairfield alone. You leave it to me."

"Very well," assented Professor Skeel.

A little farther walk through the woods brought the three conspirators to a cross-road. It was not much traveled in Winter, but in Summer formed a popular highway. The main road led back to the village, where the boys had left the railroad train, and the cross highway connected two towns—Ramsen and Fayetville.

Reaching this signboard, Murker looked around to make sure he was unobserved. Then, with a few blows from a hammer, he knocked off the two signboards. These he reversed, so that the one marked "Seven miles to

Ramsen" pointed in just the opposite direction—to Fayetville. The other board he also reversed.

"But it's the Ramsen one they'll look at if they come to Camp No. 3," said Murker, "and they're almost sure to come. Then we'll have Fairfield where we want him!"

CHAPTER XIV

THE BEAR'S TRAIL

Bert Wilson was carefully examining his camera, sitting at a table in the cozy quarters of Cabin No. 2, where he and his chums had gathered after the day's hunt. When he had adjusted the shutter, which had stuck several times of late, thereby spoiling some fine pictures, Bert took up his gun, and began taking that apart to clean it.

"I say! What's up?" questioned Tom, who was lying lazily on his back on a blanket-covered couch, staring at the flicker of the flames on the ceiling. "Getting ready for an expedition, Bert?"

"Well, I sort of feel it in my bones that I'll get a bear to-morrow, or a deer anyhow, and I'm taking no chances," was the answer.

"Going to get the game with your gun or your camera?" asked Jack.

"Both," was the quick answer. "I'll snapshot him first and pot him afterward."

"If he lets you," laughed George. "But I'd like to see any healthy bear stand for having Bert poke a camera in his face, and then shoot a slug of lead into him."

"You watch my smoke—that's all," said Bert significantly, as he went on cleaning his gun.

"What's the program for to-morrow?" asked Jack, who, like Tom, was doing nothing, and taking considerable pains at it.

"Well, I thought we'd go off on an all-day hunt again," was the young host's answer, for Tom was really in that position, it being on his invitation, through his father, that the boys had come to the hunting camp.

"That idea suits me," responded Jack. "But take along more grub than we did last time. I was hungry before we got back."

"Why don't we shoot what we want to eat?" suggested George. "I never read of a party of hunters having to depend on canned stuff or the grocery when they were really good shots, as we are!" and he puffed himself up with pretended pride. "What's the use taking a lot of grub along when you can shoot a partridge or two, and broil 'em over the coals of an open fire? Doesn't that sound good?"

"It sounds a great deal better than it really is," spoke Tom. "That sort of thing is all right to read about, but I like my game to stand a little after being killed. And it's hard to dress and get ready anything when you're on a tramp. So I think we'll just take our grub along. We'll have more time for hunting then."

"That's right," assented Jack.

Bert's interest in his gun prompted George to look after his weapon. Jack and Tom declared theirs were already in perfect shape for the morrow's sport, providing they saw any game.

"I do wish we'd spot a bear," said Jack, with an envious sigh.

"Not much chance of that," came from Tom. "I asked Sam about that, and he said while bears were plentiful in this part of the Adirondacks, at certain seasons, this wasn't exactly the time for them. They're probably in their caves, or hollow logs, waiting for Candlemas Day, to come out and look for their shadows."

"Do you really believe in that superstition—that if a bear, or a ground hog, does see his shadow on that day, there'll be six weeks more of Winter, and if he doesn't, there won't?" asked George.

"There you go again—shooting questions at us!" laughed Tom. "No, I don't believe it, but lots of folks do."

"Did Sam say anything about the chances for getting more deer?" Bert wanted to know.

"Well, yes, he admitted there were plenty this year. But I've shot mine, so I'm not interested," Tom said.

"I'm counting on a bear-skin rug to put in front of my bed," remarked Jack. "Then when I have to jump up in the cold, I can warm my feet before I start to dress."

"Nothing like comfort," spoke Bert. "Going to have your bear's skin tanned with the head on, Jack?"

"Yes, I think I will."

"Better get your bear first," said Tom grimly. "Well, let's lay out plans for tomorrow's hunt. What trail shall we take? I rather fancy, from what Sam said, that the old lumber road will be best to start on. Maybe we can make Camp No. 3 in the day's tramp, and do some hunting along the way."

"That's rather too much of a risk, isn't it?" asked Jack. "We could easily make Camp No. 3 in a day's tramp, if we started out from here early enough, and didn't waste any time following game trails. But if we try to do any hunting, we're likely to be delayed. Then we won't be able to start for camp until late. We may not reach it, and not be able to get back here and then——"

"Great Scott!" cried Tom. "Have you any more if and but calamities up your sleeve, old man? If you have, trot 'em out. We can make Camp No. 3 all right, and do some hunting, too. Why, it's a good trail once we get over the mountain and strike the road to Ramsen. That's what Sam said."

Tom spoke of going over the mountain, but what he meant was going over the ridge of the highest range which they were then among. For the mountains were all around them, differing in height and rugged appearance only.

"Well, go ahead and let's try it, then," said Jack, with a shrug of his shoulders. "And if anything happens, don't blame me!"

"We won't, as long as you don't say 'I told you so!'" exclaimed Bert. "That always makes me mad."

"All right—let it go at that," suggested Tom. "Then we'll take as much time as we want for hunting to-morrow, and strike for Camp No. 3 when we feel like it. We'll take along some grub, and make coffee as usual. That sounds good."

"And I do hope I get a bear—or deer," murmured Bert. "If I don't I'm going to——"

"Hark!" suddenly interrupted Tom. He sat up quickly, in a listening attitude on the couch.

"Nothing but the wind," murmured George, as a shutter rattled.

"Hark!" ordered Tom again.

There was some sound outside. All the boys heard it plainly, and a dog they had borrowed that day from Sam, to help them in tracking any game on the trail of which they might get, sat up and growled.

"Someone is out there," said Tom in a whisper.

"Some animal—a skunk, maybe," suggested Bert. "I'm going to stay in. I don't like him—not for a scent!" and he laughed at his own joke.

Tom, however, was softly getting up from the couch. He looked fixedly toward one certain window.

"Jack, turn the light out suddenly!" he ordered in a whisper. "Bert, have your gun ready."

"Do you really think it is—anyone?" asked Bert, as he reached for his gun, which he had finished cleaning, and put together again.

"Someone or—something," went on Tom, and his voice did not rise above a whisper. He moved slowly over toward the window.

"Here goes the glim!" Jack announced, and at once the cabin was darkened. It took but a minute, however, for the boys' eyes to become accustomed to the change, and they saw moonlight streaming through the window toward which Tom was moving. The others followed him, walking softly.

"There he goes—it is someone!" hoarsely whispered Bert, and he pointed to a black figure stealing over the snow. It was plainly in sight, for the ground was deeply covered with snow.

"It's a bear!" George burst out. "It's a bear! Where's my gun? Where do you shoot a bear, anyhow? I don't want to spoil the skin. Say, where's my gun?"

"Dry up!" ordered Tom sharply. "It isn't a bear!"

"It is so!" began George. "Where's my——"

Before anyone could stop him, or object, Bert had slipped to the door, opened it, and had fired his gun at the retreating black object.

"Look out!" Tom cried. "You might kill him! That's a man—not a bear, Bert!"

"I know it," was the calm answer. "I only fired over his head to scare him. Look at him scoot, would you?"

And indeed the black object that George had thought was a bear suddenly straightened up, revealing itself to be a man. He ran with fast strides toward the circle of woods that were all about the hunting cabin. The man reached the shelter of the black trees a little later, and was soon lost to sight.

"A man!" gasped George. "It was a man!"

"That's what it was," added Bert.

"Well, what do you know about that?" demanded Jack. "Was he sneaking around this cabin?"

"That's about it," answered Tom.

"But who was he?"

"That's for us to guess," went on the young hunter. "But I fancy I can come pretty near it."

"You mean Professor Skeel?" asked Bert.

"Him, or one of his two friends."

"But what would he, or they, be doing around our cabin?"

"That," said Tom, and he spoke more soberly than he had for some time, "that is something I'd give a great deal to learn. It's a mystery that's been bothering me for some time."

The chums looked at their friend in silence for a moment, and then Jack remarked:

"I'm going to have a peep around outside."

The others followed, two of them carrying guns. They made a circuit of the cabin in the moonlight, but no other uninvited callers were observed. There were footprints about the shack, however, which showed that the man, whoever he was, had been listening under several of the windows.

"Well, he didn't hear any secrets, for we weren't talking any," Tom said with a laugh, as he and his chums went indoors again.

"Except to say that we were going to Camp No. 3 to-morrow," said Bert.

"That's no secret."

But it was the very information the man, who had been eavesdropping under the window, had come to obtain. He ran off with a smile of satisfaction on his evil face.

"They've got nerve—firing at me!" he muttered, not thinking of his own "nerve" in doing what he had done.

The boys were rather alarmed for a while, and quite indignant. They decided to take some harsh measures, if need be, to keep Skeel and his cronies off the game preserve. And with this resolve they went to bed, for they wanted to make an early start the next morning.

Ten o'clock the next day found our four friends well on their way to Camp No. 3. They had started their hunt in that general direction. It was an hour later, when, after several false alarms, the dog gave tongue to a peculiar cry.

"What's that?" asked Jack.

"It's a bear!" decided Bert. "Sam said the dog would yelp that way when he struck the trail. Come on, fellows!"

They ran forward to rejoin their dog, that had gone on ahead. He was now barking fast and furiously, and had evidently gotten on the track of something.

"Yes, it is a bear!" decided Tom, when he had noted the tracks in the snow. "And they're fresh, too, otherwise the dog couldn't smell 'em! They won't lie long on snow. Go on, old sport!" and thus encouraged the dog bounded forward.

How the bear came to be out at that time of the year, the boys did not stop to think. But they eagerly followed the trail. It led on through the woods, and they hardly noted their direction.

At noon they stopped for a hasty lunch, grudging the time it took, for they were anxious to get sight of the big game. Once more they were on the trail.

"But it seems to be getting dark suddenly," commented Jack. "I wonder if we'd better keep on?"

"Certainly—why not?" asked Bert. "The trail is getting fresher all the while. Come on, we'll have him soon. He's a big one, too!"

Again the boys pressed forward, the dog baying from time to time.

CHAPTER XV

LOST IN A STORM

Either the bear was a better traveler than the boys gave the brute credit for being, or the trail was not as fresh as Bert had supposed. For though they went on and on, they did not see the black ungainly form of Bruin looming up before them.

They were traveling through a rather thin part of the forest then, making good time, for the snow was not so deep here. Occasionally they thought they had glimpses of the animal they sought, but it always proved to be nothing but a shadow, or a movement in the bushes, caused by the passage of some big rabbit.

"There he goes!" suddenly cried George, pointing to the left.

"Yes, that's him!" eagerly agreed Jack.

Tom and Bert also agreed that they saw something more substantial, this time, than a shadow. But a moment later the black object, for such it had been, was lost sight of.

"Come on!" cried Tom, as enthusiastic as any of his chums. "We've got him now."

They raced forward, until they came to the place where they had seen the black object, and then they noticed a curious thing. For there were two sets of marks—human footprints, and the broad-toed tracks of the bear.

"Look at that!" cried Jack. "Was that a man we saw, or the bear?"

No one could say for certain. But this much was sure. The bear's tracks led in one direction, and the man's in another.

Was the bear chasing the man, or was the man hunting the bear, was another phase of the question.

"Look here!" said Tom, who had been carefully examining the two sets of impressions in the snow. "Here's how I size this up. The bear's tracks go in a straight line, or nearly so, as you can easily see. But the man's tracks are in the form of a letter V and we are at the angle right here. The angle comes up right close to the trail of the bear, too.

"Now I think the man was walking through the woods, approaching the bear. He didn't know it until he was almost on the beast and then the man saw it. Of course he turned away at once and ran back. You can tell that the footprints that approach the bear's trail are made more slowly than the others—going away. In the last case the man was running away from the bear. But the bear wasn't afraid, and kept straight on, paying no attention to the man."

"That's good argument," observed Bert.

"Can you tell us who the man was?" demanded George.

"I'm not detective enough for that," Tom confessed. "But I don't believe the man was a hunter with a gun."

"Why not?" Jack wanted to know.

"Because if he had a gun, he would have fired at the bear, and we'd have seen some change in the bear's trail. Bruin would either have run at the shot, or attacked the man, provided the bullet didn't kill at once. And you can see for yourselves that nothing like that happened. So I argue that the man had no gun."

"Then he was Skeel, or one of his two partners," said George.

"What makes you think that?" asked Bert, curiously.

"Because we never saw either of them with a gun."

"That doesn't prove anything," Tom said. "There are lots of men in these woods who haven't guns. It might have been Sam Wilson."

"Can you tell anything by the footprints?" asked Bert.

"No. The star mark isn't there, but that's nothing. Well, whoever he was he got away, and we didn't get close enough to make out who he was."

"I tell you where you're wrong in one thing, though, Tom," spoke Jack.

"How's that?"

"You said the man came up to the bear and ran away, turning off at an angle. I don't believe he saw the bear, because we were watching the man, and we would have seen the bear if he had seen him, too. For it was right here we lost sight of the man."

"Well, maybe I am wrong about that part of it," admitted Tom, "but at least the man didn't cross the bear's trail. Something turned him back when he saw the marks of the paws in the snow."

That seemed reasonable enough.

"Well, let's follow the dog," suggested Bert. "He's after the bear, anyhow."

This was so, for the dog had not even paused at the prints of the man's feet in the snow. He evidently preferred Bruin for game.

But now it was getting so dark that it was difficult for the boys to see, even with the whiteness caused by the covering of snow on the ground.

"I say," Tom spoke, when they had gone on a little farther. "I think we'd better turn back. It will be night before we realize it, and we're a long way from either camp. It's a question in my mind whether we hadn't better start back for Camp No. 2, and let three wait for a day or so. It's going to snow too, soon, if I'm any judge."

"Why, we're probably as near to No. 3 as we are to No. 2," observed Jack. "Why not keep on? We haven't been to Camp No. 3 yet, and I want to see what it's like."

"Well, we'll leave it to a vote," decided Tom, who never tried to "run" things where his chums were concerned. "One place is as good as another to me, but we've got to do something—and that pretty soon."

"We'd better give up the bear, at least for to-night," spoke Bert, and there was regret in his voice. "But we can take up the trail to-morrow."

"Whistle back the dog," suggested George. "And then we'll decide what to do."

But the dog did not want to come back. They could hear him baying in the depths of the now dark forest, but whether he was in sight of the bear, or was giving tongue because the trail was getting fresher, was impossible to say.

At any rate, the dog did not come back in response to the whistles shrilly emitted in his direction.

"Well, let him go," said Bert. "He'll find his way to one camp or another, I guess, if he doesn't go home to Sam. He said the dog often stayed out in the woods all night, and came back in the morning."

"All right—let him go," assented Tom. "And now what shall we do about ourselves? Here comes the snow!" he cried a moment later, for the white flakes began falling in a swirl all about them.

"In for a blizzard!" commented Jack.

"Oh, not as bad as that," murmured Bert.

"Do they have blizzards up here? How long do they last? Does it get very cold? How much snow——"

"That'll do, Why!" exclaimed Tom. "We've got something else to do besides answering questions. Now, fellows, what is it to be—Camp No. 3 or Camp No. 2? We've got to decide."

"I say No. 3," called out Bert.

"Same here," echoed Jack.

"I'm with you," was the remark of George.

"Well, I don't agree with you, but I'll give in," assented Tom. "The majority rules. But I think it would be better to go back to No. 2 Camp."

"Why?" asked Jack.

"Because we know just where it is, and we know we can be sure of a warm place, and plenty to eat."

"Can't we at No. 3?" asked George.

"Maybe, and then again, maybe not. We certainly will have to hunt for it, and it's only a chance that it may have wood and food stored there."

"Sam said it had," observed Bert.

"Yes, I know. But there have been men roaming about these woods that I wouldn't trust not to take grub from an unoccupied cabin," went on Tom. "However, we'll take a chance, but I think it's a mistake."

They turned about, and headed in as straight a line as they could for Camp No. 3. They knew the general direction, and had some landmarks to go by.

The storm grew more and more fierce. The snow was almost as impenetrable as a fog, and there was a cold, biting wind. It stung the faces of the boys and made walking difficult. It was constantly growing darker.

"I say!" called Bert, after a bit. He stopped floundering about in a drift, and went on: "I say, does anyone know where we are?"

"On the road to Ramsen," suggested Tom.

"I don't believe we are," Bert resumed. "I think we're off the trail—lost!"

"Lost!" echoed George.

"Yes, lost, and in a blinding snowstorm," went on Bert.

CHAPTER XVI

THE DESERTED CABIN

Bert's words struck rather a chill to the hearts of his chums. Not that they were cowards, for they were not, and they had faced danger before, and were used to doing things for themselves.

But now they were in a strange, mountain wilderness, following an unknown trail, and night was coming on rapidly. The storm had already burst, and it was growing worse momentarily.

"Do you really think we are lost?" questioned Jack, looking about him as well as he could in the maze of white.

"Don't you?" responded Bert. "I can't make out the least sign of a trail in these woods, and we have to follow one to get to Camp No. 3, you know."

"Yes, that's right," put in George. "We are going it blind."

"We've been going according to compass, since we gave up the hunt for the bear," commented Tom.

"Well, it will be more by good luck than good management if we find either camp now," said Bert. "But come on—we've got to do something."

"Which way shall we go?" asked George. "We don't want to get lost any worse than we are."

"We can't!" spoke Bert, dryly—that is, as "dryly" as he could with snow forcing itself into his mouth. "We're as lost as we'll ever be. The thing now is to start finding ourselves."

"Let's try this way," proposed Tom, indicating the left. "According to my compass Camp No. 3 ought to lie off about there."

"And how far away?" asked Jack.

"Not more than four miles—maybe five. But we can make that in about an hour and a half, if we don't get off the trail."

"That's the trouble," commented Bert. "We can't see any trail. We are going it absolutely blind!"

And going it blind they certainly were. They were all a bit alarmed now, for they had no shelter for the night, and they had eaten most of their food.

Suddenly, as they tramped along over the snow, there came a crash in the underbrush to one side.

"What's that?" cried George, nervously.

"That bear——" began Bert, slinging around his gun.

"Don't shoot!" cried Tom. "It's our dog come back to us!"

And so it was. The intelligent and lonesome brute had abandoned the bear's trail, and had come back to join his human friends. He was exhausted from long, hard running.

"Now he'll lead us to one camp or another," said Tom. "Welcome to our city, Towser!"

"What happened to the bear?" asked Jack, as the dog leaped about caressingly from one to the other.

"Evidently nothing," Tom said. "I don't believe the dog found him. His name isn't Towser though, by the way. I've forgotten what Sam did call him, but it wasn't Towser."

"What makes you think he didn't find the bear?" Bert wanted to know.

"He'd show some evidence of it if he had," was the reply. "He'd have a scratch or two. No, I think he gave up the chase soon after we did, and came after us."

"Well, now he's here, let's make some use of him," suggested George. "Do you really think he'll lead us back to camp, Tom?"

"Well, there's a chance of it," Tom affirmed. "Let's give him a trial. Here, old boy!" he called to the dog, a beautiful specimen. "Home, old fellow!"

The dog barked, wagged his tail, and set off on a run through the driving snow. He barked loudly, turning now and then to see if any of the four young hunters were following.

"That's the idea!" cried Jack. "Come on, boys. He'll lead us, all right!"

"But where, is another question," Tom put in. "My early education was neglected. I never learned dog talk, though I can swim that fashion pretty well."

"Swimming isn't going to do any good—not in this weather," murmured Bert, buttoning his mackinaw tighter about him, and beating his arms at his sides, for they all had been standing still, and were rather chilled.

"I could talk hog-Latin," Jack said with a smile, "but I don't believe that is any good for a dog. Call him back, Tom. You seem to have more influence over him than anyone else, and he's getting too far ahead. I wonder where he's going, anyhow?"

"I don't much care—Camp one, two, or three will suit me just about now," Tom remarked, as he turned his face to avoid a stinging blast of snowflakes. "Surely the dog knows his way to all three of them, and, if they are too far, he may lead us to Sam's farm. That wouldn't be so bad."

"Nothing would be bad where there was a warm fire and plenty of grub," commented Bert. "But call that dog back, Tom, or we'll lose him again. He's off there somewhere, barking to beat the band!"

Tom whistled shrilly. A series of barks came in answer, and, a little later the dog himself came bounding through the snow. His muzzle was all whitened where he had been burrowing, perhaps after some luckless rabbit. But his bright eyes were glowing as the boys could see in the half-darkness that had fallen, and Towser, as they continued to call him, for want of a better name, seemed delighted at something or another. Whether it was the storm, the fun he had had trailing the bear, or whether he was just glad to be with the boys, and happy over the prospect of adventures to come, no one could say.

The dog barked, wagged his tail, ran on a little way, came back, barked some more, ran on again, and then repeated the performance over and over, getting more and more excited all the while.

"He wants us to follow him," decided Tom. "All right, old man, I'm with you," he said. "Come on, boys. We'll see what comes of it."

Together the four hunters set off with the dog in the lead. Truth to tell they did not feel very much like hunters that day, nor had they had any luck. Matters seemed to be going against them. And in the storm and darkness there was a distinct feeling of depression over everyone. The dog was really the only cheerful creature there, and he had spirits enough for all of them, could they but be transferred.

"Whew! This is a storm!" cried Tom, as he bent his head to the blast.

It did seem to be getting worse. The wind had a keener cut and whirled the sharp flakes of snow into one's face with stinging force.

"It's a young blizzard," affirmed Jack.

"Well, if it does this in its youthful days, what will happen when it grows up?" Bert wanted to know, as he paused and turned around to get the wind out of his face while he caught his breath. No one took the trouble to answer him.

The dog seemed impatient at the slow progress of the lads, for he was now well ahead of them. They could only tell where he was by his barks, and by an occasional flurry of snow as he burrowed in some drift and then scrambled out again.

"Better call him back again, Tom," suggested George. "He'll get away beyond us, and soon it will be so dark we can't see our hands before our faces."

"Yes, I guess I will," Tom assented. "I'd put a leash on him if I had a bit of cord, and hold him back."

"Here's some," Jack said, offering a piece. "I had it tied around the package of sandwiches."

"By the way—any of those same sandwiches left?" asked Tom.

"A few—why?"

"Because that may be all we'll get to eat to-night."

"What's that?" cried Bert. "Aren't we going toward camp?"

"That's what I can't say," was Tom's answer, as he whistled for the dog. "We may, and then, again, we may not."

"But where are we heading, then?" George wanted to know, as Tom proceeded to tie the cord on Towser's collar.

"That's more than I can say," Tom made answer. "We're in the hands of fate, as they say in books."

"Well, I'd rather hang to Towser's tail," spoke Jack, with grim humor.

"I'm sorry I got you fellows into this mess," went on Tom, as they advanced again through the storm and darkness, this time keeping the dog closer to them by means of the cord.

"What mess?" asked Bert.

"Getting lost, and all that."

"Forget it!" advised Jack. "It wasn't your fault at all. You wanted to go back to No. 2 Camp, and the rest of us favored this move. I wish, now, we had taken your advice."

"Oh, well, mine was only a guess," Tom said. "We might have been as badly off had we gone the other way. We'll just have to trust to luck. Come on. But what I meant was that coming out to-day to hunt was my proposition. I was afraid there was a storm coming."

"We wouldn't have stayed home on that account," George asserted. "We're all in the same boat together, and we'll have to sink or swim—or skate," he added, as the icy wind smote him.

It was now about six o'clock, but as dark as it would have been at midnight. The moon was hidden behind dark clouds, but of course the white snow made it lighter than otherwise would have been the case. But in the dense woods even this did not add much to the comfort of our friends, and its increasing depth made it harder to walk.

Almost before the boys knew it, they had emerged from the forest to a road. They could tell that at once.

"Hurray!" cried Tom. "Now we'll be all right. A good road to follow."

"And a signpost, too, to tell us which way to go!" added Jack.

He pointed through the storm to where was evidently a crossroad, at the intersection of which was a post with the familiar boards on it.

"What does it say?" asked Bert, as Tom stood at the foot of it.

"Have to get out the electric light," Tom said, producing a pocket flashlight. By its powerful tungsten gleam, he read:

SEVEN MILES TO RAMSEN

"That's the ticket!" he cried. "Ramsen is the way we want to go. Camp No. 3 lies in that direction. Now we're all right, boys!"

"Good old signpost!" murmured Jack.

But, had he only known it, the signpost was a "bad" one, though, as we know, that was not the fault of the post itself.

Trudging along the road was easier now, and the boys made better time. But it was tiresome work at that. And when, a little later, they saw a building looming up at one side of the road, Bert cried:

"There's our camp now!"

For a moment they thought it was, but a closer look showed that it was not. It was an old deserted hut, almost in ruins, and as Tom flashed his light within, a sorry sight was presented to the eyes of the boys.

"Let's go inside," was Tom's proposal, and his chums looked at him in some amazement.

CHAPTER XVII
SPIED UPON

"What do we want to go in there for?" asked Jack, at length.

"Because," was the rather short answer of Tom. Then, feeling perhaps that he might explain a little more at length, he turned from where he stood in the tumbled-down doorway, and added:

"Let's get in out of the storm. This is a good place to rest, away from that cutting wind. Quiet, Towser," he added, for the dog showed signs of not wanting to go in. He growled and hung back. Then he looked in the direction in which they had come, and his hair rose on the back of his neck as though he saw something the boys did not see, and resented the sight—whatever it was.

"I don't like that," commented Bert. "Dogs know more than we do—sometimes."

"Oh, come on in!" repeated Tom, and he spoke to the dog again. This time Towser followed his temporary master inside the hut.

"But what gets me is why are we going in?" objected George. "It will only delay us, and if we've got to make seven miles to Ramsen to-night, we'd better be getting at it."

"That's just it," spoke Tom quickly. "I think we can't get at it."

"What do you mean?" came from Jack.

"I mean that we can't go on in this storm. It's getting worse every minute, and we may stray off the road. We have found this shelter providentially, and we ought to take advantage of it. It will give us a half-decent place to stay, and we won't be buried in the snow which may happen if we keep on.

"Come inside and stay here, that's what I mean," Tom went on. "It might be a heap-sight worse," and he flashed his torch about the bare and crumbling ruin of the cabin.

"What!" cried Bert. "Do you mean to stay here all night?"

"Why not?" asked Tom. "It's better than being out in the storm, isn't it? Hark to that wind!"

As he spoke a blast howled around the corner of the shack, and blew a cloud of flakes in through a glassless window.

"It's a little better than outside—but not much," murmured George. "Look at those windows."

"We can find something to stuff in them," said Tom cheerfully. "There may be some old bags about. And we haven't been upstairs yet. This place may be furnished better than we think. Come on, boys, make up your minds to stay here."

"Well, we might do worse, that's a fact," slowly admitted Jack. "Say, look at that dog, would you!"

His manner, as he said this, was excited, but no less so than that of the dog. The animal brushed past the group of boys, fairly pulling loose the improvised leash from Tom's hand and stood in the doorway with bristling hair, lips drawn back from his teeth and showing every appearance of anger.

"Something ails him," spoke George, in a low voice.

"I should say so," agreed Tom, rubbing his hand where the stout cord had cut into him, even in spite of his heavy mitten.

"It's that bear!" cried Jack.

"What?" questioned Tom.

"That bear we were following," explained Jack. "It's outside now, and the dog has winded him. Where's my gun? I'm going to have a potshot at him!"

He started toward the corner where he had stood up his gun. The interior of the cabin was fairly light, for Tom had snapped on the permanent switch of his little pocket electric light.

"Hold on a minute!" Tom said, placing a hand on his chum's shoulder. "What are you going to do?"

"Don't go out," advised Tom. "I don't believe it's the bear, to begin with, and, in the second place, if it is, you wouldn't stand any chance of hitting him in this storm. And you might get lost. It's a regular blizzard outside."

"What makes you think it isn't the bear?" asked Jack, ignoring Tom's other reasons.

"Well, from the way the dog acts, for one thing," was the answer. "He didn't act that way before, when we had a plain sight of the trail, and Towser may even have come close to Bruin himself."

"If it isn't the bear—who is it—or—what is it?" demanded George.

"I don't know," was Tom's frank reply.

"Let's give a yell," suggested Bert. "Maybe it's Sam Wilson, or someone who could put us on the right road. I don't fancy staying here all night if it can be helped. Let's give a yell."

"All right," Tom agreed. "Here, Towser," he went on to the dog, "come in here and behave yourself."

But the animal did not seem so disposed. He remained in the doorway, looking out into the storm, now and then growling hoarsely in his throat, but showing no disposition to dash out. Certainly he was acting very strangely, but whether it was fear or anger the boys could not decide.

"Well, whoever it is, or whatever, we've got plenty of guns and ammunition," remarked George. "We haven't had a decent shot to-day."

Which was very true. They had had great hopes, but that was all.

"Come on if we're going to yell," suggested Jack. "And if we don't raise someone, we'll prepare to stay here. It's the best we can do, fellows."

They united their voices in a shout, and the dog added to the din by barking. He seemed to feel better when the lads were making as much noise as they could.

But the echoes of the boys' voices, blown back to them by the snow-laden wind, was all the answer they received. They waited, and called again, but no one replied to them. Nor, as at least George half-expected, did they hear the growls of a bear. The wind howled, the snow rattled on the sides and roof of the cabin, for the flakes were almost as hard as sleet. But that was all.

"Guess we'll have to put up at this 'hotel,'" said Bert, after a pause. The dog had quieted down now, as though whatever had aroused him had passed on.

"Let's take a look around and see what we've drawn," suggested Jack. "If there's any wood, we can make a fire, and there must be some of that grub left."

"There is," announced Bert, who had constituted himself a sort of commissary department. "We've got some sandwiches, and I can make coffee."

"That isn't so bad," remarked Tom. "Once we have a little feed, we'll all feel better. And in the morning the storm may have stopped, so we can easily find our road. We're on the right one, I'm sure, for that signboard said seven miles to Ramsen, and that's in the direction of Camp No. 3."

If Tom had only known about that changed signboard!

Each of the lads carried a powerful electric light, with a tungsten bulb. It was operated by a small, dry battery. It was intended only for a flashing light, of a second or so each time, but there was a switch arrangement so that the light could be held steady and permanent, though of course this used up the battery quickly.

"I'll let my light burn," proposed Tom. "It's nearly burned out anyhow, and you fellows can save yours until later."

"If we could have a fire, we wouldn't need a light," Bert said.

"That's right," agreed Tom. "Let's look about a bit."

There was a hearth in the main room of the deserted cabin, and on it were the ashes of a fire, long since dead and cold. But it seemed to show that the chimney would draw. Scattered about the room were pieces of old boxes and barrel staves, and a pile of these was soon set ablaze on the hearth.

"That looks better!" remarked Bert, with satisfaction, as he rubbed his hands in front of the blaze. "Now if we had a way of stopping up some of these broken windows, we wouldn't be so cold."

"Take some of those bags," suggested Tom, indicating a pile in a corner. It looked like the bed of some chance tramp who had accepted the shelter the deserted shack offered.

The boys soon had the broken lights filled in, and when the tumble-down door had been propped up in the entrance, the cabin was not such a bad shelter, with a blazing fire going.

"Now for a look upstairs," suggested Tom, for the cabin was of two stories, though the top one was very low.

"I'd rather eat," suggested George.

"It won't take long to investigate," Tom said.

They went up the rickety stairs, but the trip hardly paid for their pains, for there was less upstairs than there was down. Some few rags, bits of broken bottles, boxes and barrels were seen, and that was all.

"And now for grub!" cried George, when they were once more in the main room downstairs. "Let's get that coffee going, and eat what there is."

The boys carried a coffee-pot with them, and a supply of the ground berries. Some snow was scooped up in the pot, which was set on the coals to provide the necessary water by melting the white crystals. Then the packages of sandwiches, rather depleted, it is true, were set out. A little later the aroma of the boiling beverage filled the room.

"That smells fine!" murmured Jack.

"It surely does," agreed Bert. "Now for a feed."

They all felt better after they had eaten what food was left from lunch. And surely they needed the grateful and stimulating warmth of the coffee, even though it was rather muddy, and was drunk out of tin cups they carried with them. They even had condensed milk and sugar, for these were carried in a case, in which fitted the pot and the ground coffee. This was one of Tom's up-to-date discoveries.

To Towser were tossed the odds and ends of the sandwiches, and he ate them greedily, drinking some snow water which George melted for him in a tin he found in one corner of the cabin.

Then the boys prepared to spend the night in the deserted cabin. They sat about the fire, on improvised seats made from broken boxes, and watched the fire, which certainly was cheerful. They expected to only doze through the night, and hoped to get on the proper road by morning.

Suddenly the dog, which had been peacefully lying in front of the hearth, sprang up with a growl and bark. He startled the boys.

"Quiet!" commanded Tom, but the animal continued to growl.

"That's funny," remarked Jack.

"What is?" asked Tom. "Just because he barks on account of hearing something, or scenting something, that's beyond us?"

"No, not that so much, but it's a funny feeling I have," said Jack. "I feel just as if we were being spied upon."

"Spied upon!" repeated Tom. "Say, you're as nervous as a girl, old man!"

Before Jack could reply, the dog had leaped up and rushed out into the storm through a small opening where the old door was only propped against the frame.

CHAPTER XVIII
LOST AGAIN

"Now what's up?" cried Tom, as he made a rush after the dog. But he was too late. Towser was out in the snow.

"It's that bear again," George said.

"You've got bear on the brain," commented Bert.

The boys looked out and listened, but they could neither see nor hear anything, and soon the dog came back. But, even as he reached the door, he turned and sent a challenging bark toward someone—or something.

"This sure is queer," murmured Bert.

"And it's queer what Jack said," went on Tom. "About being spied upon. What do you mean, old man?"

"Just what I said," was the answer. "Just before the dog gave the alarm, I had a feeling as though someone outside was keeping watch over this shack."

"That sure is a funny feeling," commented George. "Who would it be? There aren't any persons up around here except Sam Wilson, or maybe some of those Indian guides he knows."

"It might be one of the Indians," suggested Bert. "They might be sneaking around, to see what they could pick up."

"A wild animal wouldn't make a fellow feel as I felt," decided Jack. "But maybe I'm only fussy, and——"

"You are—worse than a girl," said Tom, with a laugh that took the sharpness out of the words. "I guess it's only the storm, and the effect of being in a strange place. Now let's settle down and take it easy. There's no one outside."

Once more they disposed themselves before the cheerful blaze, the dog stretching out at full length to dry his shaggy coat that was wet with melting snow.

"I wonder what sort of a place this was?" spoke Jack, at length.

"Must have been a hunter's cabin," suggested Tom.

"It's too big for that. This looks as though people had lived in it once," declared Bert. "Besides, it's too near the road for a hunter to want to use it. I guess the family died off, or moved away, and there isn't enough population up here to make it so crowded that they have to use this shack."

"Well, it comes in handy for us," remarked George. "I could go another sandwich, but——"

"All the going you'll do will be to go without," laughed Bert, grimly. "There isn't a crumb left, but I could manage to squeeze out some more coffee."

"Better save it for morning," advised Tom. "We'll need it worse by then."

The storm still raged, but inside the deserted cabin the boys were fairly comfortable. They had on thick, warm garments, and these, with the glowing fire, made them feel little of the nipping cold that prevailed with the blizzard.

The wind howled down the chimney, scattering the light ashes now and then, and filling the room with the pungent odor of smoke. Around some of the windows, where the rags were stuffed in the broken panes, little piles of sifted snow gathered.

At times the whole frail structure shook with the force of the blast, and at such times the boys would look at each other with a trace of fear on their faces. For the ramshackle structure might fall down on them.

But as it did not, after each recurrent windy outburst, they felt more confident. Perhaps the cabin was built stronger than they thought. The dog showed no uneasiness at these manifestations of Nature. He did not even open his eyes when the wind howled its loudest and blew its strongest. And, too, he seemed to have gotten over the strange fear that caused him to act so oddly.

The other boys had rather laughed at Jack's "notion" of being "spied upon," but had they been able to see through the white veil of snow that was falling all about the cabin, they would have realized that there is sometimes something like telepathy, or second sight. For, in reality, the boys were being observed by a pair of evil eyes.

And the evil eyes were set in an evil face, which, in turn belonged to the body of a man who had constructed for himself a rude shelter against the storm.

It was such a shelter as would be hastily built by a hunter caught in the open for the night—a sort of "lean-to," with the open side away from the direction in which the wind blew. But it could not have been made in this storm, and, consequently, must have been put up before the blizzard began.

The lean-to showed signs of a practiced hand, for it was fairly comfortable, and the man in it chuckled to himself now and then as he looked over toward the deserted cabin.

The man was on the watch, and he had prepared for just this emergency. At times, when he heard the barking of the dog, a frown could have been seen on his face, had there been a light by which to observe it. But the lean-to was in absolute darkness, save what light was reflected by the white snow.

"I thought they'd end up here," was the man's muttered remark to himself, for he was all alone. "Yes, I thought they would. It's the nearest shelter after they left the doctored signboard. Naturally they turned in here. That changed sign did the trick all right. Lucky I thought of it. Now I wonder what the next move will be?"

He did not answer himself for a few seconds, but crouched down, looking in the direction of the cabin, through the chinks of which shone the light of the fire.

"They'll stay there until morning, I reckon," communed the man to himself. "Then they'll light out and try to find Ramsen. But they won't locate it by going the way that sign pointed," and he chuckled. "They'll only get deeper in the woods, and then, if we can cut out that Fairfield from among the others, we'll have him where we want him. If we can't, we'll manage to take him anyhow."

He paused, as though to go over in his mind the details of the evil scheme he was plotting, and resumed:

"Yes, they'll light out in the morning. I'll have to follow 'em until I make sure which trail they take. Then the rest will be easy. It isn't going to be any fun to stay here all night, but it will be worth the money, I guess.

"That is, if Skeel ponies up as he says he will. And if Skeel tries to cut up any funny tricks, and cheat me and Whalen, he'll wish he never had. He'll never try it twice!"

With another look out at the dimly lighted cabin, as if to make sure that none of those he was spying on had left, the man composed himself to pass the night in his somewhat uncomfortable shelter. He curled up in a big blanket and went to sleep. For he was a woodsman born and bred, and he thought nothing of staying out in the open, with only a little shelter, through a long, cold night. He was even comfortable, after his own fashion.

And slowly the night passed for our four friends in the deserted cabin.

They had managed to construct a rude sort of bed by placing old inside doors on some boxes. Their heavy mackinaws were covers, and the nearness of the fire on the hearth kept them warm. Occasionally, through the night, as one or another awoke from a doze, he would toss on more wood, to keep the blaze from going out.

The dog whined uneasily once or twice during the night, but he did not bark or growl. Perhaps he knew that the man in the lean-to was asleep also, and would not walk abroad to plot harm.

"Well, it's still snowing," remarked Tom, as he arose and stretched his cramped muscles.

"How do you know? Is it morning?" asked George, yawning.

"It's an imitation of it," Tom announced. "I looked out. It's still snowing to beat the band."

"Oh, for our cozy camp—any one of them!" sighed Jack. "Let's have what's left of that coffee, Bert, and then we'll hike out and see what we can find."

The coffee was rather weak, but it was hot, and that meant a great deal to the boys who had to venture out in the cold. Every drop was disposed of, and then, looking well to their guns, for though they hardly admitted it to each other, they had faint hopes of game, the boys set out.

As they emerged from the cabin, they were not aware of a pair of sharp, ferret-like eyes watching them from the hidden shelter of the lean-to. As the wind was blowing toward that shack, and not away from it, the dog was not this time apprised by scent of the closeness of an enemy, whatever had happened the night before.

"Well, let's start," proposed Tom. "This is the road to Ramsen," and he pointed to the almost snow-obliterated highway that ran in front of the deserted cabin they were leaving.

Their hearts were lighter with the coming of the new day, though their stomachs were almost empty. But they hoped soon to be at one of their camping cabins, where, they knew, a good supply of food awaited them.

On they tramped through the snow. It was very deep, and the fall seemed to have increased in rapidity, rather than to have diminished. It had snowed all night, and was still keeping up with unabated vigor. In some places there were deep drifts across the road.

"This sure is heavy going," observed Jack, as he plunged tiresomely along.

"That's right," agreed Bert.

"I don't see how Towser keeps it up," spoke George, for the dog was having hard work to get through the drifts.

"He seems to enjoy it," commented Tom. "But it is deep. I think——"

He did not complete the sentence, for, at that moment, he stepped into some unseen hole and went down in a snow pile to his waist.

"Have a hand!" invited Jack, extending a helping arm to his chum, to pull him up. "What were you trying to do, anyhow?"

"I don't know," answered Tom, looking at the hole into which he had fallen. "But I think we're off the road, fellows."

"I do, too," came from Bert. "It seems as though we were going over a field. Yes," he went on, "there's a stump sticking up out of the snow. We're in some sort of a clearing. We're clean off the road!"

It took only a moment for the others to be also convinced of this.

"We'd better go back," George said. "We've probably come the wrong way. I don't believe this is the road to Ramsen at all."

"The signboard said it was," Bert reminded him.

"I can't help that. I believe we're wrong again—lost!"

"Lost—again!" echoed Jack. "Lost in this wilderness!"

"It does begin to look so," admitted Tom slowly. "Where's that dog?"

CHAPTER XIX

THE CAPTURE

Towser had run off again, on one of his attempts to wiggle through a drift. A shrill whistle from Tom brought him back again, however, sneezing because some snow had gotten up his nose and into his mouth.

"Towser, you old rascal!" Tom exclaimed. "Why don't you lead us back to camp?"

"Or to Sam Wilson's," added Bert. "That would be good enough on a pinch, until we get straightened out. Home, old fellow! Wilson's farm! Lead the way!"

The dog barked and leaped about, but he did not show any inclination to take any particular direction through the snow-covered wilderness. He seemed to want to follow, rather than lead.

"I don't believe he knows where Sam Wilson's place is," was Tom's opinion, after watching the animal for a while.

"I guess he's as badly lost as we are," said Bert.

For a few seconds the boys stood there rather at a loss what to do. They had done their best, but they did not seem to be on the way to success. The storm was worse than when it first started. It still snowed hard, and the wind, while not as strong as it had been during the night, was still cold and cutting.

The boys turned their backs to it as they stood there huddled together, hardly knowing what to do next. Towser, finding he was not wanted immediately, to trail a bear or some other game, devoted his energies to burrowing in a snowbank.

"Well, I would like to know where we are," said Tom at length.

"Wouldn't it be a good idea to go back to the deserted cabin?" asked Jack.

"It might not be so bad, if we knew where it was," agreed Tom.

"We could at least take that for a starting point, and try to head for Camp No. 2," Jack went on. "I'd be satisfied with that, as long as we can't locate No. 3."

"Oh, I side with you there, all right, old man," Tom said, "but where does the old cabin lie?"

"Off there!" said Bert, pointing to the right.

"No, it's over there," was the opinion of George, and he indicated the left.

"It's right behind you," insisted Jack.

"And I should say it was in front of us," spoke Tom. "So you see we each have a different opinion, and, as long as we can't agree, what are we going to do about it?"

"That's so," admitted Jack. "But we can't stay here doing nothing. We've got to get somewhere."

"Somewhere is very indefinite," was the remark George made. "It's very easy to say it, but hard to find it. If we could only get back on the road, we could head in either direction, and some time or other we would get somewhere. But now we are in the woods and we may be heading right toward the middle of the forest instead of toward the edge. And these forests are no little picnic groves, either."

"I should say not!" Tom exclaimed. "But where is the road? That's the question."

It was a question no one could answer, and they did not try. Eagerly and anxiously they scanned the expanse of snow for some indication that a road existed—even a rough, lumberman's highway.

But all they could see, here and there, were little mounds of snow that indicated where stumps existed under the white covering. They were in a clearing, with woods all around them. If they advanced, they might be going toward the deeper forest instead of toward the place where civilization, in the shape of man, had begun to cut down the trees to make a town or village.

"Well, we sure have got to do something," Tom said, and it was not the first time, either. "We'll try each direction, fellows, and see where we come out. We may have to go the limit, and tramp a bit in each of four directions, and, again, it may be our luck to do it the first shot. But let's get into action. It's cold standing still."

They had given up all hope of game now. Indeed, the snow was falling so thickly that they could not have seen a deer or bear until they were very close to it—too close it would be, in the case of the bear.

As for smaller game—rabbits, squirrels and partridges, none of those were to be seen. The snow had driven the smaller animals and the birds to cover.

"Bur-r-r-r-r! But this is no fun, on an empty stomach," grumbled George, as he followed the others. The dog, having seen his friends start off, was following them. He seemed to have no sense of responsibility that he was expected to lead his friends in the right direction. "I sure am hungry!" George went on.

"Quit talking about it," urged Tom. "That doesn't do any good, and it makes all of us feel badly. Have a snow sandwich!"

"It makes you too thirsty," interposed Jack. "If you want to drink, we'll stop, make a fire of some fir branches, and melt snow in our tin coffee cups. If you start chewing flakes, you'll get a sore mouth, and other things will happen to you. That's what a fellow wrote in a book on Arctic travel."

"If only we hadn't eaten all the grub!" sighed Bert.

"Too late to think of that now," Tom spoke. "Come on—let's hike!"

Off they started. They decided to make an effort in each of the four cardinal points, first selecting that which one of the boys declared led back to Camp No. 2.

"If we go on for a mile or two, and find we're wrong again, back we come and try the other side," Tom explained. "But I can't see why that sign says seven miles to Ramsen, when the road is so easy to lose yourself on."

"It will take us the rest of the day to do that experimenting," grumbled George.

"Well, suggest a better plan," spoke Tom, quickly. "We're lost, and if we don't find the proper road soon, we'll be more than all day in this pickle."

George had no more to say.

The boys were now a little alarmed at their plight, for they were cold and hungry, and that is no condition in which to fight the wintry blast. But there was nothing they could do except keep moving. In a way, that was their only hope, for the exercise kept them warm, though it made them all the more hungry.

"Keep a lookout for game—even small kinds," advised Tom, as they went on. "A rabbit or a squirrel wouldn't come amiss now. We could manage to broil it over the coals of a fire, though it probably won't be very nice looking."

"Who cares for looks when you're hungry?" demanded Bert.

But game did not show itself as the boys tramped on through the snow. They went on for some distance in the direction first decided on, but could see no familiar landmarks. Nor did they reach anything that looked like a road.

"Better go back," Tom decided, and they did manage to find the little clearing again.

"Say!" cried Bert, as they stood irresolute as to which of the three remaining directions to select next, "aren't we silly, though?"

"Why?" asked Tom.

"Why, because all we had to do was to follow our trail back in the snow. That would have led us to the old cabin."

Tom shook his head.

"What's the matter?" asked Bert.

"Our footprints are blown or drifted over three minutes after we make them, in this wind and shifting snow," Tom said. "Look!"

He pointed over the route they had just come. Their earlier footprints were altogether gone. The expanse of snow was white and unbroken.

"Well, we go this way next," said Jack. "I remember because I saw that broken white birch tree. Head straight for that."

They did so, but again were doomed to disappointment. That way led to a low, swampy place, though there was no water in it at present, it having been frozen and covered with snow.

"No road here," Tom said. "Let's try some other route."

"Say!" cried Jack. "What's the sense of all four of us going in the same direction all the while? Why not try four ways at once? The one who finds the road can fire two shots in quick succession. The rest of us will then come to where we hear the shots."

"A good idea!" commented Tom. "We'll try it. Scatter now, and don't go too far. Oh, you're coming with me, are you, Towser?" for the dog followed him, evidently considering Tom his master.

The four boys now set off in different directions, and soon were lost to sight of one another in the storm. Tom was sure he was going the route that would take him to the road. He pressed on eagerly.

The dog ran on ahead, and disappeared.

"He's fond of taking a lot of exercise," was Tom's mental comment. Then he saw some bushes, just ahead of him, being agitated and he went on: "No, he's coming back. Maybe he's found something."

Suddenly the bushes back of Tom parted with a crackling of the dry twigs. The lad thought perhaps it was some animal stirred up by the dog, and he was advancing his gun, to be in readiness, when he felt, all at once, something cover his head. He was in blackness, but he could tell by the smell that a bag had been thrust over his eyes.

"Here. Quit that! Stop!" yelled Tom, and then his voice ended in a smothered groan. Something like a gag had been thrust between his lips and he was thrown heavily.

For a moment Tom's senses seemed to leave him. He could see nothing, but he felt that he was being mauled. He had a momentary fear that it might be a bear. But, he reflected, bears do not throw sacks over one's head, nor gag one. It must be men—but what men?

Vainly Tom struggled. He felt his hands being tied—his feet entangled in ropes. He fought, but was overpowered. Then he heard a voice saying:

"Well, we've captured him, anyhow."

"Yes," agreed another voice, and Tom vainly wondered where he had heard it before. "Yes, we have him, and now the question is, what to do with him."

CHAPTER XX

A PRISONER

Tom was in sort of a daze for the first few moments following the unexpected and violent attack on him, an attack culminating in his being bound so that he could hardly move.

Dimly, and almost uncomprehendingly, he heard voices murmuring about him—he could hear the voices of men above the howl of the gale that seemed to continue with unabated fury.

Gradually Tom's senses cleared. The haze that seemed to envelope his mind passed away and he began to realize that he must not submit dumbly to this indignity. He first strained lightly at his bonds, as if to test them. The sack was still over his head, so he could not see, and there was a horribly stuffy and suffocating feeling about it.

Tom's effort to loosen his bonds, slight as it was, had the effect of starting his blood up in a better circulation, and this helped him to think better and more quickly.

"I've got to get out of this!" he told himself energetically. "This won't do at all! I wonder who the scoundrels are who have caught me this way?"

But Tom did not stop then to argue out that question. He wanted to devote all his time to getting himself loose. With that in view, he put forth all his strength. He was lying on his back, in a bank of snow, he judged, and he now strained his arms and legs with all his might.

But he might just as well have saved his strength. Those who had tied the bonds about him knew their evil business well, and poor Tom was like a roped steer. Not only was he unable to loosen the bonds on his arms and legs, but he found the effort hurt him, and made him almost suffocate, because of the gag and the closeness of the bag over his head.

Then he heard voices speaking again.

"He's coming to," said someone—a vaguely familiar voice.

"Yes, but he'll have to come a great deal harder than that to get away," was the answer, and someone chuckled. Tom wished he could hit that person, whoever he was. His gun had either fallen or been knocked from his hand at the first attack.

"Well, what are we going to do with him?" asked the voice that had first spoken.

"Wait until——" but the rest of the sentence Tom did not hear, for the wind set up a louder howling at that point, and the words were borne away with it. Then, too, Tom was at a disadvantage because of the bag over his ears.

He felt himself being lifted up, and placed in a more comfortable position, and he was glad of that, for he felt weak and sick. It must be remembered that aside from a little coffee that morning, he had had no breakfast, and that he had had little or no sleep the night before. With a scant supper, a battle with the storm, the anxiety about being lost, and having led his friends, unconsciously enough, into a scrape, it was no great wonder that Tom was not altogether himself.

"But who in the world has captured me, and what do they want of me?" Tom asked himself. He had an idea it might, perhaps, be some of the half-breed Indians who had caught him for the sake of his gun and clothing. Or perhaps some trapper or guide was guilty.

But if they were after his gun, or what money he carried, or even the fine mackinaw he wore, why did they not take those things and make off into the woods? That would at least leave Tom free.

But the men remained on guard over the bound figure of the boy, now sitting upright on a bank of snow. Tom could dimly hear them moving about. They were evidently waiting for someone.

"But if they wait long enough, the fellows may come to look after me," Tom reasoned. "Jack, George, and Bert will know how to deal with these scoundrels."

Then he reflected that the other lads would not know where he was unless he fired his gun, and he could not do that. If one of the others—Bert, Jack or George—found the road, they would not know where Tom was.

"Unless the dog could lead me to them, or them to me," he mused. "I wonder where Towser is, anyhow?"

Tom's last view of the animal had been when it darted into a bush, after some rabbit, perhaps. Then had come the sudden attack. If the dog had returned, Tom did not know of it. He only hoped the animal would "raise some sort of row," as he put it.

But there was no evidence of Towser. Tom could hear only the now low-voiced talk of two men, and the rush of the wind. That it was still snowing he was quite sure, and he wondered what his companions were doing.

Suddenly he became aware of some new element that entered into his predicament. One of the men exclaimed:

"Here he comes now!"

"That's good!" responded the other, and there seemed to be relief in his tones.

"I didn't see anything of him," called the newcomer. "I saw the others—they've separated, all right, but Fairfield——"

"He's here! We've got him!" was the triumphant rejoinder of one of the men near Tom. "Got him good and proper!"

"You have! That's the ticket. Now we'll see what the old man has to say. I guess he'll pony up all right."

Tom felt a shock as though someone had thrown cold water over him.

That voice!

Tom knew now. It was Professor Skeel.

He began to understand. He saw the meaning of many things that had hitherto puzzled him. The vagueness was clearing away. The plot was beginning to be revealed.

Was this why Skeel had come to the wilderness of the Adirondacks? Was this why he and his cronies had been sneaking around the camp cabins? It seemed so.

"And yet, what in the world can he want of me?" Tom asked himself. "If it's revenge for what I did to him, this is a queer way of showing it. I didn't think he'd have spunk enough to plot a thing like this, though he certainly has meanness enough."

Tom was thinking fast. He was putting together in his mind many matters that had seemed strange to him. Certain it was that at Skeel's instigation he had been made a prisoner, and probably with the help of Murker and Whalen, though Tom had not seen their faces clearly and could not be sure of their identity.

"But what's it all about?" poor Tom asked himself over and over again. "Why should he make a prisoner of me?"

"Can we carry him?" asked Skeel's voice. "We've got to take him to the old shack, you know. Can't leave him here. Besides, there's some business to attend to in connection with him. Can you carry him through the snow?"

"Sure," was the answer. "He isn't so heavy. Up on your shoulders with him, Whalen, and we'll follow the professor. I'm all turned about in this storm!"

Tom was sure, then, of the identity of his three captors. He was as sure as though he had seen them.

A moment later he found himself being lifted up, and he could feel that the men were adjusting him to their shoulders. It was no easy task, for Tom was rather heavy, and his clothing, for he was dressed warmly for the cold, made an additional burden. But the men were strong, it seemed.

"Shall we take that off?" asked one of the men. Tom had an idea he referred to the head-covering bag.

"No, better leave it on until we get farther off. Some of the others might see him," was Skeel's answer. Tom felt sure he referred to the bag.

"I wish they'd take this gag out of my mouth," Tom mused. "I don't care so much for the bag. But my tongue will feel like a piece of leather in a little while."

On through the storm Tom was carried, on the shoulders of the two men. In fancy he could see the former instructor leading the way.

"He spoke of the old shack," mused Tom. "I wonder if he means the deserted cabin where we were? If he takes me there, the boys will have a better chance of finding me if they look."

But Tom was soon to know that it was not to the deserted hut he was being carried. For the journey soon came to an abrupt termination. The young prisoner felt himself being carried into some building, for he was lowered from the men's shoulders.

"They never could have reached the old cabin in this time," Tom decided to himself. "They must have brought me to some new place. I wonder what will happen now?"

Tom felt himself laid on some sort of bed or bunk. Then he heard a door closed and locked.

"Well, we've got him just where we want him," said Skeel. "Now we'll go ahead with our plans."

And the prisoner wondered what those plans were.

CHAPTER XXI

SKEEL REVEALS HIMSELF

"Shall we loosen him up now?" asked the voice of one of the men. Tom could still see nothing, as the bag remained over his head.

"Yes, take off the headgear, and ungag him," answered Skeel. "It won't matter if he does holler up here. No one will hear him. But keep his hands tied, except when we feed him."

Tom felt a sudden sense of elation in spite of his most uncomfortable position. At least he was going to get something to eat, and he needed it, for he felt nearly famished.

"Is the door locked?" asked one of the men.

"I attended to that," was Skeel's answer. "He can't get away from here."

"We'll see about that," mused Tom. "I'll have a good try, at any rate, the first chance I get."

He felt the fastenings of the bag being loosed, and when it was taken off, he looked about him quickly. The first glance was enough to tell him, if he had not already been sure of it, that he was in some shack where he had never been before. This was not the deserted cabin where he and his chums had spent the night. Tom glanced toward the windows, hoping to get a glimpse outside so he might determine his position, but there were dirty curtains over the casements.

His next glances were directed toward the men themselves, though he was already sure, in his own mind, who they were. Nor was his judgment reversed.

There stood Skeel, a grin of triumph in his ugly face, and there were the two other men, of evil countenance, whom Tom had seen with the erstwhile professor.

"We're going to take the gag out of your mouth," said Skeel to his prisoner. "We don't want to hurt you any more than we have to, but we're going to have you do as we say, and not as you want to. You can yell, if you like, but you'll only be wasting your breath. This is a good way from nowhere, up here, and you won't be heard. You can't get away, because one of us will be on guard all the while. I tell you this to save you trouble, for I know you, and I know that you'll make a row if you possibly can," and Skeel stuck out his jaw pugnaciously. He and Tom Fairfield had been in more than one "row" before.

"Take it off, Murker," the former instructor said to the worse-looking of his two helpers. "Let's see if he'll yelp now."

It was a relief to Tom to have the bunch of not overly-clean rags taken from his mouth. His tongue and jaws ached from the pressure and now he sighed in relief.

Tom Fairfield was not foolish. He had already made up his mind to do all he could to circumvent the plans of the plotters, and he was going to begin as soon as possible. He did not altogether believe Skeel when the latter said that shouting would do no good, but Tom did not intend to try, at once, that method of getting help.

He wanted to rest his throat from the strain, and he wanted to see how best to direct his voice in case he did feel like shouting. He had no doubt but what if he cried out for help now, the gag would be put back in his mouth. And that he did not want. He wanted to eat, and oh! how he did long for a drink of cold water.

"Guess he isn't going to yap," murmured the man known as Murker.

"So much the better," said Skeel. "Now you can loosen those ropes on his legs. He can't get away."

Tom wished, with all his heart, that they would loosen the bonds on his hands and arms, but he stubbornly resolved to stand the pain those cordsgave him, rather than ask a favor of any of the trio of scoundrels.

He simply could not endure his thirst and hunger any longer. He tried to speak—to ask at least for a glass of water, for the men could not be so altogether heartless as to refuse what they would give to a dumb beast. But Tom's throat was so parched and dry that only a husky sound came forth.

"Guess he wants to wet his whistle," suggested Whalen.

"Well, get him a drink then," half-growled Skeel. "Then we'll talk business."

Tom thought nothing ever tasted so good as that draught of water from the cracked teacup one of the men brought in from another room, and held up to his lips. It was better than nectar ever could be, he was sure.

"How about a little grub?" asked Murker.

"Oh, he could have it, I guess," Skeel replied. "Guess they didn't any of 'em have much. They were away from their camp all night, you say, and there wasn't anything in the old shanty."

"That's right," assented Whalen.

Then Tom realized that he and his companions had been spied upon, just as Jack had so strangely suspected. They had also been followed, it was evident, for the men knew of the movements of himself and his chums.

"I meant grub for all of us," went on Murker. "I'm a bit hungry myself, and it's about time for dinner."

"All right—get what you want," assented Skeel. "And give him some. One of you can sit by him, and take off the ropes while he eats. But watch him—he's like a cat—quick!"

Tom felt like smiling at this tribute to his prowess, but he refrained. It was no time for laughter.

"I've got a bit of writing to do," Skeel went on. "You fellows can eat if you like. I'll take mine later."

"All right," assented Whalen. "But what about—well, you know what I mean," and he rubbed his fingers together to indicate money.

"I'll attend to that," said Skeel, a bit stiffly. "You mind your own affairs!"

"Oh, no offense!" said Whalen, quickly. "I only wanted to know."

"You'll know soon enough," was the retort, as the former teacher moved toward another room.

"Well, I'm in on this too. Don't forget that!" exclaimed Murker, and there seemed to be menace in his tones.

"Oh, don't bother me!" answered Skeel, apparently a bit irritated.

Evidently the feeling among the conspirators was not as friendly as it might have been. It was very like a dissention, and Tom wondered if the truth of the old adage was to be proved, "When thieves fall out, honest men get their dues."

"I hope it proves so in my case," Tom reflected. "But first I would like something to eat. And I wish the others had some, too. I wonder where they are now, and what they think of me?" Professor Skeel went into another room, and closed the door after him. Murker also went into another apartment—there seemed to be three rooms, at least, on the first floor of the cabin—and presently the evil-faced man came back with a platter on which were some chunks of cold meat and bread. It looked better to Tom, half famished as he was, than a banquet would have seemed—even a surreptitious midnight school-feed.

"Help yourself," growled Murker, as he set the platter down in front of Tom, on a rough table, and loosed the bonds of our hero's arms.

"Guess I'll have a bit myself," murmured Whalen.

"Go on," mumbled Murker, his mouth half full. "The boss will eat later, I reckon."

Tom reflected that by the "boss" they must mean Skeel.

As for the young hunter, he eagerly took some of the bread and meat. It was cold, but it was good and nourishing, and seemed to have been well cooked.

It put new life into Tom at once. He would have liked a cup of coffee, but there seemed to be none. Perhaps the men would make some later. Tom certainly hoped that they would do so.

The men ate fast—almost ravenously, and Tom was not at all slow himself. He did not realize what an appetite he had until he saw the victuals disappearing.

Then, when the edge of his hunger had been a little dulled and blunted, to say the least, Tom once more began wondering why he had been caught and brought as a prisoner to the lonely hut.

"What's the game?" he asked himself.

He was soon to know.

"Well, if you fellows have had enough, and he's been fed, tie up his hands again," said Skeel, coming from the room just then. "I want to have a talk with him. You can wait outside," he added, when the ropes had once more been put on Tom's hands and arms.

Skeel waited until the men had left the hut. Then, locking the door after them, the former teacher confronted Tom. Up to now our hero had said nothing. He believed in a policy of silence for the time being.

"Well, what do you think of yourself now?" sneered Skeel, folding his arms. "You're not so smart as you thought you were, are you?"

"I haven't begun to think yet," said Tom, coolly. "But I would like to know why you have brought me here—by what right?"

"By the right of—might!" was the answer. "I've got you here, and here I'm going to keep you until your father pays me a ransom of ten thousand dollars. That will square accounts a little, and make up for some of the things you did to me. It's you against ten thousand dollars, and I guess your father would rather pay up than see you suffer. Now I'll get down to business," and he drew up a chair and sat down in front of Tom.

CHAPTER XXII

AN ANXIOUS SEARCH

George Abbot had the luck of finding the road for which he and his chums had all vainly sought so long in the storm. It will be remembered that the four boys had started in different directions, corresponding to the different points of the compass, to search for a route, either back to the hut where they had spent the night, or to one of the three camps.

And it was George who found the road.

True he did not know which road it was at the time, but when he had stumbled on through the drifting snow, fighting his way against the storm for some time, he fairly tumbled down a little embankment, rolling over and over.

"Well, what's this?" George asked himself, rather dazed, as he rose to his feet.

He had his answer in a moment.

"It's a road—I hope it's the road," he went on, as he saw that the little declivity down which he had fallen was where the road had been cut through a hill, leaving a slope on either side of the highway.

"I must signal to the others at once," George decided. His gun had slipped from his grasp when he fell, but he now picked up the weapon, and fired two shots in quick succession. It was the signal agreed upon.

The wind was blowing hard, and George was not sure that the sound of the shots would carry to his chums. He did not know just how far they were from him. So, after waiting a bit, he strolled down the snow-covered road a bit, and fired again. He repeated this three times, at intervals, before he heard an answering shot. Then he raised his voice in a yell, and soon was relieved to be joined by Jack.

"What is it?" Jack asked.

"The road—I've found it," George answered.

"Where's Bert—and Tom?"

"Haven't seen either of them."

"Well, they're probably looking yet. We'll fire some more shots and bring 'em up."

George and Jack fired at intervals, the signal each time being two rapid shots, but it was some time before they had an answer. It finally came in the shape of another shot, followed quickly by a shout.

"It's Bert," said George.

"Sounded more like Tom," was his chum's guess. While they waited, they exchanged experiences. Jack told of vainly floundering about in the drifts, while George had better news to impart.

"I fairly stumbled on the road," he said.

"Any way at all, as long as you found it," said Jack. "Here comes someone now."

It proved to be Bert, who staggered up through the storm, himself almost a living snowball.

"Found anything?" he gasped, for he was quite "winded."

"The road," answered George.

"Where's Tom?" asked Jack.

"Why, isn't he with you?" asked Bert, in some surprise. "I haven't seen anything of him."

"He's probably off searching for a highway," said George, hopefully. "We'll fire a few more shots."

They fired more than a few, but received no response from Tom, and we well know the reason why, though his chums did not at the time.

"Well, what had we better do?" asked Jack, at length. "I'm about all in, and I guess you fellows feel about the same."

"I would like something to eat," admitted Bert.

"And I'm terribly cold," confessed George, who was shivering.

"Well, let's look about a bit on either side of this road, then go up and down it a ways, and keep firing and shouting," suggested Jack. "We may find Tom. If we don't—well, I think we'd better see where this road goes."

They adopted that plan, but though they shouted vigorously, and fired many shots, there came no answer from Tom.

The exercise and the shouting, however, had one good result. It warmed George so he was no longer in danger of coming down with pneumonia.

"Well, it's six of one and a half dozen of the other," said Bert, at length. "What shall we do, and which way shall we go on this road to get to camp?"

"We'd better try to find one of the cabins," said Jack. "And I think this direction seems to be the most likely," and he pointed to the left.

"Go ahead; I'm with you," said Bert, and George nodded assent.

"What about Tom, though?" asked George, anxiously.

"Well, we can't find him. He may have gone on ahead, or he may still be searching for a road. In either case he's too far off for us to make him hear—that's evident. And we may find him just as well by trying to make our way back to camp as staying here," said Jack.

So it was decided to do this, and off they started. The storm did not seem quite so fierce now. In fact, there were indications that the fall of snow was lessening. But a great deal had fallen, making walking difficult. The cold was intense, but it was a dry cold, not like the damp, penetrating air of New Jersey, and the boys stood it much better.

They had not gone far before Jack uttered a cry.

"Here he comes! There's Tom!" he shouted, pointing at a figure advancing toward them through the mist of flakes that were still falling, but more lazily now.

"It's someone, but how do you know it's Tom?" asked Bert.

"Who else would it be?" Jack wanted to know.

"It might be—Skeel," suggested George.

"Or that—bear!" and, as he said this, Bert advanced his gun.

"Nonsense—that's no bear!" exclaimed Jack. "It isn't Tom though, either," he added, as the figure came nearer.

A moment later they all saw at once who it was.

"Sam Wilson!" exclaimed Bert. "That's good! Now he can tell us what to do, and where Tom is. Hello, Sam!" he called, for that was how everyone addressed the genial guide—even those who had met him only once or twice.

"Hello yourselves!" Sam answered in greeting. "What are you fellows doing here?"

"We've been lost, and we've just found ourselves," explained Jack. "We're on our way to Camp No. 3."

"Oh, no, you're not!" exclaimed Sam, smiling.

"Why not?" Bert wanted to know.

"For the simple reason that you're on your way to Camp No. 2," answered Sam. "You're going the wrong way for Camp No. 3."

"Well, maybe we are twisted," admitted Jack, "but as long as we're headed for some camp, I don't care what it is.

"We've been out all night," he added, "or at least sheltered in only an old cabin. We haven't had anything to-day but some coffee, and we're about done out. Isn't this storm fierce?"

"Oh, we're used to these up here in the Adirondacks," spoke Sam.

Then the boys told how they had been out hunting and had seen the signpost that informed them it was seven miles to Ramsen.

"But you went the wrong way!" exclaimed Sam, when he had heard the details. "Ramsen was in just the opposite direction."

"Then the signboard was wrong!" declared Jack.

"That's funny," Sam spoke, musingly. "Signboards don't change themselves that way. There's something wrong here."

"Well, never mind that," went on Bert. "Have you seen anything of Tom Fairfield?"

"Tom Fairfield! Why, I thought he was with you!" exclaimed Sam, quickly looking around.

"He was, but we separated to find the road," explained George, "and now we can't locate Tom."

"Well, this won't do," Sam spoke, and his voice was serious. "We will have to hunt for him right away. He hasn't had anything to eat, you say?"

"None of us have," said Jack. "That's why we were so glad to find some sort of road."

"Well, I've got my pung back there a piece," said the guide. "I have some grub in it that I was taking over to your Camp No. 2. I can give you a snack from that, and then we'll do some searching for the boy. I like Tom Fairfield!"

"So do I!" exclaimed Jack, and the others nodded emphatic agreements, with a chorus of:

"That's what!"

Never did food taste so good as that which Sam brought up from his pung. He explained that he had walked on ahead while his horses were eating their dinners from nose-bags.

"And it's lucky for you fellows I did," he said, "though of course you might have stumbled on the camp yourselves. But now for a search."

And with anxious hearts the boys took it up. Where could Tom Fairfield be? That was a question each one asked himself.

CHAPTER XXIII
DEFIANCE

Tom, a bound prisoner, watched the insolent professor who sat facing him. The latter had on his face a sneer of triumph, but mingled with it, as Tom could note, was a look that had in it not a little fear. For the desperate man had planned a desperate game, and he was not altogether sure how it would work out.

Tom steeled himself to meet what was coming. He did not know what it was, but that it was something that would concern himself, vitally, he was sure. And he was better prepared to meet what was coming than he had been an hour or so previous.

For now, though he was a prisoner, and bound, he was warm, and he had eaten. These things go far toward making courage in a man, or boy either, for that matter.

"Now," said Professor Skeel, and the sneer on his face grew more pronounced, "we'll talk business!"

"Oh, no, we won't!" exclaimed Tom, quickly.

"We won't?" and there was a sharp note in the man's voice.

"I'll have nothing to do with you," went on Tom. "You brought me here against my will, and you are liable to severe penalties for what you did. As soon as I can get to an officer, I intend to cause your arrest, and the arrest of those two miserable tools of yours.

"I'm not at all afraid—don't think it. You can't keep me here for very long. Sooner or later I'll get out, and then I'll make it hot for you! That's just what I'll do—I'll make it hot for you!"

During this little outburst on the part of Tom, Professor Skeel sat staring at his prisoner. He did not seem at all frightened by what Tom said, though the young man put all the force he could into his words. But Tom was observant. He noticed that the little look of worry did not leave the man's face.

"I'll make it so hot for you," went on Tom, "that you'll have to leave this part of the country. You'll have to leave if you get the chance, and perhaps you won't. My father and I will push this case to the end. I don't know what your game is, but I can guess."

"Well, since you can guess, perhaps you can guess what I'm going to do with you!" angrily interrupted the professor.

"No, I can't, exactly," spoke Tom, slowly, "but if it's anything mean or low-down, you'll do it. I know you of old. I've had dealing with you before."

"Yes, and you're going to have more!" the professor fairly shouted. "I'm going to get even with you for what you did for me. You caused me to lose my place at Elmwood Hall——"

"You deserved to lose it!" said Tom, cuttingly.

"And you mistreated me when we were out in that open boat——"

"Mistreated you!" fairly gasped Tom, amazed at the man's hardness of mind. "Mistreated you, when you tried to steal the little water and food we had left!"

He could say no more. His mind went back vividly to the days of the wreck of the Silver Star, when he and others had been in great peril at sea. He had indeed prevented the professor from carrying out his evil designs, though Tom was not more harsh than needful. But now he was to suffer for that.

"I've got you where I want you," went on Skeel, when Tom had become silent. "I've laid my plans well, and you fell into the trap. I won't deny that the storm helped a lot, but I've got you now, and you're going to do as I say, or it will be the worse for you. You'll do as I say——"

"Don't be too sure!" interrupted Tom.

"That's enough!" snapped the angry man. "You may not realize that you are in my power, and that you're up here in a lonely part of the woods, away from your friends. They don't know where you are, and you don't know where they are. They can't help you. Those two men of mine will do as I say, and——"

"Oh, I've no doubt but that you've trained them well in your own class of scoundrelism," said Tom, coolly.

"Silence!" fairly shouted the infuriated man. Tom ceased his talk because he chose, not because he was afraid.

Professor Skeel hesitated a moment, and then drew from his pocket some papers. Tom was at a loss to guess what they might be. In fact, he had but a dim idea why he had been captured and brought to the hut in the wilderness.

Some things the two men—Murker and Whalen—let fall, however, gave him an inkling of what was to come. So he did not show any great surprise when Professor Skeel, handing him a paper, said:

"That's a copy of a letter I want you to write to your father. Copy it, sign it in your natural hand, without any changes whatever, or without making any secret signs on the paper, and give it back to me. When I get the right kind of an answer back, I'll let you go—not before. Write that letter to your father!"

There was a veiled threat implied in the insolent command.

Professor Skeel held the letter out in front of Tom. The latter could not take it, of course, for his hands were tied.

"Oh!" exclaimed the plotter, as though he had just wakened to this fact. "Well, I'll loosen your hands for you, but you must promise not to fight. Not that I'm afraid of you, for I can master you, but I don't want to hurt you, physically, if I can help it."

Tom did not altogether agree with the professor that he would be the master if it came to an encounter. For our hero was a vigorous lad, he played football and baseball, and his muscles were ready for instant call. True, he was tired from lack of rest and the hardships he had gone through, but he was not at all afraid of a "scrap," as he afterward put it.

So, then, when Professor Skeel made the remark about the bonds, Tom was ready for what came next.

"I'll loosen those ropes, so you can copy this letter, if you'll promise not to attack me," went on Skeel.

"I'll promise nothing!" exclaimed Tom, defiantly.

"All right. Then I'll have to call in my helpers to stand by," grimly went on the former instructor. "They'll take care of you if you cut up rough."

He went to the door, and called out:

"Murker—Whalen! Come in. We may need you," he added significantly.

Tom steeled himself for what was to come.

"Take off those ropes," went on the professor, when his two mean men had come in. "Then, if he starts a row—let him have it!"

The words were coarse and rough, and the man's manner and tone even more so.

"Are we to take off these ropes?" asked Murker.

"Yes, and then stand by. I'm going to make him write this letter. That will bring the cash."

"That's what we want!" exclaimed Whalen, with an unctious smile. "It's the cash I'm after."

"You'll get none from my father!" cried Tom, beginning to understand the course of the plot.

"We'll see about that," muttered the professor. "Loose his bonds, but look out! He's a tricky customer."

"Not any more so than you are," Tom said, promptly. "And I want to tell you here and now, when you have your witnesses present—mean and low as they are—I want to tell you that you'll suffer for this when I get out. I'll make it my business, and my father will also, to prosecute you to the full extent of the law!"

"Words—mere words!" sneered Skeel.

"You won't get out until you do as the boss wants," said Whalen.

"Don't be so rough. Better give in, it will be easier," spoke Murker, who seemed a little alarmed by what Tom said.

"I'll attend to him," said Skeel curtly. "Take off the ropes. Then you read this letter and copy and sign it!" he ordered.

A moment later Tom's hands were free. He did not see any chance for making an escape then, so he waited, merely stretching his arms so that the bound muscles were more free. True, he might have made a rush on his captors, but the door had been locked, after the entrance of Murker and Whalen, and Tom did not see what opportunity he would have with three against him. He might be seriously hurt and that would spoil his chances for a future escape.

"Read that," ordered Skeel, thrusting the paper into Tom's hands. A glance showed that it was addressed to his father. It recited that Tom was in trouble, that he had been made a prisoner by a band of men who would release him only on payment of ten thousand dollars. Details were given as to how the money, in cash, must be sent, and Mr. Fairfield was urged to make no effort to trace Tom, or it would result seriously for the prisoner.

"Sign that and we'll send it," ordered Skeel.

Tom dropped the letter to the floor, disdaining to hand it back.

"What's this?" fairly roared the professor. "Do you mean you won't do as I say?"

"That's just what I mean," said Tom, coolly. "You may keep me here as long as you like, and you can do as you please, but I'll never sign that letter. Go ahead! I'm not afraid of you!" and he faced his enemies defiantly.

CHAPTER XXIV
THE ESCAPE

Professor Skeel retained control of himself with an obvious effort. Clearly he had expected more of a spirit of agreement on the part of Tom, though he might have known, from his previous experiences with our hero, that compliance would not be given. But Tom did not even take the trouble to hand back the letter. It had fluttered to the floor of the cabin.

"You—you——" began Whalen, angrily spluttering the words.

"Silence!" commanded Skeel. "I'm attending to this." His face and his tone showed his anger, but he managed to keep it under control. He picked up the letter—something of a condescension on his part, and said to Tom:

"Then you refuse to do as I ask?"

"I most certainly do! The idea is positively—silly!" and Tom had the nerve to laugh in the faces of his enemies.

"We'll make you sweat for this!" declared Whalen. "We'll——"

"Better let the boss work the game," suggested Murker. In spite of his evil face, and the fact that he was just as guilty in the matter as the others, he seemed of a more conciliatory spirit.

"Yes, you keep out of this," commanded the professor to the former employee of the school. "I know what I'm doing."

Tom wondered what the next move would be. He did not have to wait long to find out.

"Well, if you won't sign this now, you will later," said Skeel, as he folded the letter and put it into his pocket. "Take him to the dark room," he ordered. "Maybe he'll come to his senses there. And don't give him too much bread and water," and the man laughed as he gave this order. "A little starving will bring some results, perhaps. Lock him up, and bring me the key."

"All right, you're the boss," assented Murker. "I'm in this thing now, and I'm going to stick it out, but I wish——"

"You're right; you're going to stick!" interrupted Skeel. "You're in it as deep as I am, and you can't get out!"

Murker did not finish what he started to say. He shrugged his shoulders and seemed resigned to what was to come. Tom disliked him the least of the three, though the man's face was not in his favor.

"Shall we tie him up again?" asked Whalen.

"Yes, and tie him good and tight, too. Don't mind how you draw those cords. The more trouble we make now, the less we'll have to make later. Tie him up and put him away where he can cool off," and Professor Skeel laughed mockingly.

For an instant a desperate resolve came into Tom's mind to make a rush and a break for liberty. But the idea was dismissed almost as soon as it was formed.

What chance would he stand with three full-grown men to oppose him? The door was locked, and Tom's feet were still bound. He had a knife in his pocket, but to reach it, and cut the ropes on his ankles would take time, and in that time he would easily be overpowered by his captors. It was out of the question now.

"But I'm going to escape, if it's at all possible," Tom declared to himself. "And when I do get out of here——"

But he could not finish his thought. His gun and mackinaw had been taken away from him, and now when Whalen roughly seized him, and put the ropes on his wrists, Skeel said:

"Search his pockets. Take what money he has and any sort of weapons. Then lock him up!"

Tom did have considerable money on him, and this was soon out of his pockets, and in that of the professor. Tom's knife and other possessionswere also removed. Then he was lifted up, carried to another room, and roughly thrust into sort of a closet that was very dark. Tom fell heavily to the floor. His mackinaw was tossed in to him.

"He can use that for a blanket—we're short of covering," he heard Skeel say. "We don't want him to be too comfortable, anyhow."

Tom was anything but at his ease just then, but he did not falter in his determination not to give in. He shut his teeth grimly.

The door was closed and locked, and our hero was left to his not very pleasant reflections. He managed to struggle to a sitting position, and to edge over until he was leaning back against the wall. He drew his heavy mackinaw to him. It would be warm during the cold night, for that he would be kept a prisoner at least that length of time, he could not doubt.

Tom's thoughts were many and various. So this was why Skeel had followed him and his chums. This was why he had reappeared at Elmwood Hall, and had caused Whalen to ask questions about the hunting trip.

So this was Skeel's plan for enriching his purse and at the same time getting revenge. So far, fate had played into the hands of the unscrupulous man and his confederates.

"But I'll get away!" Tom told himself. He sat there in the gloomy darkness, trying to think of a plan.

Meanwhile his chums, with Sam Wilson, were frantically searching for him in the storm. Sam's idea was not to leave the neighborhood where Tom had last been seen, until they had exhausted every effort to locate their missing chum.

But it was difficult to search in the storm, and the whirl of flakes made a long view impossible. Then, too, they were in a dense part of the wilderness. Sam Wilson's farm was perhaps the largest cleared part of it, though here and there were patches where trees had been cut down.

Up and down the road, and on either side of it, the search went on. Sam Wilson was a born woodsman, as well as a hunter and farmer, and he brought his efficiency to the task.

"But it seems to be no go, boys," he said, at length.

"But what has become of him?" asked George with a look of worriment on his face.

"That's what we can't say except that he's lost," spoke Jack.

"Yes, but lost in this wilderness—in this storm," added Bert. "It's dangerous."

"Yes, that's what it is, provided he is still lost," Sam said.

"Still lost! What do you mean?" asked Jack.

"I mean he may have gone so far that he found his way back to one of the camps."

"Really?" hopefully cried Bert, who thought Sam might be saying that simply to cheer them up.

"Why, of course it's possible," the caretaker went on. "He may have gone on beyond the sound of your guns. And, unexpectedly, he may have hit the trail to one of the camps. For there are trails that lead through the woods. They're not easy to find, or follow, but Tom might have had luck."

"Then what shall we do?" asked Jack.

"Go back to Camp No. 2," answered Sam. "Tom may be there. If he isn't, we'll go to the others in turn. Let's go back. We'll drive."

So, abandoning the search for the time being, they started back for camp in the pung, drawn by the powerful horses. They were hoping against hope that Tom would be there, or that they would find him at one of the other cabins.

But Tom was still a prisoner in the dark closet of the lonely shack. What his thoughts were you can well imagine, but, above everything else stood out the determination not to give in and sign the letter asking for the ransom money.

Hours passed. Tom again felt the pangs of hunger. He had an idea the men might try to starve him, but after an interval, which he imaginedbrought the time to noon, Murker came in with some bread and water.

"Boss's orders," he growled. "I'll untie your hands while you eat, and don't try any tricks."

Tom did not answer. The bread was welcome, but the water more so. Murker left him a glass full after he had once emptied the tumbler. Then the ropes were again put on his hands, and he was left alone in the darkness.

Whether it was the same day or not, Tom could hardly tell. He must have dozed, for he awoke with a start, and he knew at once that some noise had caused it.

He listened intently, and heard a scratching, sniffing sound back of him. He could feel the board side of the shack, against which he was leaning, vibrate.

"Can it be that the boys are trying to release me?" Tom asked himself. But in another moment he knew this could not be true. His chums would come boldly up and not try to get him out in this secret fashion. The scratching and sniffing increased.

"It's some animal!" Tom decided. He edged away from the side of the closet-room, and waited. The sound increased. Then came a splintering, rending sound as of wood breaking. Tom fancied he could feel a board move.

An instant later a streak of light came suddenly into his prison. It was from the moon which was shining brightly on the snow outside, and by the light through the crack Tom could see a big hairy paw thrust in where the board had been torn off.

"It's a bear!" cried the lad. "He must smell something to eat, and he's trying to get after it. He's standing outside and has pulled off a loose board, and—by Jove! I can get out that way!" he said aloud. As he spoke the board was pulled farther loose, leaving a large opening. A sniffing snout was thrust in. Tom had no intention of sharing his prison with a bear, and, raising his two bound feet Tom kicked the animal on its most tender place—the nose. With a growl Bruin withdrew, and Tom could hear him sniffing indignantly as he scampered over the snow. But the bear had made for Tom a way of escape.

"If I could only get my arms and legs free, I could squeeze out through that opening," Tom decided. Then like a flash the plan came to him.

The tumbler of water had been left within reach. Tom kicked it over with sufficient force to break the glass. He had to make a noise, but after waiting a while, he felt sure his captors had not been aroused. They did not seem to be on guard, or they would have heard the bear when he pulled loose the outside board.

Tom's muscles were in good control, but he had to strain himself unmercifully to bend over and get a piece of the broken glass between his hands. Then he put it between his two boots, and held it there, with a sharp edge up, by pressing his feet tightly together.

You have doubtless guessed his plan. He was going to use the glass as a knife and saw the rope of his wrists upon it. This he proceeded to do. The moonlight outside, streaming in, gave him enough illumination to work by.

He cut himself several times before he succeeded in fraying the rope enough so it could be broken. Then, rubbing his arms to restore the interrupted circulation, Tom used the glass on the rope that bound his ankles. This he cut through quickly enough, and, was able to stand up. His legs were weak, and he waited a few minutes until he could use them to better advantage. Then, forcing farther off the dangling board, Tom crawled out in the snow, putting on his mackinaw when he was outside.

The storm had ceased. It was night—a night with a dazzling moon, and Tom was free. But where his chums were, or in what direction the camp lay, he could not tell.

CHAPTER XXV

THE SHOT

For a moment, after getting outside the cabin, Tom hardly knew what to do. He was at a loss in which direction to start, but he realized the necessity of getting away from that vicinity as soon as possible.

Though his escape did not seem to have aroused his captors, there was no telling when they would take the alarm and start after him. Tom looked for the bear. The animal was not in sight, though he could see by marks in the snow, where it had approached the cabin from the woods, and where it had run off into the forest again.

"Too bad I haven't my gun!" mused Tom. "But I don't dare try to get it."

Then began for Tom a time he never forgot. He set off toward the woods, wishing to gain their friendly shelter as soon as he could, but once there he was at a loss how farther to proceed.

"But there's no need to wait for morning," he reasoned. "I can see almost as well now, as long as the moon is up. I'll try to find some sort of a trail."

He staggered on, yes, staggered, for he was weak from his experience, and he had not had proper food in some time. It seemed almost a week, but of course it was not as long as that.

Scarcely able to walk, but grimly determined not to give up, Tom urged himself on. Whither he was going, he knew not, but any way to leave that hateful shack, and the more hateful men behind, was good enough for the time being.

All night long Tom kept on going. He fancied he was on some sort of trail or road, but he could not be sure. Certainly the trees seemed cut down in a line, though it was a twisting and turning one.

Then the moon went down, leaving the scene pretty dark, but the white snow made objects plain. Tom kept on until at last he was fairly staggering from side to side. He was very weak.

"I—I've got to give up," he panted. "I—I've got to—to rest."

He looked about and saw sort of a nook under some bushes. On top was a matting of snow, like a roof. Tom crawled into this like some hunted animal, and sank down wearily. He pulled his mackinaw about him, thankful that he had it with him. He must have frozen without its protection.

Again Tom was unaware of the passage of time. He must have dozed or fainted, perhaps, but when he opened his eyes the sun was shining. The day was a brilliant one, and warm, for that time of year. Tom took heart. He crawled out, and once more started on his wearying tramp. He was very weak and exhausted, and there was a "gone" feeling to his stomach.

"Or the place where it used to be," Tom said, with grim humor. "I don't believe I have a stomach left."

But he forced himself onward. It seemed that he had been staggering over the snow for a week. Time had lost its meaning for him.

"Oh, if I only had something to eat! If I only could find the camp!" murmured poor Tom.

He reached a stump, and sat down on it to rest. He closed his eyes but suddenly opened them again.

Was that fancy, or had he heard a shot? He leaped up, electrified, and then hesitated. Perhaps it was Skeel and the others after him. But a quick look across the snow showed him no one was in sight. Tom reasoned quickly.

"Skeel and his crowd wouldn't shoot unless they saw me, and then it would be to scare me. It can't have been those men who fired. It must be the boys. But where are they?" Tom looked eagerly about.

Again came the shot. There was no mistake this time. Then Tom heard a shout. He tried to answer it, but his voice was too weak. Another shot cracked on the frosty air, and then came a series of confused calls.

"There he is!"

"We've found him!"

"Hurry up!"

A mist dimmed Tom's vision. He cleared his eyes with a quick motion of his hand, and then he saw his three chums and Sam Wilson rushing toward him. They came out of the woods, and, a moment later, had surrounded him.

"Where were you?"

"What happened?"

"Where's your gun?"

"You look all in!"

Fast came the questions.

"I—I am all in," Tom faltered. "It's that rascal Skeel. I—I——"

He could not go on for a moment. Then he pulled himself together.

"Here! Drink this!" exclaimed Jack, producing a small vacuum bottle. "It's coffee and it's hot yet." He poured some out into a tin cup and Tom drank it. It revived him at once. Then, with a little more of the beverage, and a hasty swallowing of a sandwich which formed part of the emergency lunch the boys had brought with them, Tom was able to tell his story.

Hot indignation was expressed by all, and then Jack related how they had found the road, but lost Tom, and how they had met with Sam. Their trip to Camp No. 2 had been fruitless, as we know, nor were they any more successful when they came to Camp No. 3. Tom was not there. Then they started for Camp No. 1, and were on their way thither when they came upon the object of their search. On the way they shouted and fired signal guns at intervals. The dog had found his way to Camp No. 1, after leaving Tom, but the animal could not lead Tom's friends to him.

"And now to make it hot for those scoundrels!" exclaimed Sam. "We'll prosecute them not only for kidnapping and robbing you, for that's what they did when they took your gun and money, but we'll bring an action in trespass against them. That shack where they kept you belongs to the hunting club."

"And to think Tom was there all the while and we never knew it," said Bert.

"Oh, I intended to have a look there, if we hadn't found him at Cabin No. 1," declared Sam. "But now let's get busy! Can you walk, Tom, or will you wait here until I can go get a horse?"

"Oh, I'll be all right soon. I was just weak from hunger."

Soon Tom was able to proceed. They were about half way between Camp No. 1 and the shack where our hero had been kept a prisoner, and it was decided to go to the latter place and make an endeavor to capture Skeel and his cronies.

But our friends were too late. The kidnappers had fled, but Tom's gun and all his possessions, save his money, were found in the cabin. Doubtless the personal belongings were too conclusive evidence against the plotters, to risk taking, but someone had succumbed to the temptation of the cash.

"Well, I'm glad to get this back," Tom said, taking up his gun.

"Yes, and we'll get those rascals yet!" declared Sam. "I'll rouse the whole country after them!"

They went on to Camp No. 1 and there Tom had a good rest. It did not take long to pull himself together, and he was as eager as the others to start out on the trail of the scoundrels. For the time being hunting and the taking of photographs was forgotten. Sam sent word to the authorities, and a sheriff's posse was organized. It was done so quickly that Skeel and the others, who had taken the alarm and fled when they discovered Tom's escape, were apprehended before they could leave the neighborhood. The heavy storms had blocked the railroad and there were no trains. The men could not hire a sled and team and so were forced to walk, which put them at a disadvantage. They left a trail easy for the woodsmen, hunters and trappers to follow.

"Well, you got us, and you got us good!" said Murker, when they were arrested and confronted by Tom and the others. "I was afraid something like this would happen."

"Why didn't you say so, then, and keep me out of it?" asked Whalen, sullenly.

Professor Skeel said nothing, but he scowled at Tom. The plotter's plans had fallen through, and he faced a long prison term, which, in due course he received, as did his confederates. The letter Skeel had tried to force Tom to write was found on the man and made conclusive evidence against him and the others. So the scoundrel-professor was cheated of his revenge and the money he hoped to get from Mr. Fairfield.

It became known that Professor Skeel had various experiences after Tom had last seen him. The man was in desperate circumstances when he formed a plan of kidnapping Tom, and holding him for ransom. It was a foolish and risky plan, but Skeel talked it over with his two cronies anddecided to try it. They knew Mr. Fairfield was rich.

Then came Skeel's trip to Elmwood Hall. The snowball was an accident he had not counted on, and it made him more angry than ever against Tom.

Professor Skeel's injured ear, which looked, as Sam said, "like it had been chawed by some critter," was the result of a fight he had with a man before this story opened, and with which we have nothing to do. Sufficient to say that it served to identify the man, and put our friends on their guard, so that justice was finally meted out.

The trial and conviction of the men came later. After the trio were safely locked in jail, Tom and his chums returned to the woods where they had been lost. But they were better acquainted with the forest now.

"And we'll have some fine hunting!" cried Tom, now himself again.

"And get some photographs!" added Bert. "I want a view of that hut where the bear pulled the board off so you could get out."

"That was queer," said Tom, smiling. "I don't believe I'll like to shoot a bear now, after that one did me such a good turn."

"You won't have much chance," Sam said. "I guess even the oldest and toughest bear is 'holed-up' by now. Better be content with deer!"

And the boys had to be, rather against their wills. But they were made happy when each one got a specimen, though none was as fine as was

Tom's antlered head. Moreover, Bert and the others secured all the photographs they wanted.

But deer was not the only game they shot.

Rabbits, partridges and squirrels were plentiful, and the boys had more than enough for their meals. They enjoyed to the utmost the holiday time spent in the hunting camps, and Tom paid his first visit to Camp No. 3.

"Well, take it all in all, how did you enjoy it, fellows?" asked Tom, when, after a last successful hunt they were preparing to go back to home and Elmwood Hall.

"Couldn't have been better!" was the enthusiastic answer from all.

"But it was rather tough on you, Tom," said Jack.

"Oh, I didn't mind it so much, except the 'hunger-strike' I had to go on, after I escaped," was the reply. "And I had the satisfaction of besting Skeel."

"He'll hate you worse than ever," commented Bert.

"He'll be a long while getting out," Tom said. "That's one consolation. Well, here comes Sam with the pung. I suppose we've got to go back!"

And with sighs of regret at what they were leaving, real regret in spite of the hardships, the boys prepared to return to civilization, at which point we will take leave of them.

THE END